ABOUT THE BOOK

Trust or run? The wrong decision will be deadly.

After losing three loved ones, Detective Dominic Rossi is an expert at keeping his distance from all things female—that is until he meets Tessa Redman, a woman who seems mighty troubled. She's definitely hiding something from him, but that only brings out his need to protect even more.

When a hot looking detective begins snooping around Tessa's bar, she panics, believing he's there on behalf of her ex-husband—a cop on the take who she turned in—a man who swore he'd kill her.

But Dom's random tenderness awakens something deep inside her, and while he doesn't seem anything like her ex, the guy is a cop—and a rich one at that.

Only after several of her patrons are murdered and her father is killed is she forced to decide: trust Dominic or run for her life?

PROLOGUE

Charlotte, North Carolina

About time she got here. Morton Richter ducked down in his seat just as Audrey Mae Thompson and her baby boy, Bobby, rolled to a stop at her duplex. He turned the ignition key to check the dashboard clock for the tenth time in the last hour. What had taken her so long to arrive?

Better not have been another man. His pulse spiked at that thought. *Don't even go th*ere. Morton forced a calming breath. Think. She has Bobby with her, which meant she would have been visiting her mama. It was the only explanation.

He unclenched his fists, wiped his slick palms on the nubby seat fabric, and lowered his window halfway, sending in the cold air. He took another deep breath. *Shit*. Did it stink or what? It had been a bad idea to park next to the open dumpster, but he hadn't wanted Audrey Mae to spot him when she got home.

He wrinkled his nose, sat up, and placed the clunky binoculars on the top of the steering wheel, ready for a front row view of Audrey Mae in the flesh.

Damn, it was fucking cold. What'd he expect? He'd been sitting in his truck in the middle of November for three goddamn hours with the engine off.

Hold on.

Morton jerked to attention. She was getting out of her car. Just as Audrey Mae hauled little Bobby out of the backseat of her rusty, lime green VW, the front porch light flickered, and then went out. He hoped she'd remembered to pay her utility bill. It wouldn't do to keep a baby in a cold house.

Audrey Mae shifted her kid from one hip to the other as she stabbed her hand in her purse, probably looking for her house key. Good thing the moon was full so he could see her.

Morton started to slip out to give her a hand but then decided it was best to let her settle in first before he surprised her. A moment later, she slipped inside. The lamp in the window came on and cast a yellow-like glow in her postage stamp sized living room.

Through his lens, Morton watched her duck into the baby's room. As he waited for her to return, his foot tapped out a beat.

Sweet Audrey. So vulnerable. So in need of his care. Morton vowed he'd never hurt her child like his old man had hurt him. No. He'd be gentle, no matter if the kid stole his cigarettes or stashed porno mags under the bed. Kids deserved a little fun.

There. She was back with little Bobby now in his pajamas. Morton adjusted the focus ring to get a clearer image of her breastfeeding. Pride swelled. This morning he'd decided he had no choice but to take them away. Far away—where Bobby's no good father couldn't find him and abuse him.

Not wanting to waste any more time, he pushed open the truck door, and the hinge squeaked loud enough to wake the neighbors. *Damn.* If the car noise didn't alert her, the stupid mutt barking across the street would. The dog acted like someone had filleted one of its young.

"Shut up," Morton whispered in a throaty growl.

He hoped to God Audrey didn't question the dog's racket. Of course, around here, she probably didn't even flinch at a gunshot.

He tossed the binoculars behind the seat and closed the door real slow, but it still let out another groan. He needed to fix it, but not until after he took Audrey and the baby away from here.

Morton strode up to her place, wishing he'd brought a flashlight. Just his luck to step in dog shit.

He couldn't wait to see the expression on her face when she saw him in his spiffy new suit. He pretended it was his wedding suit. The flower he'd stabbed in his lapel made it look official too. It shouldn't matter to her the pink carnation was plastic.

Damn. He should have brought her flowers. All women liked flowers. And Audrey Mae was all woman.

He pressed her doorbell a couple of times, liking the sound of the chirping birds. Sweet. Like the woman inside.

"Who's there?"

Her voice came out too shrill, almost as if the sound had frightened her. Had Bobby's father come sniffing around and hurt her again?

"It's me, Morton," he said real slow, wanting to sound non-threatening.

"Go away," Audrey Mae shouted.

She couldn't mean it. The baby began to cry. "Now you've gone and upset Bobby," Morton bit back, trying not to become angry. When she didn't answer, a sharp pain stabbed him behind his eye. "Come on, Audrey Mae. Lemme in," he said with more force than before to make sure she'd hear.

He jiggled the storm door handle. *Shit*. It was locked.

"I told you I don't want nothin' to do with you," Audrey yelled back. "Do I need to get a restrainin' order or somethin'?" Her tone changed to sharp and demanding—real mean-like.

"Don't talk like that, honey. I want to help you and Bobby." He waited a beat, watching his breath frost on the glass.

She wedged open the main door and peered out. Her blondish red hair tangled about her shoulders and her jeans were a little too tight, but to him she looked like a ripe peach ready to be plucked.

"You can't come in. I told you we was finished." Audrey Mae's bottom lip firmed as she clasped Bobby closer to her chest and turned to the side.

"Please?"

God. I sound pathetic.

It was just like when he was ten, and he had to grovel in front of his dad to stop him from doing bad things to him.

"Go away!" She slammed the door in his face.

Anger rushed up his gut so fast he had to take a sharp breath to keep from ripping off the door.

"Bitch," he spat out.

Audrey wasn't any better than his no-good mama who'd ignored him when he needed her most. As he stalked back to his truck, Morton knocked the lid off from one of the trashcans. It pinged and rolled half way into the street. He hoped the whole goddamn neighborhood woke up.

Once in his truck, he stabbed the key into the ignition and took off, but he didn't go far. Oh no. Not far at all. He knew women. Audrey Mae would go running back to her mama. And he'd be right there behind her when she did.

From a block away, he pulled over to the curb where he could watch her house. He'd wait for as long as it took. He had no place else to go.

Sure enough, twenty minutes later, Audrey Mae came sneaking out with her bundled up baby and a suitcase. She looked so like his mama, all scared and whimpering, bent over like she was waiting for a beating.

What had he seen in Audrey anyway? Oh yeah. She was a woman with a child who had a bad ex hanging around—a woman who needed protecting.

Her headlights flashed on, and she raced out of her driveway, heading toward Charlotte, where her mama had an apartment. Morton wasn't sure exactly where the older woman lived, but he knew it was somewhere in town.

Keeping a few car lengths behind, he kept an eye on her as she sped up. Audrey took a corner too fast and her VW skidded toward the curb. His heart raced, fearing for Bobby's life. He wanted to yell at her for being so careless, but he knew scared women never listened.

She pulled to a stop at the signal then turned around toward the baby. She obviously had no clue he was two car-lengths behind.

Speckle-like rain drizzled on his windshield, and he wanted to warn

Audrey to drive more careful, to tell her the roads would be slick, but before he could get his hand on the door handle to jump out, the signal turned green and Audrey Mae took off, the car's rear end fishtailing through the intersection.

A van, traveling along the cross street going super fast ran the red light then slammed on its brakes. Tires squealed as the huge vehicle swerved left and then right. Not having enough space to stop, it crashed into the side of Audrey's small car.

Metal crunched, sparks flew. *Oh, shit.*

Audrey's car got squashed.

"Noooo." Morton ripped open his door refusing to believe the two people he'd wanted to protect the most might be dead.

CHAPTER ONE

Four years later

"Ohmigod," Chelsea said. Waiting for the Blue Moon's Bar to open, the waitress hopped up on the barstool and spread the Tampa Tribune on the shiny bar. "Listen to this, Tessa. A woman was shot to death in her car two nights ago on Bayshore Boulevard."

Tessa Redman looked up at the waitress and stopped polishing the counter. Bayshore was less than two miles away. "How horrible." Thinking about a killer on the loose caused a chill to race down her spine. "Maybe I'll ask Judd if I can beef up the lights in the parking lot."

Chelsea's shoulders visibly relaxed. "Great idea. I hate going out by myself at night. It's creepy sometimes."

"Tell me about it." Tessa returned to disinfecting the bar, wrinkling her nose at the strong bleach smell. Her mind reeled with the horror the woman must have experienced in the last few seconds of her life.

Tessa finished cleaning, tossed the rag into a bucket of soapy water, and then stacked the liquor bottles behind her. The crinkling of the flipped page brought Tessa back to the incident, and she stepped in front of Chelsea. "Do the police have any leads?"

The waitress ran a bright red, well-manicured nail farther down the newspaper column. "Not really. All it says is the time of death was around midnight."

"Hmm. Even at that time, I'm surprised no one heard the gunshot."

"Maybe everyone was sleeping."

"Or no one could be bothered."

Chelsea bobbed her head up and down. "I can see that." A hint of regret filled her tone. "Hey, maybe the guy used a silencer."

Before Tessa could speculate on the series of events, the doublewide front doors opened, sending in a shaft of bright sunlight through the dimly lit restaurant, silhouetting a large man. Cool, salt air from the bay filtered in along with him.

"We open at eleven," Tessa announced.

"That's all right," he replied as the doors swung shut behind him. "I just need some information."

As he neared the bar, last night's peanut shells crunched under his commanding steps. He looked down, and then returned his gaze to her face. A narrow cone of light from the overhead lantern illuminated the angle of the man's face. *Whoa*. The sharp plane of his face and powerful shoulders caused her breath to catch, and her heart did an unexpected flip—a sensation she hadn't experienced in...forever.

He held up his police badge, and her heart almost stopped before it raced, and blood rushed from her face. "What do you want?" The panic in her voice made her sound guilty, even to her.

"I'm Detective Dominic Rossi with the Tampa PD. I'd like to ask you a few questions."

The detective's piercing gaze had Tessa grabbing for the edge of the bar. "What about?"

"A woman was killed near here two nights ago. We have reason to believe she might have visited the bar before she was murdered. Were you working Wednesday night?"

Tessa nodded to Chelsea. "Would you mind seeing to the table set ups?" Her heart continued to pound.

"Okay," Chelsea said, pursing her lips, clearing wanting in on the action.

Tessa turned back to the cop, and a lump formed in her throat. "Yes, I was here."

The detective plucked an envelope from his shirt pocket, stepped closer to the bar, and slid a photo toward her. "Do you recognize this woman? I'm sorry it's rather graphic."

Tessa let out a pent up breath. Apparently this cop only wanted a name. She'd be happy to help any way she could and leaned over to get a closer view. The bone-white face of the woman resting against a half open car window grabbed the breath out of her. A trail of blood ran from the woman's blond hair ran down to her neck.

"Ohmigod." Unfortunately, the angle of the photo failed to give Tessa a good look of the woman's face. She tilted the photo toward the light hoping for a better view. "She's kind of familiar, but I can't place her." Her heart thudded at the gruesome scene.

"Her name's Keri Wilkerson. We found a set of matches on her front seat with the Blue Moon's name on it." He pulled out a notepad and flipped to a yellow Post-it tab. "It also had a phone number inside. 813-555-8395."

Her number. Goose bumps raced up Tessa's arms. "I remember her now." She'd told the distressed woman if she needed to talk to call her at home. "She was here Wednesday night."

"Do you remember if she was with anyone?"

Tessa visualized where Keri sat at the bar. "No, she was by herself. I don't remember her talking to anyone but me."

"How did Mrs. Wilkerson seem?"

Tessa pictured the woman—shoulders slumped, mascara blurred under her eyes, but dressed in designer jeans. "Sad, confused, angry."

"Did she say why?"

The larger-than-life cop lifted a lean hip onto the stool and focused on her face as if memorizing it. Tessa didn't like the scrutiny and forced a calm she didn't feel.

"Her eyes were red, and her face was splotchy when she arrived. I could tell she'd been crying. The woman, Keri, came in and ordered a double scotch on the rocks. She downed her drink in a few chugs and ordered another. I couldn't forget her. For quite a while Keri just stared, not saying a word. After about an hour, I asked her if anything was wrong, and she blurted out she'd caught her husband in bed with a man."

His brows arched. "You sure she said a man?"

"Yes. Keri suffered from overwhelming guilt, as if she was somehow to blame for her husband's deception and change of lifestyle."

The detective neatly printed her information in his pad. "Do you remember what time Mrs. Wilkerson left?"

"Not exactly, but I think it was a little before midnight, right before we close."

His face remained unreadable as he continued to jot notes. "May I have your name?"

"My name?" Her heart stuttered.

"Yes."

Did she dare tell him? "Why?"

"For the record."

"Oh. Ah, Tessa." His hand stilled in midair, obviously waiting for her last name. "Redman. Tessa Redman."

His pen went to work again, and she prayed her name wouldn't ring a bell.

"Are you the owner?" He glanced up, his piercing blue eyes locking onto her face.

"No, my half-brother, Judd Redman, owns the Blue Moon."

"Was he around Wednesday night?"

Her stomach turned queasy thinking about Judd's condition. "I'm afraid he's been in and out of the hospital for the last few weeks."

"I'm sorry." His sincere tone surprised her. "What time did you leave here that night?"

"It was after one. I stayed to work on the books since Wednesday is my bookkeeping day, or rather night."

"Can anyone vouch for your presence?"

"No." She tried not to show her annoyance. "What are you implying?"

"I'm not implying anything, ma'am, just doing my job."

As if she'd have anything to do with a murder. *Please.* Tessa glanced over to Chelsea cleaning a tabletop a few feet away, no doubt listening to every word.

The detective looked down at his hands for a split second. "I know you're not open for business yet, but could I have a drink?"

His abrupt shortening of the interview threw her. What was he up to? Was he just another cop needing to take the edge off the horrors of his job? Or was he here for another purpose?

"I'm sorry. I don't serve on-duty policemen."

He lifted his head and seemed to fight a smile. "I meant a Coke. I'll pay."

Heat rose to her cheeks. "Sure. Sorry."

Some psychologist she was going to be. She needed to be more careful about jumping to unwarranted conclusions.

Tessa drew the drink from the tap and handed Detective Rossi the glass. Their fingers touched for a brief moment causing a shock of electricity to bolt up her arm. She jumped back so fast, she felt like a fool.

The cop's long, broad fingers had unsettled her, reminding her of someone else. Tessa choked back her anxiety, picked up a clean rag, and began to polish the spotless, wooden bar again, hoping the detective wouldn't notice her discomfort. The last thing she needed was the exposure of a criminal investigation.

The detective took a large gulp of soda and eyed her above the lip of the glass. "Is there something you're not telling me?"

"N-no."

Chelsea sauntered up to the detective, slid onto the stool next to him and leaned close. "Do you have any other cases you need help with?" She ran a nail down the Pledge can, slow and easy.

Tessa made a silent promise to give the girl a bonus for distracting the policeman.

The detective scanned Chelsea from head to toe before turning back toward the bar. "No."

"Tessa," one of her cooks called, sauntering out of the kitchen, the swinging double doors clacking close behind him.

"Excuse me," she said to the detective, relieved to get away from him. "And Chelsea? Work awaits." She turned and strode toward

Roger. "What is it?" She failed to keep the exasperation from her voice.

Roger shuffled his feet from side to side and stuck his hands in his pockets. "We're out of chicken," he announced in the slowest southern drawl she'd ever heard.

"You're kidding. That's like a bar being out of beer. How could this have happened?" she whispered, not wanting the cop to overhear their conversation. She didn't need this aggravation.

"I dunno. Walt does the ordering."

She checked her watch. "And where is Walt?"

His lips firmed for a split second before shooting his gaze shot to the floor. "He's not here."

Obviously. "So what would Judd do in this case?" she asked, praying Roger would offer a quick solution.

"Get some more?"

Duh. "Look, we open in forty-five minutes. Can you run down to the store and buy whatever we need?"

Roger let out a long breath and rolled his eyes. "I suppose so."

The kitchen help around here sucked. What had her brother been thinking when he hired these guys? She made a mental note to speak with Judd. On second thought, maybe not. He didn't need the added stress when he was so ill right now. She'd have to handle the crisis herself.

As soon as Roger disappeared into the kitchen, she looked up Walt's number and called him. She kept her back rigid and turned away from Detective Rossi.

"Uh-huh?" Walt answered.

Oh God, she'd either woken him up or he had a hangover. "Walt, where are you? It's after ten already."

"Who's this?"

"Tessa. Your new boss. Remember?" She didn't wait for him to answer. "You're supposed to be at work."

"I quit yesterday." He yawned loudly into the phone. "Charley was supposed to tell you."

Charley, her taciturn bartender, wouldn't bother telling her if the restaurant was on fire. "Why didn't you tell me? Did something happen?" If she could understand his dilemma, she might be able to help.

"I'm moving back to Alabama. Sorry. Didn't my friend show up? He needs a job, and I told him to stop by."

"No."

"He's a good guy and really needs the work. Just don't judge him by his past. Listen, I gotta go."

"I don't—"

He hung up on her. Damn it. Tessa dropped the receiver back onto the cradle and swiveled on her heels. She was half way back to the cash register to check on the change drawer when the phone rang again. She threw up her hands. "What is this? I-4 in rush hour?" she mumbled as she marched back. "Hello?" This time she didn't sound so nice.

"Ms. Redman, please."

Tessa glanced toward the detective, wondering what was going through his mind and why he was still here. His elbows were planted on the counter, his gaze solidly fixed on her. Not a hint of expression laced his face.

"This is she." She kept her voice low. Maybe it was Walt's friend telling her he'd found another job. Wouldn't that suck?

"Ms. Redman. This is Grady Jankowski from the Jankowski Development Company."

Her body tensed, ready for battle. She'd needed the caller to be the cook, not the jerk who kept bugging her every few days about selling the place. She had to believe her brother would recover soon. He loved the Blue Moon, and he didn't need some sleazy developer to come in and liquidate his pride and joy.

"Mr. Jankowski, as I've told you before, the restaurant's not for sale. Please don't call here again."

"Thanks for the Coke, Ms. Redman," the detective called out as she pressed the disconnect button. She whipped around to face him. He smiled and her heart sped up. "Seeing you at work has been an enlightening experience."

Before she could question him what he meant, he tossed a few dollars on the counter and walked away.

***

"Rossi," Dom's partner, Phil Orloff, sang out as he walked into his office and tapped him on the shoulder.

"What?" Dom swiveled in his desk chair to face Phil.

"We have a homicide to solve or don't you remember?"

Dom remembered all right. He wished he could forget the way the black gunpowder stippled the Wilkerson woman's temple or the angle at which her head slumped against the steering wheel. Her vacant eyes kept haunting him. They were so much like his mom's eyes after the burglar killed her and Dad. The memory of the bullet hole in each of their heads made his stomach sick.

"Yeah, what about it?" Dom said between clenched teeth.

"Did anything at the restaurant pan out?" Phil leaned against the gray metal desk and crossed his arms, reminding Dom of a damned commando—tough and ornery.

Dom relaxed. "We were right about the victim visiting the Blue Moon the night she was murdered. Ms. Redman, the bar's manager, told me the Wilkerson woman said she found dear hubby in bed with another man the night she died."

Phil whistled. "Now there's something we didn't suspect."

"No kidding." Dom drew the keyboard closer to him, ready to work on the report.

Phil leaned closer. "I know the look on your face. What aren't you telling me?"

Dom sat up. He knew Phil's bulldog tone meant he'd never leave him alone until he gave up the info. "Ms. Redman isn't coming clean. I can feel it. I tell you, Phil, the woman looked downright scared the moment I walked into the bar. I've never seen such wide eyes. Talk about being fidgety. She couldn't wait to get rid of me."

"Well, that's because of your ugly mug," Phil answered without a trace of humor in his eyes.

"I'm serious."

"So am I." He flashed a smile then sobered. "Did you run her name?"

"Of course, but nothing popped up." Dom leaned back in his chair.

"Did you check to see when the autopsy would be back on Keri Wilkerson?"

"I did. You should have the results by the end of next week."

"Next week?"

"The woman's only been in the morgue two days," Phil said. "You know how overloaded they are."

"I know, but just this once—" Dom waved a dismissive hand. "Never mind. Did you get anything on the victim's relatives?"

Phil straightened, pulled out a notepad and riffled through the tattered pages. Dom shook his head. The guy needed to get some kind of PDA.

"It's here somewhere," Phil said then smiled. "Yup. Here it is. Only living relative in the area was her husband, Taylor Wilkerson, aged forty-five. I checked out his alibi. He was at the Tampa Art Museum fund raiser until 10:30 p.m. before heading to a party on Davis Island until 2 a.m."

Dom whistled. "On a Wednesday night? Even I'm too old to be partying that late on a work night, and I'm ten years younger."

Phil chuckled. "You? Party? When was the last time you had fun? As in F-U-N?"

Ever since Lisa died, Phil was always worried about him, but he wouldn't confide in his partner if he ever did go out. The whole precinct would have a memo detailing his actions by morning. "None of your business. What else you do you have?" Dom kept his tone even.

"I can take a hint," Phil said. His grin did nothing to calm Dom's stomach. "Let's see." He ran a finger down the pad. "Jimmy finished canvassing the neighbors, but as you might expect, nobody saw anything." Phil looked up.

"No surprise. See what dirt you can dig up on Wilkerson's love interest."

"I'm on it." Phil shoved off Dom's desk and strode back to his own.

Dom studied Keri Wilkerson's file again. There wasn't much he could do until the reports came in. As his palm brushed his short-cropped hair, he contemplated his next move.

The smell of burnt coffee wafted over to him. What he wouldn't give for a cup of his specially mixed Kenyan blend right now, but he'd have to settle for the crap Sergeant Cantori was brewing—that or toothpicks to keep his eyelids open.

As he picked up his blue coffee mug, the exact color of Tessa's eyes, he could almost see her glaring at him. Pretty eyes, but one that held a well of guilt. Her knee-jerk reaction to his simple questions implied she was troubled. Now all he had to do was find out why.

CHAPTER TWO

Dear Audrey Mae,

I've moved again. This time to Tampa. You would have liked it here, all warm and sunny, with sandy beaches for Bobby to play on. I know I said I wouldn't move again, but I had to leave Atlanta. Detective Lowell, some Atlanta PD dick, was asking too many damn questions. Don't get me wrong. I'm not sorry for what I had to do. As a matter of fact, it felt real good to kill those three drunks—one for each year you and Bobby have been gone. No one should have to go through what I went through after that alcoholic asshole stole you from me.

I can't wait till I join you in heaven. Then we can be together forever and no one, and I mean no one, will ever hurt you or the baby again.

Forever yours,

Morton

***

When a guy in a torn t-shirt with more tattoos than skin strode into the Blue Moon at lunchtime, the hair on the back of Tessa's neck stood up. Tattoo boy stepped up to the cash register next to the bar where she was counting the change, and she hoped he couldn't see the tension lacing her fingers. With the way her luck had been going this week, she half expected him to pull a gun and rob the place.

"You Tessa Redman?" His voice held a hard, defensive edge.

She closed the register and looked up at his face. "Yes."

"I'm Mick Stukes," he said over the noise of customer conversations and the ice clinking in glasses. "Short-order cook."

Her relief was palpable. "Oh, you're Walt's friend." She wanted to ask what had taken him so long but decided she was glad he'd arrived at all.

He shrugged. "Sure, whatever." He fidgeted with the stud collar on his wrist. "I heard you might need a cook, and I could use the job."

His hand shook slightly as if he could use a fix too, but she tried not to judge. "Do you have any experience?"

His eyes darted around the bar as if trying to decide whether to tell the truth. "In the pen I had to feed a couple hundred men three squares a day."

A convict? In her place? Her brother would die.

She stopped short and amended the image. Judd, her now reformed half-brother, would have a fit. There, that sounded better.

Mick's glance locked onto the hardwood floor as if he found the darkened grooves fascinating. Two couples piled in the nearly full restaurant, and Chelsea shuttled between two tables so fast she knocked over one of the saltshakers, which was very un-Chelsea like. Roger had been his usual slow self in the kitchen not helping the dire situation.

"Why don't we slip into my office?" Tessa certainly didn't need the world to know she was interviewing an ex-con.

She turned away from tattoo boy and could feel him hover behind her as she walked with false confidence down the dim hallway.

"It's not what you think," he said with such unexpected emotion her heart clenched.

"What am I thinking?" she asked as she pushed open the door to her workspace.

When she turned to sit in the chair behind her desk, she saw a scared kid before her.

"That I'm a hardened criminal you can't trust."

"Go on."

He wrung his hands. "I'm not going to tell you I'm not guilty, because I am, but I had a good reason to assault that man. He was hurting my sister."

Her heart swelled. Tessa's older sister's rape in high school was never far from her mind. If only Judd hadn't been away at school at the time of her attack, her sister wouldn't have run away from the nightmare.

"Protecting your sister speaks well of you," she said. "I have to know, though, are you doing any drugs? I don't condone that kind of behavior, and I don't want it around my restaurant."

He looked her straight in the eye. "No, I don't do drugs. I swear."

She believed him. He seemed like a good kid who'd had a bad rap, and she could relate. He thrust a crumpled paper at her that listed his work experience. After a few more questions, she handed him an application—needing his name, address, and driver's license number.

"When can you start?" she said. Normally, she was a thorough person, but with the way the problems kept flying at her the last few days, Tessa decided she didn't have the luxury of interviewing a ton of prospective cooks.

"Now, I guess."

"Good. I'll start you off at minimum wage. If you prove you can do the job, I'll give you a raise. How does that sound?" She prayed she wasn't making a stupid mistake.

His smile came out genuine. "Thanks. Walt told me you were cool." He pumped her hand with enthusiasm.

"Let me show you to the kitchen."

***

When Dom's eyes refused to focus on the information his team had unearthed on the Wilkerson murder, he placed the reports in alphabetical order with the rest of the pending cases, and then stretched to get the kinks out of his neck and back.

It was time to visit the Blue Moon again. He'd waited over a week to check up on Tessa Redman, wanting to give her time to forget him, but that wasn't nearly long enough for him to forget her.

Tessa had looked scared, like his little brother had when the foster home explained no one wanted both a nine year old and a six year old. It didn't matter they were brothers. Geez. Dom had almost peed in his pants when the social workers told him the bad news.

He'd argued with them. Boy, had he argued—or rather begged and cried—all night in fact. It would have been enough to make his papa proud, but it hadn't done any good. In the end, Dom stayed in Connecticut and Alex had been whisked away somewhere. If he had a dime for every dollar he'd spent on P.I. fees looking for his kid brother, he'd be rich.

Life wasn't fair sometimes.

Dom's stomach suddenly grumbled. Crap. He'd been too focused to eat. Every time a case stymied him, he'd work non-stop, not taking the time for lunch or dinner, almost as if his sacrifice would help bring the criminal to justice that much sooner. It never worked however, but he didn't change his habit.

Now was as good a time as ever to see what interesting tidbits he could unearth at the Blue Moon. If he was lucky, he might find a customer who'd noticed the Wilkerson woman conversing with someone. He needed a clue to help him find the bastard who'd killed her. As of seven p.m. today, his team had squat.

Dom exited the station, surprised at the unusual bite in the air. November was unusually cold this year, signaling a cool front was moving in.

Half way to the restaurant, the skies opened up, turning the evening a dark, battleship gray. The dried love bugs on his windshield smeared as he turned on the wipers. He'd been meaning to get new ones, but with the rash of recent cases, he hadn't taken the time to shop for a pair.

Dom clocked the drive to the Blue Moon to be right around seventeen minutes. When he pulled into the hard-packed, dirt lot, it was close to seven thirty, and he was surprised to find the place full. The restaurant must do a good dinner business or else lots of people had a bad drinking habit.

A neon blue moon lit up the front of the old wooden structure. The name flashed in white, then blue. Only tonight it read, Blue Moo. The *N* was out.

Seagulls squawked above the outdoor patio that overlooked the Bay. They'd be disappointed if they expected food tonight. It was too chilly for sitting outside.

Along the side of the restaurant, he spotted a sharp looking Chris Craft pulled up to the dock. What he wouldn't give to take a spin in that beauty. Maybe in about twenty or thirty years when he retired he'd live his dream of sailing the ocean.

He shook his head at the fantasy and eased through the Blue Moon's double doors. The contrast from dark to light wasn't as stark as the first time he'd come. Now wall lights, in the shape of anchors, filled the restaurant with a nice glow. Rather homey, if you liked the house-boat theme.

His gaze zeroed in on the bar, hoping to spot Tessa. No luck. Instead he found Mr. Clean bartending. Shaved head, well over six-four, his muscles bulging beneath an out-of-place bowling shirt.

"Table for one, sir?"

Dom hadn't noticed the hostess until she spoke. Pretty girl, but too skinny for his tastes. "I think I'll sit at the bar, thanks."

Even though his back would be to the tables, he figured he'd be able to pry information from the bartender. Only four of the ten bar stools remained open. He slid onto the stool at the end, not wanting to be sandwiched between two patrons.

Dom flagged the bartender.

"Whatllya have?" the giant asked without a hint of welcome.

"A Guinness draft." Dom disliked the taste of ale, but ordering the brew would ensure he'd hold fast to his no drinking rule. He'd been really dumb-ass-stupid in his twenties, and the scars on his neck and chest from the knife fights were a constant reminder of what could happen when one took bets after drinking all night.

The giant plunked down a tall glass of the dark beer in front of him, sloshing part of the contents down the sides. The guy didn't offer an apology or clean up the mess. Dom grabbed a paper napkin and soaked up the spill.

"Want to run a tab?" Mr. Clean asked.

"No." Dom fished a twenty out of his pocket and tossed it on the bar. "Is Tessa working tonight?"

If Dom hadn't been looking for it, he would have missed the stiffening of the man's back. "She's in her office tending to the baby."

Baby?

The image rocked him. Tessa was a mom? He never would have guessed. Her skittishness sent out a message she wasn't comfortable around men, or was it just being around him? Hell, maybe she hated cops.

Her defensiveness hadn't been his imagination. When her fingers brushed his hand, she'd jumped, her eyes had visibly widened, and her jaw had slackened. Her response had been too strong to ignore. Or did she have a husband lurking in the background? Maybe one who abused her? At that thought, a surprising surge of anger welled up before he could squash it.

"You from around here, young man?"

Dom swiveled to his left. As if someone had pulled a magic trick, an old woman replaced the young professional in the seat next to him. Short, white curly hair capped a lined, but lively face, her eyes sparkling with intelligence. It must be his lack of sleep that made him miss the sleight of hand.

"Yes." He turned his shoulders to the bar and took a sip of the tart beer to avoid further conversation.

"Then you must have heard about the terrible tragedy on Bayshore last week. Such a shame. A woman gunned down like that. Tampa didn't used to be like that when I was growing up, you know."

His ears perked up at the topic. "I'm sure it wasn't. Did you know the victim?" he asked with false innocence.

"Not personally, but I saw her here the night she, ah, died. Madge, that's my friend, and I even commented on her agitated state. Poor dear. Looked like she'd lost her best friend."

Dom's heart sped up at his luck. "You saw her here? Did she stay long?"

She grabbed his forearm with gnarled fingers that ended in red spikes. "Oooh, you sound like a cop." She let go and leaned toward him as if she were imparting top-secret information. "Well, my friend and I left around ten thirty and the woman was still here. The paper said she died around midnight or so. You do the math."

Dom had to smile at her way-too-youthful turn of phrase. "Did you see her talking to anyone?" He'd wondered if Tessa had told him the truth.

"Just Tessa. She's running the bar now that her brother is ill." She batted her eyelashes. The older woman searched his face then ran a gaze down his chest and stopped at his crotch.

He felt like a damn horse for sale.

"Oh, where are my manners? I'm Eleanor Stablein."

"Dominic Rossi." They shook hands.

"Rossi. Such a nice name. Italian?"

He sucked in a calming breath. "Yes."

"I just love Italy. Have you ever been?"

"No."

"You should go, you know." Eleanor let go of his arm and glanced to the far end of the bar. "Have you met her?"

"Who?" Maybe Eleanor was senile.

"Why Tessa, of course." She turned back to him and swatted his arm. "Pay attention. You'll never get a woman if you don't listen."

Her chiding forced a chuckle. "Yes, I've met her. Once."

"She's a real doll that girl." She cocked a brow. "Don't you think?"

Tessa had hardly been a doll with him. "Why do you say that?"

"How many women do you know would give up her life's dream of becoming a psychologist to help out a brother—a half-brother to boot? And to care for his baby while he waits for a liver transplant? Why the girl is practically a saint. Can you imagine doing something like that for someone?"

As a matter of fact he could. He'd be willing to give up everything for his brother—if he ever found Alex again.

Eleanor shook her head, thankfully not pressing him for an answer. "Poor, Tessa. This whole bar business has her in such a frazzled mess. Why Madge and I had to babysit Mandy just this past weekend when her sitter couldn't make it. If only Judd's wife hadn't run off like she did, Tessa wouldn't have to play mom. Of course, she's doing a wonderful job, but the baby and the Blue Moon are hard to juggle." She tapped a nail on his chest. "I see your finger doesn't have any gold around it. Why, she could use a nice man to help her out. Do you work?"

"Yes, ma'am, I work."

Great. That's all he needed. An interfering matchmaker. However, a clearer picture of Tessa developed. Apparently, she wasn't married and was devoted to her family. His dark mood lightened at the thought.

"And what exactly do you do, Dominic?"

Before he could make up an occupation that would keep her talking, a tall, elderly woman with short, bright orange permed hair approached them.

She gave Eleanor a hug. "There you are. Sorry, I'm late, but—" Her mouth turned up in a smile. "I didn't know you'd met someone. Oh, don't let me interfere."

Did Eleanor have a habit of picking up younger men? Younger, as in forty some odd years younger?

Eleanor grabbed his hand. "This is my new friend—" She paused.

Had she forgotten his name already? She seemed too sharp. "Dom. Dominic Rossi," he answered, hoping to pry information from the newcomer. "A pleasure to meet you. Can I buy you ladies a drink?"

"Oh, that's so sweet of you, but we must be going," Madge said. "I just came to pick up Eleanor. We're going to the movies."

Eleanor hopped off her perch with surprising agility, and then let go of his hand.

"Well, Dom, I hope we see you around. Madge and I come here all the time." She winked. "And do check out Tessa. She's quite the find."

Dom smiled. He liked the old biddy, but not her suggestion to scope out Tessa. He'd had enough heartbreak in that department to last a lifetime. Being engaged, then losing Lisa to cancer, cured him of any hope for a happily ever after.

"Don't like the ale?"

Dom spun around. The giant was standing in front of him casting a disapproving eye. "I was distracted."

The man grunted. Figuring he had Mr. Clean's attention, Dom

reached into his pocket and removed a photo of Keri Wilkerson. "Do you recognize her?"

He glanced once at the photo. "Nope."

"Mind taking a closer look?"

The giant shrugged. He leaned over, grabbed the snapshot from Dom and held it up to the light. "She don't look so good."

"She's dead."

"You a cop?"

No use lying. "Tampa Homicide. Dominic Rossi."

He shrugged. "My old man was a cop in Ohio," the bartender said with little affection.

"You didn't want to follow in Dad's footsteps?"

"Hell no. My dad was a real dick."

Dom had no ready retort. He scooped up Keri Wilkerson's headshot and slipped it in his breast pocket for safekeeping.

"Hey, Charley, my man," a short, stocky patron shouted from the other end of the bar. "Can I get some service over here?"

"Be right there, Mr. Dirkman."

Charley narrowed his eyes at Dom, as if to give a warning before rushing away. Dom bet the laconic giant rarely moved with such speed. It was surprise that Charley wasn't interested in further conversation with him. Most people brushed him off once they found out he represented the law.

Dom took another small sip of beer for show and suppressed a groan as the cold brew slid down his throat, quenching his thirst. He missed the taste of beer sometimes, but he didn't regret his change of lifestyle—at least most of the time.

Dom closed his eyes to soak in the mood. The place seemed noisier and the smells more intense than before. Robust conversation and easy laughter helped him relax. Eleanor's flowery perfume lingered around him, while the aroma of fried chicken filtered out of the nearby kitchen. He liked the atmosphere here since there was something down to earth about the place.

He turned his back to the bar, wanting to get a feel for the clientele, to see why a seemingly rich housewife would come here alone.

Safety, he decided. The place had an intangible aura of comfort that permeated the place, as if Mr. Clean would rush to the rescue if anyone bothered a customer.

As he was checking out the place, Chelsea turned toward him, stopped short, and then made a beeline in his direction, swaying her hips in an exaggerated fashion. He could have told her to save her effort for a more worthy cause, but he didn't want to hurt her feelings.

"Hey, there. I see you're back," Chelsea purred as she crossed into his personal space. "Trying to solve more cases?" She ran a finger down his arm as her mouth formed a pout.

Dom leaned back against the bar and planted his elbows on the counter to give him some distance. "Chelsea, isn't it?"

She beamed. "Yeah, you remembered! Can I get anything for you?" Her seductress tone turned bubble-gum cute.

His first instinct was to say, Tessa, but instead asked for a menu. "What's your specialty?" he asked as he pursued the long list of items.

"Why Detective Rossi, whatever do you mean?"

"I was asking what food is the restaurant known for?" He wasn't into kinky. At least not with Chelsea.

"Oh. Well, that would have to be our world famous hamburgers. They're delish." She straightened her shoulders in an obvious attempt to show off her ample breasts.

"I'll have one but hold the cheese." He didn't bother looking over the menu. He wanted Chelsea away from him. She drew too much attention, and he wanted to remain unnoticed for as long as possible. Dom wasn't ready yet to face the nervous Ms. Redman.

***

"Tessa," Chelsea whispered as she slipped into the office. "You won't believe who's here."

From Chelsea's excitement, Tessa guessed some hot, rich stud had arrived. Good for her. Chelsea could use a new beau to distract her.

"Who?" Tessa whispered back, not wanting to disturb Mandy. The baby had finally fallen asleep after fussing for over an hour.

"Detective Rossi."

Oh, God. Ice poured through her veins. "He's here?" She'd

answered all of the detective's questions last week. Why had he returned?

"Yeah. He's sitting at the bar next to the door. He's looking real hot. Black dress pants, maroon fitted shirt open at the throat and—"

"I know who he is." Tessa had been too anxious to think about him as a man or to notice how broad his shoulders were. Right. "He's so not your type," Tessa blurted.

If the detective fell for Chelsea, he'd be around all the time, and she didn't need the law around with her ex-husband cop turned con searching for her. Police stuck together.

"Oh, I don't know about that." Chelsea ran a hand over her pulled back hair.

The man had to be more than ten years older than Chelsea. What was the girl thinking? "Well, thanks for letting me know, but I really don't care what he does in his spare time," Tessa said with amazing calm.

Chelsea giggled. "I'd better put in his order."

"Good idea."

No sooner had Chelsea disappeared and Tessa had settled comfortably at her desk when the door nudged open. Tessa jumped. She grabbed her heart when she saw it was only Roger. "You scared me."

"Sorry. Were you expecting someone else?"

"No."

"We, uh, need some help in the kitchen unloading a couple of crates."

Her pulse slowed to normal. "Okay. I'll send Charley in to help."

"Thanks," he answered in his usual monotone.

The man needed a life she decided—or something to jumpstart his heart.

Look who's talking? School had occupied all her time until three weeks ago. Now the restaurant had become her life. She hadn't shopped or gone to the movies once in that time.

Tessa jumped up from her seat. Damn. Now she'd have to make a public appearance and be under Detective Rossi's watchful eye.

She took two deep breaths and plunged into the restaurant, eyes focused ahead.

CHAPTER THREE

Ralph Ferino was pissed. First, it had taken him three straight days to drive from Colorado to Tampa. He'd battled a blizzard, and then a hail-storm with ice so big it pummeled the car. The hood looked like Al Capone's gangsters had used it for machine gun practice. Not that it mattered. The heap was a rental.

What irked him was the fact he didn't have enough money to buy his own car. But hell, he'd only been out of jail a short while. Nobody, and he meant nobody wanted to hire an ex-con. It didn't matter he had been a decorated police officer. The fact he'd been incarcerated cancelled all the good he'd done in his life.

He figured as long as he was now an official outcast, he was going to make sure the bitch who'd made him one paid big time. Tessa Marie Redman Ferino would be ever so sorry she'd double-crossed him.

The second he was released, he started his search for her. He'd checked out all their old haunts in Denver, but she'd vanished. Then he smartened up and paid his former partner a visit. It hadn't taken long to convince Smithers to hack into records at every state university for a Tessa Redman or a Tessa Ferino.

Bingo. Tessa was registered at the University of South Florida in Tampa. It actually surprised him that she actually had the guts to finish pursuing her Ph fucking D in psychology. She'd sure taken her sweet time when they were married, always having an excuse as to why she couldn't have a full time job.

The Florida part he expected. Her half-brother and dad lived in the area. Dumb bitch.

Why not change your name, girl? She had to know he was going to come after her. And here she was supposed to be the smart one. Hadn't he taught her anything?

He'd called information in Tampa, but they didn't have a Tessa Redman listed, so at least she'd done one thing right.

Now that he was here, he needed to find her exact location. He could stop at the restaurant, sure, but there was no way Judd would give up his own sister. And in the off chance she was there, Ralph wanted their first confrontation to be private—as in no one around to hear her scream when he did wonderfully-painful-things-to-her-body kind of private. As to what he'd do first? Satisfy his needs. That was a given. Three years was a long time to go without a woman. Then he'd make sure she never told on anyone again.

He had thought his best bet was the USF registrar's office—wrong. The tight-lipped bitch wouldn't give him any information. She said personal information was for the student only. He wanted to belt her one, but with twenty witnesses, he restrained himself.

He'd left the university too tired to think and had found a sleazy looking motel a few streets away. He checked in with cash. Always cash. Never credit cards. He wasn't stupid like most of the criminals he used to catch. Of course, he had to use his fake credit card for the rental car, but he had no plans to use that piece of plastic again.

He was smart. Tony the Forger had made a new set of credentials complete with a new name. It might have been for naught since the motel clerk had barely looked at the ID. Good thing since the photo wasn't a good likeness anyway.

After a few hours of sleep, Ralph opened his eyes, refreshed and ready to begin his quest to find his holy grail—Tessa.

First stop—dear old daddy Redman's place. The guy would talk, and if he didn't, he'd suffer. Big time.

Ralph had been to his father-in-law's beach house only once, right after he and Tessa had married. He didn't have to look farther than a phone book to find Dan Redman's address. Sorry bastard.

The roads to the beach hadn't changed much except for an addition of a few high rises along the way. He was pleased he located the place without much trouble, especially in the dark.

Dan's place had one lone light at the front door. With only the half-moon to light the area, Ralph couldn't tell much, other than the place looked like it could use a paint job and a landscaper. The small home wasn't worth the concrete it was made out of, but the property was probably worth a mint being so near the beach and all. It didn't look like Tessa's dad had fixed anything after the last set of hurricanes either. Two of the shutters hung by a nail and covered part of the window.

Ralph decided it would be wiser to park about two blocks away and walk to Dan's place since he didn't want the neighbors to remember his car if things got ugly.

With the television blaring, Ralph knew the old man was inside.

It took a full minute for Dan to answer. Was the old guy deaf or something? When his ex-father-in-law cracked finally open the door, fear laced his face the moment recognition hit.

"Ralph? Is that you?"

Good. He wanted him on edge—and very fearful.

Ralph had to admit he was a little surprised to see him in a wheelchair. While he wondered what had happened, he didn't care enough to ask.

"Sure is. Long time, no see, Dad."

The old man's lips thinned. "What do you want?"

Ralph barged in, not waiting for an invitation and checked out the small space. "I see things haven't changed." No housekeeper or significant other came charging out of a side door, implying he lived alone.

"Get out." Dan's pronouncement came with some authority, which Ralph respected. Not that it would change the outcome of the visit.

"I need to find your daughter." Ralph fingered Tessa's photo displayed proudly on the mantel. She was still beautiful. "I see she cut her waist-length hair."

"Yes. Now leave. Please."

"When was the last time you saw her?"

"Not in over a year," he spit out.

"Now that's bullshit, and we both know it," Ralph said evenly as he turned to face the old man. "I happen to know she's registered at USF, not even an hour from here."

His face blanched. "Look, she doesn't want to see you anymore. She has a new life."

Ralph laughed. "Tessa, a life? You're lyin', old man."

Dan wheeled over to a side table and picked up the phone. Ralph couldn't have that. He pulled out a knife and flicked open the blade. "Why don't you put that down?"

Dan's jaw slackened and did as Ralph asked. "What are you going to do?"

The pathetic man firmed his jaw and stabbed a fist in the air. Like that was going to scare him.

"Well, I'm not leaving until I know where I can find my lovely wife."

"She's not your wife anymore."

His tone was getting a little too aggressive for Ralph's tastes. The man needed to be taught a lesson.

"A mere technicality," Ralph explained as he stepped toward Dan, brandishing the blade.

Ralph jumped behind the guy's wheelchair, and before Dan could get his hands on the wheels to spin around, Ralph pressed the blade hard against his Adam's apple. The old man grabbed Ralph's knife hand with both of his and tried to pull the blade away, but it didn't do any good. Three years in prison made a man strong—stronger than any cripple.

"She's at the Blue Moon," Dan said with a strangled cry.

"Good. I like a man who cooperates." Ralph let up on the pressure. A little. "But why would she be there? Shouldn't she be studying?"

"Judd's in the hospital. She had to take over for him."

Interesting. With a flick of the wrist, he sliced his former father-in-law's throat. The last thing he needed was for him to warn the bitch. Ralph wiped the excess blood from his blade on Dan's shirt and stored the knife back in the sheath.

Now to get what he'd come for—Tessa's address. He decided it was best if he made Dan's death look like a robbery. Not that a real robber would break into this dive, but he'd attempt to make it look real enough to fool the local cops.

Ralph headed into the bedroom, glad he felt nothing over the old man's death. In the past he would have, but the joint taught him survival, not sympathy.

One good thing would come from the old man's demise. Tessa would suffer. She loved her dad. She loved him more than she'd loved her own husband. Bitch. He'd make her pay for the agony he'd gone through in jail.

The time he'd spent in the Colorado penal system gave him plenty of time to think about how he wanted to live his life after prison—or A.P. as he called it. So far everything had gone according to plan.

Just thinking about seeing Tessa gave him an added jolt of pleasure.

Ralph donned a pair of latex gloves and refocused on the task on hand. The desk drawers provided fifty bucks in cash but no address. Shit. Wouldn't a father have something with his daughter's address? Guess he had no need to write when they lived close.

Ralph didn't figure anyone would be stopping by tonight to socialize with dear old Dad, but he didn't need to be staying there for a prolonged visit either. Time was up. Except for the money and the photo of Tessa, he'd found nothing.

Well, almost nothing. He'd found out where she worked. That counted for something. Ralph decided he'd wait for her outside the restaurant and follow her home. Simple as 1-2-3.

He could just picture the look on Tessa's face when he announced, "Honey, I'm home."

He swallowed his chuckle as he snuck out of the old man's house and headed back to Tampa. Time to take care of Tessa.

**

Knowing Dominic Rossi was anywhere in the vicinity set Tessa's nerves on edge. The odd sensation infusing every inch of her body wasn't her usual one of fear, but she refused to analyze the mixture of excitement and trepidation.

Tessa marched up to Charley and touched his arm, keeping her focus only on him.

"What is it?" he asked with concern in his eyes. "Is the baby okay?"

"Yes, Mandy's asleep. Thanks for asking. Roger needs help in the kitchen. I'll watch the bar."

Obviously relieved, he dropped his clenched fist. "Okay."

Tessa avoided making eye contact anywhere near the door. Because she suspected the detective's gaze was on her, her hands began to sweat and her pulse turned erratic. To help with the jitters, she busied herself straightening the liquor bottles, while keeping her back to the patrons —and to Detective Rossi.

"Hey, sweetcakes," a familiar voice called. "Can I have another drink?"

Hackles rose up her spine at the nickname, but she turned around to face the pain-in-the ass, Bob Dirkman. "Scotch, Bob?"

"You got it baby. On the rocks."

He was on the rocks, all right—with his wife. That was his problem —or most of it, anyway. Tessa didn't want to get into another pity party with the washed up salesman tonight. She wasn't in the mood to play shrink, nor was it the right time to confront Bob about his inappropriate name-calling, especially with Detective Rossi watching. She didn't want any of his attention on her if she could help it.

Her hand shook as she poured Bob his drink, but at least she didn't spill any. When she set the glass in front of Dirkman, he grabbed her hand.

"Thanks, darling."

"I'm not your darling." She pulled away and turned from him again, fuming. Be nice. Without patrons like Bob, she wouldn't make money —money her brother needed.

"Hey, you're a woman," Bob said, seeming to ignore her brush off. "Can you tell me why Brenda would want to go off like she did?" He took another chug of his scotch. "How could she just leave me with three kids? Is this a natural thing to do when a gal turns forty?"

The man was drunk, but the sadness in his voice made her answer.

"I don't know, Mr. Dirkman. Women do crazy things just like men sometimes do." She knew she sounded tired, but at least she was trying to answer him honestly.

He took a long drink from his glass. "Tell me something else then. And be honest. Am I attractive? Or am I too fat?" He patted his stomach as though he needed to test if his belly had gotten any larger since he'd walked in.

She didn't want to go there. "What do you think?" Answering a question with a question was the safety net for all psychologists.

"Well, I've gained a few pounds over the years," he replied. "But hell, I've worked hard and deserve a little relaxation on the weekends. Brenda never understood that. You want to relax sometimes too, don't you?"

"Sure." Not needing this right now, she walked toward the cash register, scanning each drink along the way to see if anyone else needed a refill.

"Hey, I was talking to you. Don't turn your back on me," Bob yelled.

Her face heated up like a bad sunburn. She closed her eyes to regain control before facing him. She walked back to where he sat and kept her voice low. "Maybe you should go home to your children, Mr. Dirkman."

He leaned over the bar, grabbed her upper arm and gave a good yank. "Don't tell me what to do. You sound like my wife."

"Let go, Mr. Dirkman," she said between gritted teeth as she tried to pull away from him.

His fingers released their hold and Tessa moved back. She rubbed her upper arm and bet his fingers had left welts. Jerk. If Judd were here, he'd know how to handle this guy—but he wasn't and sadness swept through her.

Mr. Dirkman sucked in an audible breath when Charley material-ized out of nowhere and grabbed him in a chokehold.

She rushed up to him. "Charley, it's okay," she cried. For a moment she believed the bartender might break the guy's neck.

"Let...me... go. Ple-ease." The poor man's eyes practically bugged out.

Charley dropped his arm. "Don't ever touch her again."

Mr. Dirkman coughed and ran a hand over his reddened throat. "You guys are all crazy. I'm outta here."

Tessa said nothing as he raced out of the bar, half running, half stumbling. He hadn't paid. Damn.

The place had gone quiet, and all eyes were on her.

"Excuse me, I need to see to Mandy."

Could she die or what? Maybe, just maybe, she hadn't handled the situation as well as she could have.

Hurry up, Judd. Find a liver and come back.

She placed an ear against the office door and didn't hear a peep from the baby. Just as well. In Tessa's agitated state, she'd probably wake her niece. She decided to check the kitchen. Roger had needed help unloading some food, and she wanted to see if Charley had finished the task.

That wasn't entirely true. She needed something to do, and this was all she could think of to occupy her time. She stepped inside the hot kitchen filled with the wonderful aroma of dill and garlic. Tessa leaned against the wall. Seeing Charley grab Mr. Dirkman had shaken her. She appreciated the bartender coming to the rescue, but she hated violence. The way he'd grabbed the man's throat in a death grip had freaked her out.

"You okay, Tessa?" Roger asked in his slow, metered speech.

She was surprised he'd even noticed. "Yes, I'm fine."

Mick stopped chopping the celery in mid stalk and glanced up. "Who screamed?"

She'd screamed? Here she thought she'd only grunted or worst case, let out an audible gasp. "I guess I did."

"You should have seen Charley the second he heard you," Mick said. "I didn't think a guy his size could move that fast. What happened?"

"Nothing, really. Mr. Dirkman was drunk. He grabbed me and Charley stopped him."

His brows furrowed and his mouth pinched. "Does this kind of thing happen a lot? Because if it does, I could take a spin out to the bar every once in a while to make sure nothing happens to you."

Mick's eagerness to protect made her want to chuckle. Although he was scrawny, she bet jail had given him plenty of muscles and fighting know how.

"That's all right. But thank you anyway. I need you in here more. I can take care of myself." Unless Ralph shows up.

She wondered if her ex had changed much since his stint in the pen. Mick seemed unscathed by his whole ordeal. Maybe Ralph had mellowed too. Right, and the bank would forgive her hundred thousand dollar student loan.

Roger dropped an order at the pick up window and buzzed one of the waitresses.

Once Mick returned to chopping the celery, the kitchen seemed to return to normal. They didn't need her around to distract them. It was only ten p.m., but maybe she'd call it an early night and take Mandy home. The baby's cold seemed to be worsening.

***

Dom had wanted to rush to Tessa's aid the second the drunk grabbed her, but the moment he'd pushed back his chair, Charley had come lumbering out of the kitchen and attacked the guy.

After Dickman, or Dirkman, or whoever he was, stalked off, Tessa ran into the kitchen for a few minutes, and then ducked into what he guessed was her office. She'd been in there for quite a long time. For he knew, she'd snuck out a back entrance he didn't know existed.

Hell. What was he doing here anyway? He'd found out a lot in this one visit. Perhaps he should come back tomorrow when Tessa might be more willing to answer some questions. Tonight was not a good time for her.

As he stood to leave, the object of his interest slipped out of the back room with a tiny baby in her arms, and his gut clenched at the tender sight. The way she held the fussy baby and the slight stain in her cheeks, stirred emotions he'd truly believed long dead—empathy and caring. The last person he'd tried to protect had been his brother, and look where that had ended up?

Charley hustled over to her. The huge amount of concern from the big man didn't seem to fit with Dom's impression of the giant. Was there something between them? Tessa was well educated, whereas Charley seemed...what? Coarse and crude?

Hell, who was he to talk? He only had a two-year degree, hadn't read a fiction book in years, and had never traveled out of the country. From the classy way Tessa spoke, he'd bet she'd done all of the above many times.

When Tessa leaned close to her bartender and whispered something to him, Dom's blood pulsed. He didn't like those two together for some reason—call it gut instinct.

Charley nodded and Tessa scurried out the front door, not talking to anyone.

Dom threw another twenty on the bar to cover his half-eaten dinner. Worried about her safety, he followed her out, careful to remain unnoticed.

Was Tessa in trouble? Is that why she'd been so nervous when he'd asked her the simple questions about Keri Wilkerson? Something was going on with her—something bad.

***

Mandy wasn't just a little sick, her pale skin and shallow breathing convinced Tessa Mandy was a lot sick. The baby was cold, then hot, and then cold again. How had Tessa believed she could care for a six-month old child?

She'd called her friend, Annie, for advice. Not only did her friend have two little kids of her own, she ran the women's shelter and dealt with sick families all the time.

Bathe her in cool water, give her a children's Tylenol, and put her to bed, Annie had advised. If the baby wasn't better by morning, take her to the hospital.

Hospital? No way. Not if she could help it. Tessa hated that place. Only sick people went there. It was a stupid thought, but right now she wasn't in the mood for logic.

Fear had a hold on her and wouldn't let go—fear for Mandy, fear

Ralph might find her, fear that... hell, she didn't know what to call it. Just plain fear.

If only her mom hadn't run off with another man when Tessa was twelve, she might not be in this mess. How was a girl supposed to learn motherly things without a mother? Not from her dad. He was clueless. Still was when it came to giving advice about anything other than how to run a restaurant, he was great.

Tessa stepped outside to a miserably rainy night and sheltered Mandy from the elements the best she could. The dampness made the all ready cool air, colder.

She quickly scanned the parking lot as she approached her car, checking for any strange person waiting to attack. Tessa couldn't get the photo of Keri out of her mind. Had the dead woman's husband followed her from the Blue Moon before he murdered her a few miles away? Or was a homicidal maniac on the loose?

A woman couldn't be too careful, especially at night—alone—in a secluded parking lot that needed to be better lit. It didn't matter the lot was mostly full. A shiver snaked through her.

She unlocked her car door and immediately checked the backseat before strapping in Mandy. She'd seen too many movies where the villain hid in the back and attacked the woman from behind.

Tessa finally admitted it. Her nerves were shot and had been for days. Over the last three days, the number of hours of sleep she'd had was in the single digits, which meant her mind hadn't been able to function normally anymore.

Her restlessness had begun the moment the detective had asked her about Keri. Seeing Detective Rossi brought back bad memories—memories of Ralph. If only she hadn't caught her ex accepting a bribe, she might not be hiding in a town far away from Colorado.

Mandy sent out a wail, and Tessa looked down at the water stained seat. Dampness seeped through the back of her shirt and rain had splattered on the child. Dear Lord. How long had she been standing there getting soaked?

"Shh. Take it easy, sweetheart. Aunt Tess will get you home and take care of you."

She slipped in the driver's seat determined to focus only on her niece. After tapping her heels against the metal edge of the doorframe to remove the clumps of mud dangling from her soles, she swung her legs into position.

After shutting the door and locking it, she cranked the key. The engine turned over in protest, and when it threatened to die on her, Tessa pumped the gas pedal until the engine stopped chugging. Being in debt sucked.

As she pulled out of the lot, a car pulled in. For a second, the driver looked like Ralph, but then she decided it couldn't be. Her imagination was out of control.

Focus on the road and getting home and not on Ralph.

Gandy Boulevard had fairly heavy traffic for a Saturday night. Good. Lots of cars gave her a sense of security. Four lane roads didn't bother her; it was the two-lane, unlit streets that caused goose bumps to tickle her arms.

As she headed to her small rental house, she sensed someone was following her, yet when Tessa peered into the rear view mirror, all she saw were headlights. How did anyone distinguish one car from another at night?

Mandy fussed and Tessa pressed her foot to the accelerator.

Less than twenty minutes later, she pulled into her driveway. The dead end street appeared to be deserted. Neither of her neighbors' lights was on, disturbing her a little. Glenda, the busybody across the street, was always home. Maybe she'd finally gone to her daughter's in Michigan like she said she'd been meaning to do.

Tessa snatched Mandy from the back seat and hustled into her house then flicked on every light in the place. The only reason she'd rented the dump was because utilities were included in the rent. Wouldn't the slumlord have a big surprise this month when he saw the bill?

A clap of thunder came out of nowhere, jump-starting Tessa's heart, and Mandy began to cry.

A second later the lights went out.

CHAPTER FOUR

When the phone rang, Dom pulled the pillow over his head, refusing to answer it. It was six in the morning on a Sunday, for God's sake, his day off.

The phone continued to whine. "All right, already." He took a peek at the number. Yup. He'd guessed right. The station was calling. Hell, he was still working the Keri Wilkerson case and didn't need any more distractions. Sure they were perpetually short-handed, but did the Force have to dump yet another case on him?

Dom gave up any hope of sleep and answered with a less than civil tone. "What?"

"Hi, sleepy head. Phil, here. I thought you'd want to know. This morning, a paper boy spotted a wheelchair-bound man with his throat slit."

"Where?" He knew he couldn't say no if he was needed.

"Indian Rocks Beach."

He slumped back onto his mattress. "Good. It's out of our jurisdiction."

He'd been about to hang up when Phil continued. "I know, but Anderson heard the call on the scanner on his way into work this morning. Does the name Redman ring a bell?"

Dom shot up to a sitting position. "Any relation to—"

"Yeah, it's Tessa's dad. That's why I thought you might want to use your day off to check it out."

He scratched his stubbled cheek. "Are you thinking there's a relationship between this and the Wilkerson case?" Or had his partner guessed Tessa Redman intrigued him?

"I know it's a long shot, but both are related to the Blue Moon in some way."

"You might be right. Give me his address." Dom reached over to his side table, grabbed his pad and favorite Cross pen and took down the information. "I'll be in touch." He hung up.

Wow. Tessa's dad was dead. How horrible for her. His first instinct was to comfort her, but he quickly decided he wasn't any good with the living—only the dead. Tears and sadness were sledgehammers to the rock façade he'd carefully erected over his heart.

Dom slipped on a pair of jeans and his Save the Whales T-shirt he'd been given when he donated blood. Crime scenes tended to be messy.

Since he didn't want to waste time grinding beans and brewing a cup of java, a drive-thru would have to suffice.

After waiting in a short line, he scarfed down an egg and sausage croissant as he headed over to the Gulf side. Boy did the greasy fare taste good. Without thinking, he pinched his stomach to see if the fat he'd just eaten had caused any damage. Not yet, but it would soon if he didn't watch his eating habits.

As he drove across the water, the big, yellow sun sent colored streaks across the Bay. He'd forgotten the beauty of the drive, but he didn't have the luxury right now to soak in its serenity.

Once he crossed the bridge, Dom turned onto Indian Rock's road and found Dan Redman's place with ease. The entire Indian Rocks police force appeared to be there. He pulled in behind one of the cruisers and jumped out, and held out his badge as he approached.

He recognized one of the men. "Hiya, Jack."

"Rossi. What brings you to our side of the Bay?"

"Another one of my cases might be connected to yours."

Jack shouted over to one of the officers. "Hey, be careful with the window. Don't smudge the panes. We might get prints." He shook his head. "Rookies."

"I hear ya. Say, would you mind if I have a look around? The deceased's daughter is of interest to me." That came out lame, but he decided not to clarify.

Jack Watters checked his notes. "Tessa Redman?"

"Yeah, that's her."

"We haven't contacted her yet."

Well he wasn't volunteering. "I think she'll take this hard."

"So you don't think she's involved?"

"Not a chance."

"How does this case match up with yours?"

"Last week we found a woman murdered execution style in her car on Bayshore. She had Tessa's phone number scribbled on a Blue Moon match cover. That's where Tessa works."

"That's it?"

"Kind of weak, huh?"

"I'd say, but be my guest." Jack waved him to go in.

"Thanks."

Before Dom could enter, two men popped out of the front door with the body on a gurney. He didn't need to see her old man in the flesh. A cut throat was a cut throat. This, thankfully, was a totally different M.O. from Keri's murder. Still, he wasn't so naïve to think killers always murdered in the same fashion. Someone could have done both.

He stepped into Tessa's dad's house and noted the musty smell, and then let the chaos register. Books were strewn on the floor and pictures were smashed. It looked like someone wanted something specific and wasn't after valuables. The antique clock on the mantle would have brought a pretty penny, and yet it was untouched. Of course, the thief might not have seen the value in antiques. Dom's mom had loved them.

"What do you think?" Jack asked as he stepped behind him.

"Doesn't look like your typical robbery. I wonder what the guy was after."

"Beats me. I had the same gut reaction to the place. I'm hoping forensics can do its job." He grabbed Dom's shoulder. "I know it's our responsibility to tell Ms. Redman about her dad, but it would save us time if you could notify her. It'll probably be tomorrow before we have the time to stop by and ask her questions."

He'd ask Shelley Armwood. Not only was she an excellent officer, she had a good touch with people. "Sure."

Having done all he could, Dom headed back to Tampa. He was halfway across the bridge when his phone vibrated against his leg.

"Rossi."

"Dom, listen," his partner said. "We just received the tox screens back on Keri Wilkerson."

"'Bout time." Dom changed lanes and passed a motorcyclist who seemed more interested in sightseeing than making it across the bridge in a reasonable time.

"You know as well as I do that Tallahassee is backlogged."

"Yeah, yeah." Some things never changed.

"Get this," Phil rushed on. "She had a blood alcohol level of—are you ready?"

And if he weren't? "Hit me."

".12."

"Can we say a little drunk? I'm not surprised since she'd found her husband in bed with a guy. Anything else?"

"Her system had an acceptable level of anti-depressants. That's all. What did you find out about Tessa's dad's death?"

"Whoever did it made it look like a robbery, but I'm thinking it was murder. No respectable thief would think there was anything of value in the place. One stroke of luck—Jack Watters is lead on the case. I'll know the results as soon as he gets them."

Phil must have put his hand over the receiver because Dom could hear a muffled answer to someone else's question. "Sorry about that. Say, are you going to talk to Ms. Redman about her dad's death or leave it to Jack's people?"

"I'm going to volunteer Shelley to break it to her." Dom rolled down the window to breathe in the much-needed refreshing salt air. "She has the gentle touch. I thought it would save Jack's team some time."

"You're out of luck. Shelley's on vacation and has been for three days."

"Shit."

"I guess that means it's you. I don't envy you, partner."

"Thanks, Phil." Dom tossed his phone on the seat. Tessa wasn't going to like seeing him again.

***

Tessa had just finished feeding Mandy when someone knocked on her door, and every nerve tensed. No one came to her front door on a Sunday morning. Her nerves were already shot from losing power last night for an hour. Her mind had come up with all sorts of nasty scenarios until the utility company fixed whatever had been broken.

She placed the baby on her hip and lifted the kitchen curtain to check the driveway where a shiny red truck was parked on the street. Tessa leaned more to the left and identified Detective Rossi at her front door.

Oh God. How had be found out where she lived? Her heart pounded against her ribs. He knocked again. She debated not answering until Mandy let out a wail, no doubt clueing him into the fact she was home. Not only that, her car was sitting smack dab in the middle of the driveway.

"Coming," she called out. "It's okay, Mandy." Tessa gave the baby more formula, hoping to calm her.

When she pulled open the door, Detective Rossi was running a hand over his neatly trimmed hair, glancing off to the side. "Detective."

"Oh, Ms. Redman. I'm sorry to disturb you. May I come in?"

Could she say, no? "Of course."

"I really wish I didn't have to be the one to tell you, but I'm afraid someone broke into your father's house last night and—"

Reflexively, she grabbed his arm. "Is he okay?" Her pulse spiked.

"I'm afraid not. There's no gentle way to tell you. He's dead."

Her head swam, and then her knees buckled. Tessa would have crumpled to the ground had his strong arm not wrapped around her waist and caught her and the baby.

"I gotcha." He led them to the sofa and slowly lowered her to the seat.

Mandy fussed. Tessa's gaze dropped to her brother's beautiful, alive child. Her father was dead, and she choked out a sob. "How? When? I spoke with him yesterday and he was in fine spirits."

When Detective Rossi handed her a clean handkerchief, Tessa dabbed her eyes, but her vision remained blurred. The tears refused to stop.

"An intruder broke into his house. We're not sure of the sequence of events, but the paperboy spotted him this morning. His throat had been, ah, cut." He glanced downward.

She sucked in an audible breath, and her already rapid pulse escalated. She feared her heart might break in two. "Did he suffer?"

"No. The cut looked clean." His Adam's apple bobbed in his throat. "Can I get you something to drink?"

Wasn't she the hostess? At the moment, all she could think about was Dad in his wheelchair trying to defend his property. Why hadn't he given the criminal what he'd wanted?

"Yes, thank you. The kitchen's through there." She pointed to the archway.

Tessa tended to Mandy while the detective banged open a few kitchen cabinets, obviously looking for a glass. She was tempted to tell him he'd find it above the sink, but she needed the extra moment of solitude. Why would someone want to harm an old man in a wheelchair?

Putting on her psychologist's hat, she ran through the stages of grief as an exercise to gain control. Not that everyone went through these steps in the same order, but Tessa knew she had to shift her focus to the concrete or she'd lose her composure completely.

She'd zipped through the denial stage and went straight to anger. Mandy squirmed under her clenched fists. "Oh, sorry, hon."

Tessa studied the baby. Mandy had finished her bottle, and her coloring had improved since last night once her fever broke.

The detective returned a moment later and handed her a glass of ice water. "Thanks." Tessa held the glass tight, not wanting her shaky hand to lose its grip.

"I know this is a terrible blow to you," he began, "and I hate to impose, but the sooner we can begin working on the case, the sooner we can solve it. Was there anything of great value in the house an intruder might have wanted?"

Mentally, she searched each room but came up empty. After a moment of silence, it occurred to her something wasn't right. "My dad lives, or rather lived, in Indian Rocks Beach. Why would you be investigating a crime across the Bay?

He stuffed both hands in his pockets and spread his legs. "One of the men at my precinct heard the police call on the scanner. When the name Redman came up, he recognized the name and contacted me. He knew I was working on the Wilkerson case, and I guess he figured—"

"I see." She didn't really.

"Back to my original question. Why would someone want to rob your dad?"

She shook her head. "I don't know. There was little value in the house. I had to send him money monthly just to pay for his medication."

"Did your dad have any enemies?"

This question was more preposterous than the last. "No. Everyone loved my dad. He played cards with some friends a couple nights a week, but other than that, he kept to himself."

"Did he play last night?"

"Normally he played on Saturday night, but not last night. One of the men was out of town, and another was sick."

The detective walked to the front window and planted his hands on his hips, looking as if the answer lay outside.

As if a thunderbolt crashed to the earth, she knew who'd killed her father. "Ohmigod, it was Ralph."

Mandy started to cry, and Tessa's stomach threatened to revolt. Before she could stand up, Detective Rossi flew to her side and lifted Mandy from her arms. Tessa didn't even look at him as she raced into the bathroom and vomited.

Tessa had never been surer of anything in her life. Ralph had killed her father. He must have wanted to know where to find her. Her gut told her she'd be next.

The contents of her stomach came up repeatedly until there was nothing left of her breakfast. A soft knock sounded at the bathroom door a few moments later.

"Are you all right?" Detective Rossi's voice had softened almost to a whisper.

Something stirred in her. Other than Charley, she couldn't remember the last time someone had spoken to her in such a kind manner.

"Yes, I'll be out in a minute."

Now embarrassed, Tessa rinsed out her mouth and wiped a drop of food from her shirt. The mirror reflected a frightened-looking woman —one who could scare even the most secure child.

She hand-pressed her pants and stepped back into the living room. "I'm sorry," Tess said, not daring to look at him.

"Don't be."

She looked up at his comforting tone and caught his half smile. Somehow that one look helped repair the ache in her heart.

"I was nine when I lost both my parents," he said. "I understand endless grief." His voice trailed off as his gaze grabbed the floor.

She didn't think he'd meant to tell her but was glad he had. Tessa wanted to ask what had happened, and how he'd handled the crisis, but she forced herself to turn off her incessant need to heal others. She had to think of herself for a change.

Knowing Detective Rossi grew up without a family made him more human, and it had been hard for her to think well of the police after she'd been conned by her husband.

Detective Rossi placed Mandy over his shoulder and absently patted her back, looking as if he'd been a father many times.

The idea of him as a dad jolted her. Tessa blurted out, "Are you married?"

He jerked out of his daze. "No, why?"

Once again, heat raced up her face. "The way you hold Mandy, I thought you might have a child."

"Oh, that. One of my foster parents had a baby when I came to live with them. I was used to caring for her."

She couldn't imagine being in foster care. True, her dad had raised her after her mom stormed off, but at least she had one real parent.

This awkward conversation only had one residual benefit. It had made the horror of her father's death recede for a few moments.

"Do you mind taking a seat?" he asked.

She wanted to ask why, but she didn't have the energy to argue. "Sure. I don't think my legs can take standing much longer anyway." She slipped down to the sofa's edge and laced her hands together. As if clairvoyant, Tessa knew his next question.

"Who's Ralph?" he asked.

She was right. Tessa closed her eyes for a moment and took a deep breath. "My ex-husband."

"And why do you think he killed your dad?"

"Because he was trying to find me."

Detective Rossi parked himself at the end of the sofa, as if being in her proximity made him uneasy. "Why would he kill someone for an address? Couldn't he look you up in the phone book?"

"For starters, my number's unlisted for that very reason. No number, no address. As to why he would kill my dad, it's simple. He wants me dead. Very badly."

Tessa was surprised when she received no reaction to her bomb-shell announcement.

"And yet you married him." His statement held no judgment.

She'd questioned her unfortunate choice many times. "Yes. He used to be a Vice cop, so I trusted him."

This time, Rossi's eyes did flash with surprise. Mandy wriggled in his arms, but he kept his gaze tightly on Tessa. "Want to tell me about it?"

No. "What good would it do if I did?"

She could tell he wanted to shrug, but instead he answered. "It might help me find the guy. Maybe we can tie him to your father's death and put him away for life."

If only. "Fine. His name is Ralph Ferino. He worked in Denver for five years."

Detective Rossi's brows shot up. "Go on."

"We married when I was in graduate school. I thought it was love at first sight. Ralph was supportive of me getting my PhD in psychology, but school took a lot of my time—a whole lot. I guess it's partly my fault he spent more and more time with his friends. About a year into our marriage he began to gamble. Living on one salary was more than he could handle."

"I know quite a few of the men in the precinct who gamble, but they're not killers. I went once to the Indian Reservation and played a little roulette, and I'm no murderer."

She shook her head. "It's not the same thing. It wasn't really the gambling that turned him into a killer. He lost a lot of money in a short period of time. To make up for his losses, he started taking bribes."

The detective returned to his stoic posture, showing no outward reaction other than to clench his fist on Mandy's back. "How did you find out about the bribes?"

"I happened to pick up the extension in the bedroom one night and overheard a conversation." She held up a hand. "I know. Who has a land line anymore? Anyway, I've regretted that move every day since. I waited for Ralph to tell me about his problem, but he never did. In the end I called the precinct and reported him."

"I see."

Tessa expected to see hate in his eyes, but instead she saw a man who was trying to understand, and she wasn't quite sure how to handle his reaction. The other cops' wives told her she was lower than scum to turn on her husband. Ralph was a decent man, they'd claimed.

They had no idea.

"I don't think you could understand what it was like watching a good man turn bad," Tessa said, encouraged by his willingness not to judge. "My husband conveniently lost evidence, evidence that would have put a rapist behind bars for a long time. My sister had been raped thirteen years ago, and it tore our family apart."

"Is she better now?"

Had his gray eyes not held a pained expression, she wouldn't have answered. "Better, yes. Over it, never. Actually, she left home after the incident and never contacted us again. It hurts sometimes to think of her alone and without a family."

"Did Ferino's case ever go to trial?"

"Yes. He was found guilty and sentenced to three years. Ralph believes I'm solely to blame for his situation."

"When was the last time you saw him?"

Tessa didn't have to search her mind for long. "That would be four years ago, on September 19th at 2:30 p.m."

"That memorable, huh?"

"Yeah, that memorable." The sparkle in his eyes helped erase a bit of the hate that lay in her belly. Hate not only for Ralph and everything he stood for, but hate for herself for being such a sucker for the charming man. Every synapse in her brain bought his I-believe-in-justice speech. She'd been such a fool.

Detective Rossi handed her back a quieted Mandy and withdrew a pad from his pocket, and then carefully wrote down the information. They sat in silence until he seemed satisfied with his notes.

"One more question," he said, pen poised to add the rest of her story. "Did your ex ever send you any threatening letters from prison? Anything that would indicate he planned to harm you?"

Ah, the rub. "He sent letters, but I burned everything he wrote without opening a one."

The detective made a note of her comment in neat handwriting. "Do you know when Mr. Ferino was released from prison?"

"Three weeks ago yesterday."

More jotting. "If your ex-husband was responsible for your father's death, why do you think he waited three weeks before coming down the Florida?"

"Who says he waited?" A chill ran down her spine thinking the man might have been in town all this time.

"You have a point." The detective stood, the interview obviously over. "Again, I'm sorry for your loss." Dominic Rossi sounded sincere. "Would you like me to call someone to stay with you? It's standard policy."

"Thank you, but I'll be fine."

As he headed for the door, Tessa realized she didn't want to be alone but talking to some policewoman wouldn't help either. The problem was she could hardly ask him to stay. She was a big girl and could take care of herself and hadn't taken lessons in shooting a gun for nothing. Of course, she didn't own a weapon, so maybe her I-can-handle-anything plan wasn't foolproof.

With his hand on the knob, the detective turned back to her. "You might want to install an alarm system."

"It's a rental unit. I don't think the landlord would approve."

"Then maybe you could ask someone to stay with you—or you could stay with a friend or relative until we resolve your dad's case."

"I'll think about it."

Besides Annie, she'd not made many friends since moving to Tampa. Annie had her hands full already, what with a husband, two kids of her own, and countless number of women she was trying to help at the local women's shelter.

"You can always call me." He printed his cell number on the back of his card and handed it to her.

When Detective Rossi closed the door, Tess felt more alone than ever before. She stood there facing the door trying to get a grip on what he'd told her. Between her mother splitting years ago, a now dead father, and a half-brother about to die if he didn't find a liver, the isolation nearly squeezed the life from her.

As she headed into the kitchen for another drink, she stopped short. Oh, no. She'd have to break the news to Judd. He would be devastated too since he and Dad were so close. Poor Judd. It was bad enough he'd lost his mom when he was only five, but to find out someone murdered his father might cause his shaky health to take a dive. If it turned out Ralph had been the killer, she might never be able to face her half-brother again.

***

Dumb cop. The guy had left Dan's place and driven directly to Tessa's home. How sweet was that? No doubt the cop had gone there to tell her of her father's death. Ralph was sure she was in her small hovel bawling her eyes out over her loss. He loved it.

Ralph wanted to confront her, right here, right now, but even he realized the timing sucked. The police might send in a support group, and he couldn't chance running into them.

There was no doubt in his mind she'd figure out who offed her dad. And the best part? She couldn't do a damned thing about it. Nope. He'd covered all his bases. He'd even thought to burn his sneakers so the police wouldn't arrest him for having shoes that matched any prints left in the house. And his car tires—the ones that surely had made an imprint in the soft sand? Not a problem. He'd swapped them out with similar tires on another car. The owner would never catch the difference. Given he'd tossed his knife in the Gulf, the murder weapon would forever remain a mystery.

The cover-up move he was most proud of though was changing hands when he sliced Dan's throat. Naturally left-handed, he'd switched to his right when he did the deed.

Ralph let out a laugh, jumped in his car, and raced back to the motel for a quick snooze. For some reason, an immediate resolution didn't matter anymore. He wanted to savor his time when he tortured his prim and proper Tess.

CHAPTER FIVE

Dear Audrey Mae,

I'm getting closer to the quota I promised you. Only two more to go before the month is over. The guy I did in tonight deserved to die. Not only did he drink too much, he bothered people I care about. And you know how I feel about abuse. I couldn't let him die like the rest. No, a bullet to the head was too good for this guy. But don't you worry about me, I was real careful. The only thing I feel bad about was that his kids might find him all cut up and bleeding. But such is life, or should I say death.

I wanted to leave a note so his family would know why I had to kill him, but then I figured the police might trace the paper or something. You know how good they are these days with all that forensic stuff. Damn CSI.

Soon, my sweet, I'll be reunited with you and Bobby in heaven.

Sincerely,

Morton Richter

***

Dom sat as his desk, strumming his fingers against his Formica desk, waiting for the Denver police to fax him a picture of Ralph Ferino. Everything Tessa told him about her ex-husband had panned out. The guy was a scum, a turncoat, and a loser—at least according to Ferino's commanding officer. How had Tessa ever married the guy? She must have been heartbroken when she learned what a jerk the guy was. It had to be tough to be a wannabe psychologist.

According to Ferino's superior, Tessa's husband had taken bribes all right, but the Denver squad had only been able to nail him for one involving a rapist. How could the man live with himself aiding someone like that?

The shrill ring of his phone set his already frayed nerves further on edge. "Rossi."

"Jack Watters, here. Thought you'd like to know, we dusted for fingerprints at the Redman residence, but the place was pretty clean. The killer must have used gloves."

Damn. "Anything else? Tire tracks, shoe prints, trace evidence?" His muscles tensed.

"Nada. Your average Joe parks along the street for beach access, so taking casts of them won't help. I wanted to check to see if you'd spoken with his daughter."

Dom swiveled his chair away from the precinct office window since the shifting sun was streaming right into his eyes.

"I did. She took it hard too. She's convinced it was her ex-husband who did the deed. Claims he's out to get her, but since the ex doesn't know where she lives, Ms. Redman believes he might have been trying to squeeze the information out of her dad."

"Does she have any evidence to this fact?"

"No, but get this. Her ex got out of prison three weeks ago. I'm waiting for a fax of the guy's photo right now. And the worst of it? He was a dirty vice cop from Denver. Tessa Redman was the one who turned him in."

Jack whistled. "Send the stuff over when you receive it."

"Will do. Let's keep each other in the loop."

"You got it."

He'd hoped Watters and his men would have come up with something. If and when they do, it would be sweet if it pointed the finger away from Tessa's ex. She didn't need the anxiety of believing he was around and possibly out to harm her.

The lost, frightened, and tormented look on her face when he'd told her about her dad still haunted him. Usually he focused his efforts on the facts of the case and worked hard to ignore the people. Their grief was too much to handle on a daily basis, but with Tessa, he had the urge to protect.

If Ralph Ferino was after her, as an officer of the law, Dom needed to watch her back.

"This yours?" Captain John Leffers stood next to his desk with a fax in his hands.

Dominic pulled himself back to the job. He spotted the name Ralph Ferino at the top. "Definitely. It could be the killer in a murder over in Indian Rocks."

Leffers snickered. "What, don't we give you enough work to do?"

"Actually I thought the guy might be related to the Wilkerson case, but I can't find the thread to connect them."

"Good luck. When you have time, you might want to look at this. It came in an hour ago. Bill Murtz is lead on this one. You and Phil will be assisting." He tossed a folder on Dom's desk.

"It's my day off," Dom complained to his boss's retreating back. No surprise, the boss didn't respond.

Dominic picked up the fax and studied Ralph Ferino's photo. Tessa's ex was a good-looking guy in a surly sort of way. Dark hair, tanned skin, a rugged jaw line, and brows that shaded his eyes. He could see why Tessa might be attracted to him.

An odd sensation he refused to acknowledge stirred in his gut. It couldn't be jealousy since he hardly knew the woman.

Dominic shoved back his chair and marched over to the fax machine. Should Ferino be the intruder/murderer in the Redman case, Watters should have a picture of him. Killers often visited the site a second time to revel in their handiwork. Rossi wanted the Indian Rocks force to keep an eye out for the guy, and stop him before he did anything else dangerous, assuming he murdered Tessa's dad.

After he faxed over the photo to Jack Watters, Dom picked up the case file the Captain had dropped without fanfare on his desk. He flipped opened the cover and a familiar face stared up at him. Bob Dirkman's face to be exact. "Holy shit."

"What's that?" Phil asked.

Dom looked up. "Shouldn't you be playing golf or something?" The two partners kept the same workdays.

"I switched with Flynn," he said, leaning over the desk to look at the file. "It's his mom's birthday today. Remember I called you this morning? I was here."

"Yeah." Dom thought it sweet the kid cared about his mother. If Dom had a mom, he'd celebrate her birthday too.

"It's the guy from Tessa's bar. He was harassing her last night, and now he's dead. Something's going on with the bar I don't like."

"I'd say. You gonna tell Ms. Redman?"

"Not right now. She has enough to deal with. Besides, what's she going to do besides worry?"

Phil leaned a hip on his desk and crossed his arms in his proverbial commando pose. "You know, if people learn that whoever visit the Blue Moon end up dead, her business is toast."

"You got that right. We can't let the press get wind of the connection. Come on. We're on."

"We're covering this case?" Dom asked.

"You guessed it."

The ride to Dirkman's house didn't take long, especially since the traffic was light on a Sunday afternoon.

The medical examiner's mobile unit and two squad cars sat in the driveway, so Dom parked on the side to give the ME an escape route. As soon as they stepped over the yellow crime scene tape and entered the house, Bill Murtz exited a back room. "Thank God, you are here. I'm going crazy keeping all the neighbors out of the house. Don't people understand what the yellow crime tape means? I never thought I'd ever clear the place, what with trying to get his three kids to safety."

How horrible. "What do you know so far?" Dom asked.

"The ME and CSU team are in the room now. It looks like another execution style killing. The vic's throat was slashed. That's it."

Could it be the same MO as the Redman case? "Was anything taken?"

"Not that I could tell. The back door was jimmied open, so we might find some footprints on the way into the bedroom. If we're lucky, we'll be able to lift a latent print somewhere. The team is dusting now. Go ahead and look before they take the body away."

Dom and Phil donned sanitary footgear, pulled on rubber gloves, and then followed Bill into what he guessed was the master bedroom, which wasn't much bigger than his small den.

"Hey, Chris," Dominic said to the coroner. The doc was dressed in white scrubs, head-to-toe. "This is getting to be a habit." They'd worked the Wilkerson case together.

"Ain't that the truth?"

"You know time of death?"

"From the rigor, I'd say 2 a.m. last night."

Dom turned back to Murtz. "Was Mrs. Dirkman here?"

"No. She was staying at her sister's place. The sister vouched for her. The three kids were upstairs, nestled tight in their beds when their dad was hit."

"Who found the body?" Phil asked.

"The eldest daughter, Jenny. She's twelve."

"Mother, Mary and Joseph," Phil burst out.

The air squeezed out of Dominic's lungs. He visualized his parents in their bloody bedroom and visibly shivered. "Who's with them now?"

"Mrs. Dirkman. She came right over when we called."

"Was she upset?" Dom asked, realizing if they were estranged, the wife might not show much emotion.

"I'd say. Her grief looked genuine. If you've seen enough, how about canvassing the neighbors to ask if they heard anything last night?"

"Sure. We'll get right on it." Dom turned to Phil. "Ready?"

"As ever."

***

Tessa couldn't take the silence anymore. Mandy was asleep, and the television held no interest. She jumped at every noise, even though she knew full well the wind and rain were rattling her windows and not some criminal trying to break in. All Tessa could think of was how terrified her father he must have been when Ralph showed up—or whoever had taken his life.

Tessa called Annie, needing to talk to someone. Dang, she didn't answer. "Annie, it's Tessa," she said, leaving a message. "My father, he, uh, was murdered yesterday. Don't worry. I'm fine. I just need to talk to you."

She hung up and debated calling Judd, but after looking at the clock, she figured he might be asleep. Who did that leave? Crap. No one. She'd been too busy studying for her PhD to connect with more people. Something was wrong when a psychologist shut herself off from those she was trying to help most.

Going to the bar was out of the question. Ralph might guess she'd be there. Of course, he would have no way of knowing Sunday was her day off. Lucky for her, the bar was closed Monday. By Tuesday she'd have to face the crowds and chance running into him since she couldn't hide forever.

Aw, hell. Maybe Ralph wasn't in Florida after all, and she was only imagining he was out to get her. It wouldn't be the first time stress put strange thoughts in her head.

She snapped her fingers. She could call Marli, the one friend she had in Denver. Marli's husband had worked with Ralph and had supported Tessa's decision to turn him in. He might know of Ralph's whereabouts.

Tess dialed and waited.

"Hello?"

"Marli? It's Tess Redman."

"Ohmigod, Tess, it's so good to hear your voice. I thought you'd dropped off the face of the earth. How are you?"

"Okay, I guess. I wanted to let you know my dad was murdered last night." The silence on the other end hung in the air like poison gas. "Marli, you still there?"

"Yes, yes. I'm in shock, that's all. I never met your dad, but I know how close you two were. I'm sorry."

"Thank you." Somehow relating the horror of his death lessened her loneliness.

"Do the police know who did it?"

"Not yet, but I have a hunch it might have been Ralph."

"Ralph? As in ex-husband, Ralph?"

"Yes."

"Geez, Tess, you think it could really be him? Sure, he might have taken a few bribes, but do you think he's capable of murder? That's a pretty big step. Remember, the guy was a cop who had decent principles at one time."

"I realize that, but don't you remember the way he acted at the trial?"

Her friend took a moment before answering. "I have to admit he did seem a little pissed at you."

"You think? When the bailiff dragged his sorry ass out of the court room, he mouthed something to me."

"What?"

"'I'll kill you for this, bitch.'"

"Ohmigod. But Tess, we all say things we don't mean when we're being punished."

"Maybe. Do you have any idea if he's anywhere near Denver?"

"I really couldn't say, hon. Ethan told me he'd been released, and to be honest, I never asked about him."

"But can't you see the man's a menace?"

"I know, I know, but murder?"

"Yes, murder. He had issues you didn't know about and ones I only found out about after I married him. I wanted to warn you. He might hassle your family in order to find out where I am. I never thought of the ramifications of my actions to anyone else."

"Nonsense. You had to turn him in, but don't worry about us. We can take care of ourselves. Ethan's a cop, remember."

"I know, but still." Tess needed her question answered. Now. "Do you think you could ask Ethan if he knows where Ralph might be?"

"Of course, I will. Hold on."

Marli's muffled voice came through the line. Intermittent words filtered through. "I'm back. Ethan said he hadn't heard anyone mention his whereabouts, but that doesn't mean Ralph's left town or that he's coming after you. Ethan said he'd try to find out something and get back to you."

"Tell Ethan, thanks."

"Hey, just promise to keep in touch. This once every three years thing doesn't work for me."

At that, Tessa had to chuckle. "I agree. I promise to stay in touch."

After the call, Tessa felt a connection that had been missing in the last few years. She missed Marli and the old life—the life before Ralph ruined it.

A strong knock sounded at her door, and Tessa's heart dropped to her stomach.

Before she could ask who it was, the person called, "Tess, it's me."

She jumped up and threw open the door, her heart beating a tad too fast. The rain slanted in, carrying with it cold air that smelled refreshingly good.

Normally not a demonstrative person, Tessa couldn't help but throw her arms around her friend. "Come in, come in."

Annie hugged back. "Oh, Tess. I came as soon as I heard. I'm so sorry about your dad."

Tessa motioned Annie over to the sofa. "I'm still in shock," she confessed. "If Dad had died of natural causes, I'd be upset, sure, but it's the way he died that keeps tormenting me."

"Oh, you poor thing." Her friend wrapped an arm around her shoulder.

Next to the tall, statuesque Annie, Tessa felt small.

"You shouldn't have come," Tess said. "Not in this weather. I can't believe Tony didn't throw a fit." Annie's husband was terribly possessive and rightfully so since always Annie threw caution to the wind when it came to helping people.

"I had to come. You're my friend, and don't worry, Tony understands, but I promised him I'd only stay a little while."

"Tell him thank you. You don't know how much I appreciate it."

Annie grabbed Tessa's hand and drew her down to the sofa. "Tell me what happened."

"All I know is that someone broke into Daddy's house. This morning, a paper boy happened to look in the front window and spotted him with his throat cut." Tessa couldn't control her right hand from grabbing her own throat and massaging her neck. "The police think the attack was motivated by robbery."

Annie squeezed Tessa's left hand. "How utterly terrible for you. Do they have any clue who it might be?" Her voice helped soothe part of Tessa's anxiety.

"None. But Annie, I think it was Ralph."

Besides the people in Denver and her family, only Annie knew of her ugly past. "Your ex?"

"Yes. He's been out of jail for three weeks. Maybe he thought Dad would tell him where I lived." Someone had to believe her.

"I thought Ralph was in Colorado."

"Was, being the operative word. I know Ralph. He'd go to any length to get back at me for stealing his life. You didn't see his eyes at the trial. I've never seen such hate before."

"Oh, Tessa. If that's true, you've got to leave town."

"Leave? You know I can't do that. Who would run the bar?"

"Don't you have a manager you can trust?"

Tess ran her fingers through her tangled hair that desperately needed cutting. She hadn't had time for something as luxurious as a haircut.

"No. I'm the manager. If Judd thought someone else could run the Blue Moon, he would have put him or her in charge."

"Then shut down the restaurant for God's sake. Your life's worth more than money."

"I can't. Judd's medical bills are huge. We need the income."

Annie shook her head and blew out a loud breath. "I'm sorry Judd is ill, but speaking of him, how is he taking your father's death?"

"I visited him this afternoon. I had expected him to break down when I told him about Dad, but he didn't cry or anything. He just stared at me like I was making it up."

Annie rubbed Tessa's hands. "Don't judge him. People grieve in many different ways. Sometimes it takes days, weeks, even months for grief to show."

"As a psychologist I know that, but emotionally I guess I wanted someone who could sympathize with what I was going through."

"I'd feel the same way if anything happened to Tony or the girls."

Annie leaned back on the sofa. "Didn't you tell me some liver patients have memory issues when the waste products back up in their system?"

"Yes, but he was lucid today."

Annie grabbed her hand. "It must be terrible seeing Judd like this."

Maybe it was Tessa's imagination, but the circles under her friend's eyes appeared darker, and there seemed to be more lines around her mouth. Tessa wanted to cry for her.

"It is. I have to be strong for Mandy's sake. I can't run away and pretend nothing happened."

"Maybe you should get a roommate," Annie offered.

Tess had been alone for so long, she wasn't sure she could share her space with anyone. Logically, it made sense, but emotionally, she wasn't ready.

"Detective Rossi suggested the same thing. The idea holds some appeal, but I haven't exactly taken the time to make a lot of friends. You're it, kiddo."

Annie's lips turned up at the corners, reminding Tessa of the Mona Lisa. "How about Chelsea?"

Tessa shook her head. "I'm not sure about that. She's kind of wild. And she's just a kid."

"Chelsea is twenty-three, just six years younger than you. I'd hardly call her a kid. And she's street smart. You should think about it. Besides, wouldn't you feel safer with someone in the house? If Ralph did come by, I bet he'd think twice about trying something."

"This is only a two bedroom. One for Mandy, one for me."

"Maybe you and Mandy could share a room."

"That's not a bad idea, but I doubt Chelsea would want to move again. Didn't you tell me she moved out of the shelter right before getting the job at the Blue Moon?"

"Yes, but I know her. She'd love it if you asked. The worst she can say is no."

When a sharp crack of thunder dimmed the lamp next to the sofa, Tessa jumped.

"Hon, I better get back before Tony has a fit. Think about what I said. Remember, you can always come to the shelter if things get bad."

Annie's sincere offer gave her comfort. "Thanks, Annie. You're the best."

Once Annie left, Tess sat in the dimly lit room thinking about her life. She had to make some kind of decision about whether to keep the restaurant open or close it, before she went crazy. If she wasn't already.

* * *

This weather sucked. Ralph didn't know why he wanted to watch Tessa's house. He'd been about to confront her when some tall bitch stopped by. As he waited for the visitor to leave, he had the idea that the best way to punish Tessa would be to drive her crazy a little bit at a time. Scare her to death, and make her think he was going to kill her at any moment. Eventually, he'd have to, but for now, he'd work on ways to bring her to her knees. Literally.

CHAPTER SIX

Being at work two days after she'd learned of her father's death was harder than Tessa had ever imagined. She'd tried to be cheerful in front of the customers, but near closing time, she had to force herself not to break down when someone offered her his condolences.

Everywhere she looked, she saw her dad's little touches—the bar mirror he'd spent a week searching for, the big wooden sailboat hanging from the ceiling that took three men to put up, the crab traps he'd won in a poker game. Each decoration had a story, and remembering those stories tore her soul apart.

The lack of sleep and a half eaten meal didn't help her fragile state of mind either. She should have taken the time to eat better, but eating would have meant she'd have to stop working—and stopping meant she'd have time to dwell on how and why her dad had died, and whether Ralph had been responsible for her father's death.

Anger at her dad's untimely death bubbled up inside threatening to put a hole in her gut. It was easy to preach forgiveness to help a person move past her sorrows, but actually doing it was hell, if not impossible.

On top of everything, she had to deal with those two developers earlier this evening. She was still pissed they didn't understand the word, no. Of course, she could use the money. Who couldn't? She had mega school loans and Judd's transplant costs to consider, but her family's happiness took precedence over everything else in her life. Judd had told her he wouldn't sell under any circumstance, and she wanted to abide by his wishes.

Then Chelsea had told her the detective had stopped by before Tess had come in to work. He warned the workers to be careful. Bob Dirkman was dead. How terrible was that? Not that she liked the drunk, but no one deserved to die in his own house, asleep in bed. His poor kids were the ones who would suffer a lifetime because of his absence.

At first she was put off Detective Rossi hadn't told her personally, but she reasoned he might not have wanted to dump two pieces of bad news on her. His caring helped heal her.

Then a slow, chilling fear started at the base of her spine and crept up her back threatening to paralyze her. Keri Wilkerson had visited the Blue Moon, Bob Dirkman was a regular at the Blue Moon, and her dad had built the Blue Moon. All three had died within days of each other. There had to be a connection. Ralph wouldn't have any reason to harm Keri or Bob Dirkman. So who did?

"You wanted to see us?" Charley asked.

Tessa jumped at the intrusion. It took a moment for her to realize what her bartender had asked. "Yes."

Dear Charley. He'd insisted on coming to work on his day off so Tessa could leave if she needed to. She was lucky to have him.

"Gather around, everyone," Charley boomed. "Tessa needs to talk to us."

Her support staff slowly moved surrounded her—Mick and Roger from the kitchen, Chelsea, Krystal, and Barb from the floor. There was no sign of the two bus boys, but she figured they were still loading up the dishwasher.

Tessa drew in a deep breath to gather the needed courage to get through the next few minutes.

"I wanted to thank all of you for your kindness during my time of need. I really appreciate you all for pitching in."

Mick stepped forward and placed a hand on her arm. "Just ask. We're here for you."

Tessa knew what a lucky person she was to have such a devoted staff. At first, she'd questioned her decision to hire the ex-con, but he'd worked out fine. No, more than fine. His work ethic was impeccable, which meant a person could improve his life after being in prison.

She pulled a torn picture from her pocket. She thought she'd thrown away of every photo of Ralph, but this one had been stuck in a book.

"This isn't a very good likeness, but I have reason to suspect this man murdered my father."

Mumblings echoed in the near empty bar, as she passed around the picture. "Let me explain." As hard as it was to discuss her failed marriage, in a way, it brought closure. "So if any of you see this man hanging out around here, would you let me know?"

Mellow Roger stepped forward. "If you're sure he's the one, I can arrange for some of my buddies to keep watch in the parking lot," he announced in a slow, metered tone.

How sweet. "No, Roger, that's all right. I don't want us to take any action against him. The police can handle it."

"If he hurts you," Charley said in a deep, threatening tone, "you promise to let me know."

"I will, but I'm not asking any of you to play hero. That's what the police are for." Suddenly self-conscious with everyone staring, she waved them away. "Let's clean up and get out of here."

As the staff scattered, a sense of safety blanketed the place. At least when Tess was at the restaurant, she'd be safe from Ralph.

***

Dom didn't know why he was parked down the street from Tessa's house at three in the morning. He should be asleep in his big, comfortable bed. His captain sure as hell hadn't ordered the surveillance, and his body had protested every time he tried to get comfortable in the front seat, but his gut told him it was his duty to keep her safe.

Tessa's big blue eyes kept appearing in his mind every time he closed his. He could tell she fought to stay strong, not wanting her dad's death to cripple her, but behind her mask, Dom had seen fear.

Although he had no proof Ralph Ferino murdered her dad or was even in Florida, Dom believed Tessa when she told him her ex wanted to do her harm.

Her kitchen light blinked on, and he straightened. Three a.m. All he could think of was that Mandy was demanding some food. Dom wanted to assure her she'd be safe, and to let her know he, not Ralph, was outside watching to make sure her ex didn't come for a visit, but given how skittish she was, if he knocked, she'd freak.

It pissed him off he'd been unable to trace Ferino's whereabouts once the felon was discharged from prison. It was as if the guy disappeared completely. Most likely he bought a fake I.D. and used cash to prevent the police from tracing his location.

Cops understood the law, and criminals prided themselves in outsmarting cops. The two together were a lethal combination.

Dom had other cases to work besides the Wilkerson case and Bob Dirkman's murder. Not getting a good night's sleep wouldn't help him keep sharp, but he couldn't let this killer get near Tess. If he spent every night here then so be it.

Dom rolled down his window to listen for any oncoming cars. Once her light flicked off, he stretched out in the cab the best he could and prayed the boogieman would stay away until he could find a way to nail him.

**

Dom leaned back in his office chair and suppressed a yawn. "Did Mr. Wilkerson's lover give you anything?" he asked his partner.

"Not much. After Taylor Wilkerson's wife came home a day early from her business trip and found them in bed, the mood evaporated."

"I can imagine." Dom took a sip of his tepid coffee. "This stuff tastes like shit. Who made it?"

"Cantori, who else?"

"No kidding. Did this lover boy produce an alibi for the time after the wife stormed off?"

"The usual. He went home and watched television. Alone. No

witnesses." Phil held up a hand. "And before you ask, I did ask around. The old lady next door said she saw lights on at his place."

"Good job."

Dom's phone rang. "Rossi." Phil picked up the Wilkerson folder.

"Hey, hey. Long time no see."

"Trace? That you, buddy?" The call brought a smile to his lips. When Trace had first joined the force in Tampa, Dom thought he would be the younger brother he never had—until Trace screwed up, that is.

"Sure is. I won't keep you as I know you're knee deep in cases, but I'm coming to town for a week and was wondering if I could crash at your place?"

Dom's guilt surfaced. "Sure man. Did Emma kick you out?"

"As a matter of fact, she did."

He'd only been kidding. "Sorry, to hear it."

"We'll talk when I get there, but I'm hoping I might convince the Captain to give me my old job back."

"You're kidding, right?"

"Nope. I know I screwed up before, but Emma made a new man out of me. I'm not a stupid thirty year old anymore."

That might be true. "I'll let the Captain know the prodigal son has returned."

"See you in about three hours. Key in the same hidden spot?"

The guy was always pushing the envelope, so maybe he hadn't changed. "Sure, but it takes close to eight hours to get here from Atlanta."

"I know. I had a head start. I'm past Jacksonville as we speak."

"How did you know I'd be around?"

Trace laughed, and the sound conjured up some good times and some times he'd rather forget.

"You're always home."

True. "See you when I get off work."

"Can't wait, man."

Dom hung up, and Phil cocked a brow. "Who was that?"

"Your predecessor."

"That guy? I thought he got booted out of here for pulling some crazy stunt."

"He was. Trace didn't fight the accusation though, because his fiancé wanted to live near her parents in Atlanta. Now she's told him to take a hike, and he wants to return here."

"As your partner?"

Dom held up a hand. "No way. The guy is loads of fun, is amazing at gatherings, and incredible at analyzing trace evidence—hence the nickname—but as a partner, he was challenging. No. I'm afraid you're stuck with me."

Phil smiled. "Good."

"Now, let's get back to work. I'm guessing you have your finger on the Dirkman case?"

"Have I ever let you down?"

Though Phil said it in jest, Dom could tell his question was serious. "Never."

His partner jumped off Dom's desk and headed to his own.

***

When Dom pulled into his driveway, a souped up Chevy Avalanche sat in his drive. Trace sure went all out in the vehicle department. Hopefully, it was a present from Emma. By now, she must have finished her internship and was probably raking in the dough at one of the local hospitals. If she had bought it for him, Dom was surprised she hadn't asked for the truck back.

His front door popped open and Trace strode out, beer in hand, and a grin wider than Tampa Bay. "Howdy, partner."

Despite some of their differences, Dom was glad to see his old friend. They shook hands, and then Trace pulled him into a short bear hug. He guessed his former partner had forgiven him.

Dom stepped back. "You're looking well rested. A little pale from lack of sun, but otherwise fit."

"Atlanta's been good to me, but it's time to move on. Say, I'm starving. Want to grab something to eat and catch up on old times?"

"I know just the place."

After Dom cleaned up, he and Trace headed to the Blue Moon.

"This place looks like a dump," Trace said, as they pulled into the dirt parking lot.

"Not on the inside. I think you'll like it. The manager is part of a case I'm working on." Dom filled in Trace as they headed to the entrance.

"I hope the food's good."

"I can vouch for one or two menu items."

Dom flicked a glance at the bar as they entered and caught sight of Tessa, her elbows resting on the counter, talking to a man. His stomach churned. Dom chalked it up to hunger and not to anything akin to attraction.

"Two for dinner?" the too thin hostess asked. She was the same one who'd been there the last time Dom had come.

"Sure."

"Table or booth?"

So many questions. Dom nodded to Trace to let him decide.

"Booth," his friend answered.

Once they were seated, Chelsea rushed over. She looked at Dom, smiled, and then shot a glance over at Trace. Her eyes widened in obvious appreciation.

She turned back to Dom. "Detective, you didn't tell me you had such a handsome friend."

Dom swallowed a smile as Trace's eyes widened. "This is Hamilton Lowell, but he goes by, Trace. Trace, Chelsea."

She brushed a wisp of blonde hair out of her face. "Nice to meet you. I'm free Monday, Tuesday, and Friday if you're going to be around."

Now it was Dom's turn to be surprised at her brash overture. Usually, he took the initiative to ask women out. Maybe times had changed since Lisa had died.

"Well, Chelsea," Trace said. "I may have to take you up on that, but I'm only staying for a week right now. I hope to move here though."

She giggled. "I'll be here. Now can I get you fellows something to drink?"

Trace ordered a beer and Dom a Coke.

Trace leaned back in the booth and stretched his arms along the wooden back. "Wow. I'm likin' this place. I hadn't planned to score this trip, but it looks like I might get lucky."

"I see you haven't changed since you left."

Trace threw him an exaggerated frown. "Ouch, good buddy. Maybe you ought to try it. Might lighten you up. How long has it been since you've had any?"

Dom debated lying, but he was too tired to make the effort. "Not for a while."

Trace raised a brow. "Now why am I not surprised? I understand you had to go through a time of mourning after Lisa died, but you have to move on. It's been over three years."

"I have moved on." Discussing his love life, what there was of it, wasn't on his list of must dos.

"Excuse me, Mr. Rossi."

Dom looked up. Eleanor and Madge hovered over them. He couldn't believe he hadn't seen them sneak up nor smelled Eleanor's overpowering, flowery perfume, until now.

"Ladies, how nice to see you, again." He meant it. They took the focus off his life.

Eleanor leaned forward. "When we spoke the other day, you seemed like you were interested in what goes on at the bar. And if you're back, I'm guessing you took notice of our Tessa."

He didn't know how to answer her, so he kept quiet.

"Well, I thought you would want to know what we overheard last night," Eleanor continued. The proverbial image of a cat with yellow feathers sticking out of its mouth came to mind.

Trace couldn't keep the smirk off his face. "Ladies, why don't you join Mr. Rossi and me?"

Dom was grateful for any insight the ladies could provide, but a little annoyed Trace hadn't asked him first. But, that was Trace.

Both Dom and Trace scooted over to give the ladies some room. Madge sat next to Dom, and her powdery scent made his sinuses revolt. He sneezed. "Excuse me."

"You're excused. Eleanor, you go first, and then I'll fill in," Madge said.

"Okay. Well, last night two gentlemen came to the Blue Moon. They wore beautifully tailored suits and subtle colored ties with pale, silk shirts. Their hair was trimmed short in the back with the most divine thick hair on top. Why, I'd go to their hairdresser if—"

"Eleanor," Madge chided.

"Oh, sorry. I do get carried away sometimes. Anyway, we couldn't help but stare. A little young for us, but it never hurts to check out the goods."

"Of course not," Dom chimed in, suppressing a smile.

"Anyway, Barb waited on them. They didn't want dinner, only a drink."

Dom was tempted to check his watch, but he figured that would be rude. Eleanor did have a way of extending a story.

Madge placed a hand on Eleanor's arm. "What she's trying to say, in a very long-winded way, is that two men, who we later found out were developers, stopped by to speak to Tessa about selling the place."

Now that was news. "And what did she say?" Dom asked with sincerity.

It was Eleanor's turn to answer. "She said, no, of course."

Trace leaned forward. "And how far away were you ladies that you could hear their conversation?"

Dom would have been willing to bet they'd planted microphones under each of the tables to listen in on the patrons' discussions.

"Well, we were real lucky. The booth behind them vacated right after they sat down, and we asked to move there. We could hear everything they said."

"Did you happen to learn their names by any chance?" Dom asked.

"Why, Mr. Rossi. What do you take us for?" Another rhetorical question, no doubt. "Of course, we did. The tall, good-looking one called himself Grady Jankowski. He runs the Jankowski Development Company, which recently purchased the fifty acres on either side of this place in order to put in high rise luxury condos, some townhomes, and four office buildings. He'll have a marina, retail stores, and walking paths. Why if we had the money, Madge and I would move in."

The woman was a walking ad. "Why did Tessa say she wasn't interested in selling? Was it the price?"

"Oh, no. Judd's the real owner and she knew he'd never sell. The other gentleman actually did most of the money talk. I think he was the accountant. We unfortunately missed his name. But it sounded like something-mino. Maybe Polkmino or Bulmino."

Palomino? "Well, you ladies are quite the sleuths," Dom commented. Both smiled as if he'd made their day. "Let me ask you something," Dom said. "How would you describe everyone's mood during the talks?"

Madge wiggled her fingers indicating she wanted to answer. "Yes, Madge," Dom said.

"At first, the two men were very friendly, but Tessa wasn't in the best of moods. Poor thing. I can't imagine why she even came to work. Her father had been murdered just the other day." She took a deep breath. "Oh, you don't look surprised."

"No, no, I'm too shocked to look surprised," Dom answered, hoping the ladies wouldn't be able to figure out his convoluted logic.

"Anyway, I digress. Once Tessa left them, we could tell neither man was happy with the outcome. Mr. Jankowski was particularly upset. He even raised his voice to Mr. Whatevermino."

"You don't say."

"Yes," Madge continued. "Barb told me afterwards they didn't even leave her a tip. Can you imagine? Taking out their anger on the poor girl."

Last time someone gave Tessa a hard time, Charley, the bartender had come to the rescue. He wondered if Charley had been aware of the interaction.

"You two don't happen to know how much he offered Ms. Redman for the bar do you?" The higher the price, the more they wanted the place.

"Why yes. Two point four million dollars."

Trace whistled. "And this woman, Tessa, turned them down?"

"Yup. Just like that," Eleanor said, snapping her fingers with an impressive pop. "But then again, she's not the owner. Judd, her half-brother, is."

Madge checked her watch and nudged Eleanor. "We'll be late if we don't go now, dear. You know how angry Jacque gets when we come in after he's already taught the first eight counts."

"My yes. You'll have to excuse us, boys. We have our weekly dance lesson to attend. It's a great way to meet singles." Eleanor winked.

They slid out of the booth. Eleanor then leaned over the table. "You never did answer my question last time, Mr. Rossi."

"What question?"

"What do you do for a living?"

He debated whether to answer truthfully. They might be more forthcoming knowing he was a real detective. "I'm a homicide cop."

Eleanor sprang back, turned to Madge, and held out her hand. Madge fished out a dollar bill and slapped it into Eleanor's hand.

She turned back to Dom. "I knew it. I told her you were a hardcore detective, but she said you looked like a stockbroker. I won, I won."

With that revelation, the two ladies disappeared out the door.

***

Chelsea plastered her back against the kitchen wall and closed her eyes. She'd never been this overwhelmed by a man in her life before. Trace, whose five o'clock shadow gave him that sexy Brad Pitt look, was the most gorgeous creature she'd ever seen. Even the Rock would be jealous of Trace's physique. And those eyes—deep Caribbean blue like the color of the water near St. Johns. Oh, my. Chelsea placed a hand on her chest to keep her heart from busting through her chest. The best part was there was no little tan line where a ring would be. He was single. Whoopee.

"You okay, Chelsea?" Mick asked.

She opened her eyes. Mick was dipping chicken strips into a gooey batter. "I just met the man of my dreams."

"I hope he's better than your last no good boyfriend."

She held up her index finger to her lips. "Not so loud. Nobody but you knows about Randy."

"Okay, but what do you know about this new guy? He could be an abuser too."

"No, I can tell he's nice."

Mick shook his head. "Aren't they all at first?"

"I'm glad I'm not jaded like you. I may have had a string of bad partners, but I've learned my lesson."

"You ask him out yet?"

She was tempted to lie, but she decided he'd find out sooner than later. "Of course. When I see something I want, I go for it."

Mick smiled. Despite the tattoos and gaunt face, Mick was cute in a strange kind of way. He stepped over to the sink and washed his hands. Then he sauntered over to her, looking a little bit guilty.

Roger ducked into the storage room, and then mumbled something about not being able to find the tomatoes.

"Say listen," Mick said, dropping his gaze to the floor. "I really hate to ask, but I'm in a pinch, and you're the only friend I have right now."

She hated the you're-my-only-friend line. It meant guilt would tear her up if she turned down his request. "What do you need?"

He jabbed his hands into his pockets and his scrawny chest hollowed more. "My baby sister is in trouble."

"What kind of trouble?"

"She's only fifteen, and she got knocked up."

Oh God. Chelsea wished she couldn't relate, but she could. Good thing her parents could afford the best of care when she found herself prego. They'd whisked her off to a clinic where she had an abortion in the morning and was home by noon. No one, and she meant, no one ever knew.

"I'm so sorry, but what can I do?"

"I need two hundred for the abortion. Can you help?"

"Oh, Mick. I'd love to, but I'm strapped." Sad part was, she wasn't lying. "I had to pay my rent two days ago, my car payment is due in two weeks, and I have a Visa bill you wouldn't believe."

"Come on Chelsea. I promise I'll pay you back with my next paycheck. My mom will kill her if she finds out what my sister's done."

"What about the boyfriend?"

His laugh contained no mirth. "Splitsville."

"I can give you fifty, but that'll tap me out. I'm serious. Why don't you ask Tessa? She's a softy."

"No way."

"Okay, then how about Charley? He doesn't look like he ever spends money. I bet he has plenty stashed away."

"That guy? He scares the shit out of me—and I'm a hardened criminal." A small glint of humor sparked from his eyes.

"Look, if I get any big tips tonight, they're yours, okay?"

He nodded. "You're the best, Chels."

"But ask Charley. Seriously. He'll give you the money, I bet."

"I'll think about it."

Tessa barged into the kitchen. Damn. Chelsea had nowhere to hide.

"Three of your orders are up," Tessa said, her voice strained. "Let's go."

"On my way." Chelsea faced Mick and mouthed. "I'll see what I can do."

CHAPTER SEVEN

Captain John Leffers strode over to Dom's desk. "I thought you'd be interested to know someone robbed the Blue Moon last night. I know you think the place is connected to a few of your murders."

Dom's pulse jumped. "What time was this?"

"Three this morning. Thief got about $350. The big damage was to one of the plate glass windows that faces the water."

Dom held in his sigh of relief, and then let his breath out in short puffs. Tessa surely wouldn't have been around that late. "Was the place alarmed?"

"Yes, and that's how we found out about it. The security company notified us. We were there in less than eight minutes, but it was enough time for the thief to pry open the desk drawer and take the day's receipts."

"Who's the primary?"

"Cantori."

"Thanks, I'll talk to him."

Noting Cantori wasn't at his desk, he called Vince for an update.

"Cantori here."

"Vince, it's Dom. What do you have on the break-in at the Blue Moon?"

"The Captain mentioned it might have some relevance to your murder investigation, though I don't know how. This didn't look like a professional job, I'll tell you. The guy used a rock to break the back window. From all the crack marks, it took him quite a few tries before the pane broke."

"Was anyone inside during the robbery?" *Please say no.*

"Not that we could tell."

"Go on," Dom prodded.

Over the phone, Dom heard the crinkling of flipping pages. "Okay. Walters called the manager, a Ms. Tessa Redman. She's on her way in now. Apparently, she left the nightly receipts in her desk drawer. When we checked her office, nothing looked out of place other than a splintered drawer where the lock had been. The cash box she kept inside is missing."

"I'm on my way."

"We have everything under control, Dom," Cantori said, sounding as if he didn't need or want any interference.

"I'm sure you do. I just want to..." How could he phrase it? Give moral support to Tessa. "To get a handle on the type of person who might have done this. Whoever broke in might be our killer."

"Be my guest."

Dom gathered his notebook, and then straightened his desk before he headed to the Blue Moon.

When he arrived, two squad cars were pulled up near the front door, and Tessa's faded, blue Toyota was the only other car in the lot.

Dom parked next to her and rushed inside. He hadn't expected the anger to grab a hold of him the moment he saw her sitting alone at one of the tables with her head in her hands with Mandy asleep in some sort of rocker by her side.

The chair squeaked as he pulled it out to sit across from Tessa. She looked up at him, and then glanced to the baby who seemed blissfully unaware of the intrusion.

"Detective."

Her eyes were bloodshot and her cheeks tear stained. His sympathy welled. "You can call me, Dominic. Or Dom for short." Rattled by her slight smile, the statement escaped before he had a chance to think.

He shouldn't have jumped from formal to casual so fast. Tessa Redman was a victim, not a girlfriend.

A long silence stretched between them, and he was glad she hadn't suggested he call her by her first name. The line in the sand remained partially intact.

"Ms. Redman, do you have any idea who might have done this?"

She shook her head. "It has to have been a personal attack against me or Judd. I know you expect me to name my ex-husband, but this isn't his style."

"I have to admit, he was my first suspect. Is there anyone else you can think of who would rob you? Someone desperate for money?"

She laughed, but it held little joy. "Detective," she glanced at her hands. "Dominic. Every waiter, waitress, cook, and bartender needs money. Probably every person in the Blue Moon's employ could benefit from an extra $350. You know how it is? Policemen are in the same spot financially."

She looked up at him expectantly, and he had to give her the pat answer. "You got that right."

"Why are you here? I thought you were a homicide detective." She clasped a hand over her mouth. "You think this is related to Keri and Bob's murder, don't you?"

"I don't know what to think. I was hoping you could give me some guidance."

She looked toward the bar and he sensed a deep pain from within her. "I would if I could."

Dom wanted to take hold of her hand and extend some form of comfort, but his action might be misconstrued.

"How are you holding up?" he asked.

"As well as can be expected. It's not every day you find out someone is sitting at your bar one moment, and then shot in the head an hour later. Then you're told your father had his throat cut, probably by your ex-husband. When you think everything bad that could happen has, a second patron is murdered in his bed. If that isn't bad enough, I'm robbed. How do you think I'm holding up?"

Her hands trembled, and her escalating voice shook. No one should have to experience this much tragedy in the span of a few weeks. "Amazingly well."

Dom didn't think she expected his answer. "Thank you." She glanced at her watch. "Do you think I can go home? I have to get ready for work. The restaurant opens in a while."

"Not if the Sergeant and his men aren't done. I'm sorry."

She shoved back her chair. "You can't hold me if I'm not a suspect." Her sudden anger confirmed her fragile state.

"We're not holding you. We might need information."

Mandy opened her eyes, and when she began to cry, Tessa leaned over the baby and tapped the child's nose and blew a puff of air into her face. When Mandy continued to fuss, Tessa hauled her out of the constraining basket-like contraption and placed her over her shoulder.

She searched under the table. "Drat."

"What?"

"I left Mandy's diaper bag in the car."

"If you give me your keys, I'll grab the bag," he offered.

She held his gaze for a moment. "Thank you, again." She pulled her purse up to the table and attempted to retrieve the keys, but with Mandy wiggling so much, she couldn't keep a grip on her purse.

"Here, I'll take her," Dom offered, not wanting to look through Tessa's bag.

As if she'd done it a hundred times before, she handed him the baby. The moment he placed Mandy on his shoulder, the baby began to settle.

The child's added weight sent a longing through him so strong he almost squeezed her too hard.

"Here," Tessa said, holding out her keys. "On second thought," she added, pulling back her hand, "I'll get it myself. Mandy seems happier with you."

He'd noticed that too.

Tessa disappeared. Dom grabbed Mandy under the armpits and lifted her up. Her eyes widened, then she smiled. His heart pinged.

***

Tessa snatched Mandy's diaper bag from the backseat and rushed inside. Dominic's unexpected visit actually helped calm her. She never would have thought she'd welcome his presence, but she felt safer when he was around. It was as if Ralph wouldn't dare come near.

As she stepped into the darkened restaurant, Mandy's laughter reached her. In a million years, she wouldn't have anticipated the staid detective would be playing with a child. Her insides melted.

Before she reached the table, Officer Cantori stepped in front of her.

"Excuse me, ma'am, but we'll have to fingerprint each of the workers."

She wanted to cry. "Why?"

"To eliminate their prints from the around the cash register, the entry door, your office and—"

She held up a hand. "I understand. Half of the staff should arrive shortly, and the second shift comes in at four."

"Do you want to explain to your staff the need for the procedure, or would you like my team to handle it?"

Although she wasn't up for the hassle, there would be less complaining if she softened the blow first. "I'll do it."

"Thank you."

Dominic followed her with his gaze as she approached the table. She pulled out her chair and when she sat down, he handed her Mandy. "What was that look for?" she asked.

"I didn't know I was giving you a particular look. What I was thinking was how well you're dealing with this situation. I can see a little tic around your eye and how your hands bunch up at your side every time an officer approaches, both indicating you're using all your strength to keep your composure, yet you've been cordial to both me and to Officer Cantori. A lesser person would have cracked."

He didn't paint a particularly appealing picture, yet his tone implied he meant it as a compliment. "Thank you, I guess."

"Listen, why don't you head home, rest, then come back when you're ready. Cantori can take your prints later. I'll speak to your workers if you like."

She leaned back in her chair, and her jaw relaxed for what was probably the first time that day. "I should be the one to explain to my people why they have to be fingerprinted."

He raised a brow. "I'll be gentle, I promise."

Tessa took a minute to think, but her weary body won the battle. "I appreciate that. I'd love to finish washing up, have breakfast, and drop Mandy off at my babysitter's."

"You go ahead. I'll be here when you get back."

She smiled, hoping the worst was over.

Every bone in her body must have gained an extra pound since yesterday since it took all her energy to load Mandy into the car seat and drive home. The sun filled the cloudless sky with brightness, and the cold front that had rolled in the last few days seemed to have left. Tessa couldn't have asked for a more perfect November day, yet a pall hung over her head.

Her cell phone chimed halfway home.

"Hello?"

"Tessa, it's Chelsea."

The girl sounded nervous. "What's wrong?"

"I'm at work and heard about the robbery. I can't believe it."

"I'm amazed myself."

"I have a hunch who might have stolen the money."

The car ahead of Tessa slowed, and she almost hit its bumper. "Who?"

"Mick."

"Mick? Just because he's been in jail doesn't make him an automatic suspect."

"Mick's been in jail?"

Damn. Tessa thought Mick had told her given the two of them seemed so chummy. "Yes, but that doesn't matter now. What makes you think it's him?"

"Because yesterday he asked if he could borrow money. Something about his sister needing an abortion."

Her mind raced. "It could be a coincidence, but I'll mention it to the detective." How could she have been so wrong about her new hire? Her gut instinct told her she could trust him. *Well, that should have given me my first clue. I trusted Ralph too and look where that got me.*

"Okay, but don't tell Mick I suspect him."

"Of course not."

Tessa disconnected and drew her attention back to the heavily trafficked road.

Ten minutes later she pulled into her driveway. No sooner had she shut off the engine when her neighbor, Glenda Robertson, from across the street eased open her screen door and waved. "Yoohoo, oh, Tessa," she yelled in her usual singsong voice that had turned old real fast.

Tessa forced a weak smile and waved back. She so did not need the busy body right now. Glenda waddled across the street, grabbing closed her bathrobe, her pink flowered nightgown peeking out underneath.

"Hi, Glenda. Give me a sec to get Mandy."

Glenda stepped closer to the car and looked in. "She's such a doll."

"That she is."

Tessa gathered her niece along with the diaper bag and waited to see what her neighbor wanted.

"Can I come in for a moment?" Glenda asked. "I need to tell you something."

"Sure, but I have to return to work in a bit and drop Mandy off at the sitter's."

"This won't take long." Glenda kept looking down the street as if she was expecting someone.

"Come on in then." Tessa grabbed her key and unlocked the door. Tessa put down the car cradle, unstrapped Mandy, and then gathered her niece in her arms. "What can I do for you?"

"You know since Harold died I don't have much to do. I like to look out the living window to make sure everything is as it should be."

"Yes, I've seen you." It bothered Tessa knowing the widow watched her every move.

"This morning, you left earlier than usual."

Is that what the old lady wanted? "Yes, the police called." Glenda's mouth dropped open. "The Blue Moon was robbed last night."

"Oh, dear. I'm so sorry. Well maybe that explains the man who was snooping around your place after you left. It was probably a policeman looking to tell you."

"A policeman?" She fought to keep her composure. "Was he in a cruiser?"

"No, it was a tan colored car. Rather nondescript, really. I couldn't find my binoculars. Otherwise, I would have looked at the license plate."

"What did this man look like?" Please don't make it be Ralph.

"Well. Let me see." She placed a forefinger on her lips. "Ordinary. Medium height, medium build, short brown hair." Glenda dropped her hand and made a fist. "I'd know him if I saw him, I think. I'm not any very good at describing a person. The doctor said I have the beginnings of cataracts, but..." She waved a hand. "That's not important. The man I saw had his back to my house most of the time, so that was the problem."

"Hold on." Tessa placed Mandy in the playpen, and then grabbed her purse. She fished out Ralph's photo. "Is this the man?"

Glenda studied the old picture. "Gee, I don't know. I really didn't get a good look at him. I just saw him sneak around to the back of your house. He was only here maybe five minutes."

"Thank you for telling me. I'll certainly call the police and ask if they sent an officer." Tessa reached out and grabbed Glenda's hand. "And thank you for keeping an eye out for me."

"You're welcome, dear." Color flushed her face as she smiled. "Just so you know. Remember I told you I wanted to visit my daughter? Well, I'm leaving this afternoon. Would you mind taking a peek at my place? One can never be too careful."

"I'd be happy to."

Tessa showed her to the door and ushered her neighbor out. The moment Glenda was gone, Tessa pressed her back against the wall and took a deep breath, trying to calm her racing heart. Why was this happening to her?

Dominic. He'd know what to do. She rushed to the phone and found the detective's cell phone number. She dialed, then paced, waiting for him to pick up.

"Yes."

"Dominic?"

"Tessa?" With that one word, Tessa felt as if a security blanket had dropped from the sky and wrapped around her.

"Yes. I'm so sorry to bother you, but my neighbor just told me some man was snooping around my house this morning."

"What time was this?"

She reran the conversation. "I forgot to ask. Glenda said it was after I left this morning. She thought it was a policeman driving an unmarked car."

"I never asked for surveillance. Could it have been Ralph?"

"It's possible, though when I showed her his picture, she wasn't able to identify him." Tessa checked Mandy to see she was happy in her playpen. Given the baby was playing with a rattle, she dared to peek out the window.

"I'm in my car now. I should be there in twenty minutes."

As happy as she was to have the added protection, she didn't want to disturb him for what could have been a Tampa Electric man checking her meter or a repairman sent by the landlord. Surely, old Mr. Reynolds would have let her know though if he'd sent someone to do work. "I'm leaving shortly anyway. I hate to disturb you."

"Tessa. Trust me. Take your shower and get ready. When I arrive I'll have a look around. I'll feel better if you let me do this."

His tone was more like a friend than a police detective. "Thank you."

"Now do your thing."

She had to chuckle at his take-charge approach. "Fine. See you in twenty." Make that more like thirty, unless he used his siren.

Feeling better than she had in a while, she gave Mandy her pacifier and headed to the bathroom, pulling off her clothes as she went. Not wanting her nickel ring to slip off when she showered, Tessa placed the memento on her dresser.

She dashed into the bathroom. Needing the heat, turned the water to hot. When the temperature reached the desire temperature, she jumped in, and the soothing flow sluiced over her body. Tessa grabbed the lavender scented body wash and poured a handful over her skin. For the briefest second she imagined her hands were Dominic's, and a swift surge of excitement speared her between the legs.

Her eyes flew open, and she immediately rinsed away the flowery scented soap. What had she been thinking? She'd made the mistake of falling for a suave cop long ago—never again. Dominic wasn't anything like Ralph though. Her ex had been confident and cocky to the point of being obnoxious when he drank. Tessa believed Dominic to be quite the opposite—confident yes, but in a controlled sort of way. The few times Dominic had come to the bar, she'd seen him have only one beer.

Mandy let out a scream. Yikes. How long had she been in the shower? After turning off the water, she stepped out, and toweled dry. She raced back into the living room and saw her niece had tossed her precious teddy bear on the floor. After retrieving it, Mandy settled down. Tess checked her watch. Twenty minutes had passed. Oh my.

Faster than Superman changed into his cape, she jumped into a pair of jeans, a scoop neck white tank top and covered up with a striped shirt. After she slipped into her backless sandals, she dabbed on a little makeup. Boy, did she look beat. Dark circles, saggy cheeks, and dropping eyelids. She definitely looked twice her age.

Tires crunched in her drive. He was here. Tess couldn't believe she was actually excited. *It's not a date, Tessa Jean.* So as to look busy, she grabbed the phone and speed dialed her babysitter, Colette.

"Hi, Tessa. I've been waiting for you. Are you coming?"

"Actually, I'm in quite a bind. The Blue Moon was robbed last night and the police need me to help. I'm in a hurry. Is there any way you could you come over and pick up Mandy? I'd really appreciate it."

"Sure. I'll hop in the car now."

"You're the best. Thanks." Tessa hung up and set the phone on the kitchen counter.

When she heard the detective's knock, she ran a hand over her hair, pressed her lips together to make sure her lipstick was smooth, and opened the door.

His eyes widened in appreciation. Dominic cleared his throat. "I'm going to take a look around and see if I can spot anything. I'll be back in a moment."

"Fine. I'll leave the door unlocked."

Just as she closed the front door, her phone rang.

She dashed to the kitchen. "Hello?"

"Tessa, it's Glenda, from across the street."

How many Glendas did she think Tessa knew? "Hi, Glenda."

"I just wanted to make sure you were okay with that man at your house."

Tessa chuckled. "Yes. He's Detective Rossi with the Tampa Police. Any time you see his red truck, you can be assured I'm safe."

"Okay. I just wanted to check."

"Thanks, Glenda."

Tessa considered herself lucky to live near such a caring neighbor, even if she was a born snoop. Colette would be stopping by, which meant Tess needed to clean up Mandy and gather the baby's gear.

She was almost finished, when Dominic stepped into the room. She turned and felt the room shrink. She hadn't heard him enter the house.

"See anything?" Tess pretended as if she wasn't worried, but inside she was scared to death.

"I'm not sure. The place isn't in the best condition. The back window looked as if someone tried to pry it open with a screwdriver."

"Those marks could have been there before I moved in. I've never checked."

"I think you should have protection."

"Protection. Okay. I'll buy a gun."

Dominic held up his hands. "I wasn't talking about that kind of protection. A gun in the wrong hands can do a lot of damage. Especially to you."

"I know how to shoot. I took lessons."

He cocked a brow, and the left side of his lip curled up into a half smile. She wanted to drown in his look of appreciation at her accomplishment. Tessa blinked, and when she stepped back, Dominic moved forward.

"If you don't mind, I'd like to have a man stationed outside your house for a while."

"Your department will okay the expense? I thought that unless I was personally attacked they wouldn't authorize it."

"True, but I'm going to try to convince my Captain that you need to be watched."

"Would your man drive a police car?"

"He can, if it would make you feel more secure."

"It would, but..." She studied her hands.

He moved closer. "Now Tessa."

She met his gaze. Uh, oh. Dominic looked as if he wanted to kiss her, and that simply wouldn't do.

She took a step back. Suddenly, Tessa couldn't think of anything to say. Dominic reached out and brushed a strand of her hair behind her ear, and his one touch melted every defense she'd stored up.

As if her life came crashing down, a watershed of tears leaked out of her eyes. She didn't sob nor did she make a sound, but it was as if the dam had crumbled.

Before Tessa could get past him to the living room, she stumbled. As if he could move at the speed of light, Dominic's strong arms wrapped around her.

On instinct, she grabbed his biceps and looked up, his lips inches from hers. She wanted to let him take care of her, let him tell her everything would be all right, but she couldn't. What if he turned out to be like Ralph?

CHAPTER EIGHT

Welcoming blood infused Tessa's brain, and red flashing signals bombarded her. Being in Dominic's arms made her too vulnerable and way too dependent on him. She gently stepped back. "Thank you."

"Your face turned so white I thought you were about to faint."

"My legs turned to rubber. I'm sorry."

Dominic lifted her chin. "Tessa, you have nothing to be sorry about. None of this is your fault."

"I know." He dropped his hand and his wonderful warmth left her. "But I can't help feel I'm responsible for Ralph being in jail."

With a hand to her lower back, Dominic led her over to the sofa, his gentle touch tempting her resolve. More than anything she wanted to bury her face in his chest and cry her heart out, but she refused to give in. If she let herself start, no telling when she'd stop.

"Sooner or later, Ralph would have been caught, Tessa. Bad cops always slip up at some point. You saved his department a lot of time and energy by turning him in when you did."

"I keep telling myself that. Then I think of poor Dad and how he died because of me."

"You have no proof of that."

She'd been through this argument so many times she'd almost memorized it. "I know."

"I'll be right back."

A well of emptiness swallowed her at being left alone. "Where are you going?"

"To answer the door. Didn't you hear the knock?" He spoke in a slow, soothing tone as if she'd witnessed a horrible scene.

"No."

Dominic opened the door. Colette took a step over the threshold. "Hello." Her gaze shot to Tessa for a split second before returning to Dominic. "Who are you?"

"Detective Rossi."

Thank goodness he kept his tone authoritative, all the good it did. Colette stared at Dominic as if she'd never seen a good-looking man before.

"Colette?" Tessa said to break up the peep show.

Her babysitter turned toward her. As if she'd suddenly lost interest in the man at the door, she rushed over to Tessa. "I can't believe your place was robbed. You weren't hurt were you?"

"No. I wasn't even there when the thief broke in," Tessa said trying not to sound peevish. Not that she could blame the twenty-one year old from ogling the handsome detective, but did the girl have to run her gaze from his head to his crotch and back again?

Tessa nodded to Dominic who remained by the front door. "The detective is going to make sure nothing else happens to me or the Blue Moon." Partly a lie, but Tessa wanted the boundary lines drawn. Dominic didn't need the chirpy young lady fawning all over him.

"Nice to meet you." At least the girl had the sense to turn a slight shade of red.

"Colette, would you mind seeing to Mandy? She's in the bedroom," Tessa asked.

"Oh, sure. You told me on the phone you were in a hurry. I know you have a lot to do with the police. If you need me to keep Mandy overnight, I can. She won't be any trouble."

Dominic stood with his arms crossed. "How about if Ms. Redman calls you when she's ready to pick up her niece."

Colette broke into a broad, toothy smile. "Oh, I get it. Maybe you don't want Mandy disturbing you." She winked at Tessa. "You just let me know when you want me to bring her back."

It was Tessa's turn to blush. "It's not like that Colette. My neighbor saw a man snooping around the house, and the detective here came to check it out."

"Oh."

"But I appreciate your flexibility."

"No problem." The babysitter gathered Mandy and her gear. "Give me a call," Colette called as she headed to her car.

"I will."

Once Colette left, Tessa chanced a look at Dominic. He had the nerve to smile, and her heart skipped a beat. It wasn't something she'd seen him do before—and it wasn't an ordinary I'm-being-polite smile, but one that spoke of intimacy.

"Well, that was awkward," Tessa said knowing it was better to face the situation than avoid it.

"Indeed." He cleared his throat. "Why don't I drive you back to the restaurant?"

"I'd rather drive myself if you don't mind. In that way, I can leave when I want."

"I can drive you home when it's time to leave."

Tessa wasn't ready for around the clock protection. "I don't want you to go to any trouble." She held up a hand. "Besides, I feel perfectly safe at the Blue Moon. As a matter of fact, when I showed everyone Ralph's picture and explained he might have killed my dad, each of the men tried to play the hero, claiming he'd take care of my ex if he stepped foot in the restaurant." She shook her head.

"What exactly did you tell them?" His brow furrowed, and the sudden change in demeanor made her tense her fists.

"That the police would handle Ralph Ferino."

His shoulders relaxed. "Good. That was smart thinking. Since you insist on driving yourself, would you mind if I followed you to the restaurant to make sure you get there okay? Trace, my friend from Atlanta, and I will stop back tonight for dinner and make sure Mr. Ferino doesn't bother you. Trace and Chelsea have a date, I believe."

Tessa smiled, for what felt like the first time in a long while. "I think she likes your friend, but tell him to treat her well."

Dominic nodded. "If nothing else, Trace is a gentleman."

"I'm glad." Tessa stood, grabbed her bag and followed the detective out, not happy about her growing attraction.

***

"Will you hurry up," Dom said as he leaned against the bathroom jamb. "I'm starving, Trace. You know Chelsea's not going to notice if you're wearing the white shirt or the blue one. Hell, the way she looked at you, I think she'd rather you come without a shirt at all."

Trace preened in front of the mirror. "Look who's talking? You must have changed three times."

"Well, I'm undercover. I don't want anyone knowing I'm a cop."

"You can fool all of the people some of the time, some of the people all of the time, but you can't fool me," Trace quoted.

"I don't think Abe Lincoln would have liked the way you butchered his saying."

Trace dabbed on Dom's most expensive cologne. "He won't care."

"Hey, don't use all of that stuff. It ain't cheap."

"You're the one with the trust fund."

Dom had been through the argument many times before with Trace, but it didn't stop him now. "Just because I can afford it doesn't mean you should abuse my generosity."

Trace put down the glass bottle and raised his hands. "I'm done."

"About time."

Dom wasn't sure why he was agitated. Maybe it was the fact Trace was going out with Chelsea after she finished her shift, and he'd be going home alone.

Dom could pull another all-nighter at Tessa's house, but Trace would find out, which meant Chelsea would eventually know, and he had no doubt she'd tell Tessa. Knowing her, she'd balk at having him outside her place every night and ban all future surveillance.

Her noisy neighbor might even call the police on him. Then how would he explain his presence to the Captain? Half the precinct had commented on his piss poor mood lately. He didn't need Leffers on his ass too. If only the department wasn't in its perennial budget crunch the Captain might have been able to pay him to watch Tessa.

"Ready?" Trace asked.

"Yup.

The parking lot at the Blue Moon, or rather the Blue Moo, seemed quite full for a Thursday night. He was pleased Tessa was part of a successful business. Although if she and her brother succumbed to the developer's offer, he bet the developer would raze the place.

When they walked in, the hostess didn't even ask where they wanted to sit. "Come this way."

She seated them in a booth in the far corner of the restaurant.

"Let me sit facing the door," Dom said as Trace started to sit in the best seat.

"Sorry. I keep forgetting I'm not on the job. Old habits die hard."

"You got that right. Look," Dom said nodding to the front of the restaurant, "The front line has already notified the General you're here."

"Hi, Trace," Chelsea said. "Detective Rossi." Her tone cooled dramatically between the two names. "What can I get you?" she asked Trace.

"Why you, darling."

Oh, boy. Trace poured on the southern accent as if he'd actually grown up in Atlanta instead of West Tampa.

Chelsea bit her lower lip. "You'll have to wait until I clock out."

"For you, darlin', I'll do anything. In the meantime, I'd like a draft beer—whichever you think is the house best."

Dom raised two fingers, figuring Chelsea had forgotten him. "Coke here."

"Be right back." She winked at Trace and took off.

When she was out of earshot, Trace whistled. "I'm goin' to get lucky tonight."

"Looks like it."

Dom didn't want to discuss Trace's evening of hot sex. Instead he pulled out his notepad.

"Why don't you make it real obvious you're a cop?" Trace said in a loud whisper.

"I don't give a rat's ass if the world knows who I am." Dom lowered his voice.

"You've changed your tune."

"Look, it's possible we have a serial killer on our hands."

That got Trace's attention. His specialty included the deviants of the world. "Tell me what you have so far."

Dom leaned forward, happy to share his investigation with his former partner. "In the last two weeks we've had three people murdered. While we had forty-two in the county last year, we've already had fifty-five since January. None of the three are domestic violence or gang related that we can tell."

"Hell, Atlanta had four times that many."

Dom scrubbed a hand over his head. "That's Atlanta. This is Tampa. There's an evil person out there. I've no proof, but Tessa is convinced her ex-husband killed her dad."

"Could he have killed the other two victims?"

"Not likely. Her ex is from out of state and probably wasn't in Florida at the time of the first two murders. He was a dirty vice cop who was recently released from of jail. There's no connection between the last two deaths and this guy that I can find either. And trust me, I've looked."

"How can you rule out domestic violence as a motive?" Trace asked.

"Tessa was working when her dad was killed. As for the other two, both prime suspects had airtight alibis."

"Were all three victims found under the same circumstances?"

"No. Bob Dirkman was asleep in his bed when someone cut his throat, and there was no robbery attempt. Tessa's dad's throat was also cut, but this time the killer made it look like a robbery. The first person murdered was a woman who was shot in the head on a busy thoroughfare. It appeared as if she'd pulled over on the side of the road and rolled down her window. Given it was chilly, I'd say she willingly spoke to the killer before he popped her one in the head."

"And I guess you have no trace evidence, no weapons, and no other suspects?" Trace leaned back in the booth and stretched his arms out on the leather seat.

"Not enough for us to go on."

"We had a cold case in Atlanta last year that still bugs me. I finally had to let go of it a few months ago. We had three murders right in a row, kind of like you. As a matter of fact, it was last November, and all three victims were parked on the side of the road. Each was shot in the head at close range."

Dom stiffened. "Could you prove the same person committed all three crimes?" His pulse sped up at the similarity.

"No. All three were shot with a different weapon."

"Damn."

Chelsea came up to their table and set down the drinks. "You boys ready to order?"

"Give us a minute, hon, will ya?" Trace said as he snaked his hand up to her waist and squeezed.

"I'll give you anything you want." Chelsea smiled, turned, and sashayed to another table.

Dom watched his former partner carefully. "You don't have the least bit of guilt leaving Emma and hitting on Chelsea, a girl much younger than you, do you?"

"For one, Emma left me, and secondly I'm only twenty-nine. I hardly call the age difference, whatever it is, a problem."

"Fine." Dom didn't know why he even brought up the subject. Maybe he was trying to protect Chelsea despite her being the pursuer.

Dom looked over the menu, but nothing appealed to him. All he could focus on was the case. "Back to your Atlanta murders. If I take out all the domestic violence cases in Hillsborough County, I can't recall the last time we found someone shot in the head. And you said you had three in one month?"

"Yup."

Dom's mind sped through all the possibilities. "Could you ask someone to send down the case files? I'm thinking there may be a connection."

Trace laughed. "You're reaching, Dom, but I'll see what I can do."

Dom caught Chelsea's attention. She trotted over, and they gave her their orders. While Trace flirted with her, Dom took notes on who sat at the bar. While he didn't know any of their names, he wrote a brief description of each person.

Two businessmen who seemed to be enjoying themselves sat nearest the cash register. Next to them was an older man who was by himself. Overweight, balding and hunched over his drink, his gaze didn't extend past his beer. The seat next to him was vacant. Four men, all around thirty, hovered in the middle. They acted as if they were either close business associates or good friends. Dominic studied their ring fingers, but none sported wedding bands. Of course, the lack of gold didn't mean they were single. They were probably out for an after dinner drink. At the far end of the bar sat two women in their mid-forties, dressed in work suits, who chitchatted. Kind of late for an after dinner drink, but they too might be conducting business.

As Dom rescanned the bar area, a skinny guy in an apron exited the kitchen. Tessa scooted over and spoke with him for a minute. Once he disappeared back into the kitchen, she returned to the cash register. The Jolly Green Giant continued to serve the drinks in a professional, yet none too friendly manner.

Too bad he and Trace were so far away from the bar. The distance prevented hearing any conversations. Maybe after dinner Dom would have to join the drinking crowd and get in on the action.

***

Tessa couldn't keep focused. Her gaze kept wandering to the back of the restaurant where Dominic sat nursing his Coke. He kept flipping through his notepad, making notes and checking out those at the bar as if he were some big casting director looking for the perfect leading man or woman.

The evening had been uneventful until some drunk started to make a scene.

She sidled up to Charley and kept her back to the man. "Who's the man in the faded blue shirt?"

"Doug Walsh. He's a royal pain in the ass, if you ask me."

"Thanks." So that was Doug.

Tessa remembered Judd talking about this guy. Real smart, talented computer programmer, but he had the unfortunate knack of pissing off his bosses. Then they'd fire him, and he'd go on a drinking binge.

Eventually, his wife would show up and drag him out of the bar. Tessa could only hope she showed up soon.

It was time for a little intervention.

"Hi Doug," Tessa said in a non-confrontational tone.

Doug's lip turned up in a sneer. "Who are you?"

"I'm Judd's sister." Her announcement seemed to get his attention. "Where's Judd?"

"You didn't hear? I'm afraid his liver condition has worsened. He's been in and out of the hospital in the last few months. I'm taking over for him."

A flash of concern filled his eyes. "I'm sorry."

"Thanks. I'll tell him you said hello. So what brings you here tonight?" She wasn't in the mood to play therapist, but if it quieted down the guy, she'd listen.

Doug ran a hand over his unshaven chin. "I lost my job today. Fucking assholes will be sorry when they have no one to fix the Project Management system when it goes down."

She didn't dare ask for specifics. "So how's your wife taking the news?"

His eyes narrowed. "How do you know about my wife?"

"Judd's talked a lot about you."

"Oh, yeah? Well, I guess he's been out of the loop. Grace left me six months ago."

"I'm so sorry." Open mouth insert foot.

He slammed his empty glass on the bar. "You can make it up to me by pouring me another drink."

"We're about to close, Doug. Why don't you come back tomorrow? The first one will be on the house."

"What is it with you people? This is a bar, isn't it?"

Tessa leaned toward him, aware of the notice he'd brought. "I think you've had enough. I'd like you to leave," she said between gritted teeth. Yes, she knew as a therapist she should be nicer, but at the moment, she didn't feel congenial.

Before Doug could voice his opinion regarding her lightly veiled threat, Chelsea touched Tessa's arm. "I'm going, if it's okay with you." Tessa turned. Chelsea nodded in Trace's direction, and he waved.

Her aggravation whooshed out of her at the happy sight. "Sure, hon. Have a good time on your day off. And remind me to ask you about something." Tessa had decided to see if Chelsea would be willing to move in with her. She would feel safer with a roommate.

"Okay."

"You heard the lady," Charley said. "Get going."

Doug held up his hands in apparent surrender. "If I can't get another drink, I'm outta here." He shoved back his chair and nearly stumbled.

"Be careful, Doug." Tessa watched him leave and blew out a sigh of relief.

The kitchen door banged open, and she turned around. Mick waved to her. "I'm off, if that's okay."

"Sure, is the kitchen clean?"

"You betcha."

She waved him close. "Say, a rather inebriated customer just left. If you hurry you'll see him. He's a little shorter than you, big belly, and thinning brown hair. Would you mind following him for a few miles to see if he's capable of driving? I couldn't handle another tragedy."

"And if he starts to swerve?"

"Good question. Maybe flash your lights and hope he pulls over."

"That or call the cops." His jaw clenched.

"Now you're thinking."

"Well, I guess I'll see you tomorrow."

"Thanks, Mick."

Her new short order cook had been a good find. Trusting her instincts had worked.

Charley tossed down his rag on the bar. "Time to close up, I guess."

Her bartender looked tired. "Why don't you call it a night? I'll finish straightening up."

"You sure?"

"Yes, you go on." She was sure Dominic would stay until she locked the doors.

Charley nodded and picked up his keys. "See you tomorrow, then."

***

Chelsea gathered her purse and sauntered back to Trace's table. "Ready when you are."

A slow, lazy smile filled his face. God, he was the sexiest man she'd ever met.

He turned to Detective Rossi. "Don't wait up for me, Dom. Chelsea and I plan to spend the day together tomorrow."

The detective didn't look pleased, but too damn bad. It wasn't as if he'd taken her up on her offer to go out. Besides, she kind of figured he had the hots for Tessa. He must have since he was always looking at her as if he was sizing her up—or was it gobbling her up?

Chelsea turned to keep from giggling. Tessa and the detective. Now that would be a pair. They were perfect for each other. Both were straight-laced and uptight, but as they say, there's a mate out there for everyone.

Trace stood and wrapped a possessive arm around Chelsea's waist, just as Mick shot through the kitchen door and stopped short when he saw her. She smiled and waved at her friend. No use pissing him off.

The greeting wasn't returned. Sheesh. What was up with people? Couldn't a girl have a little fun? "Let's get out of here."

Chelsea grabbed Trace's hand and led him out to the parking lot. As she neared her car, Trace turned her around and hovered over her.

"I've wanted to taste you all night."

"Oooh, Trace. You say the nicest things."

"This your car?" he said, nodding to her ten-year old Mazda.

"Temporarily." She didn't want him to think she was nearly penniless, which she was.

He grabbed her face with two hands and gently moved her backwards until her butt hit the car door. She closed her eyes and waited for his lips to touch hers. Then with the gentlest of touch, Trace kissed her. She parted her lips in invitation, and he delved in. Whoa. Every juice in her body electrified. What he did to her couldn't be described, but it was amazing. He tasted of sweet beer and smelled rich and sultry. Yum.

Chelsea drew her hands around his butt and squeezed his hard orbs. What a fine, fine ass he had.

Her tongue darted in and out of his mouth, trying for as much contact with him as possible. His erection pressed against her belly, and her heart pounded in her chest as her breath sped up. Chelsea moved her hands up to his back and drew him closer, flattening her breasts to his chest. She wanted all of him—now—in the parking lot, in the backseat of her car, on the hood. She didn't care where.

Screeching tires raced past them, and Trace stiffened. He took a step back.

"What the fuck?" he said following the car's path out of the lot. "The guy nearly hit the light pole. Shit."

Chelsea needed Trace to focus on her, not on some stupid drunk. "Don't worry. It's just some idiot racing back to his wife." She leaned up and kissed his lips, but he kept his head averted.

"Who's behind him?"

She glanced at the white truck that had a cab on the back and shrugged. "How should I know? I don't know what people drive."

Trace seemed to lose focus on the crazy guy and pulled her toward him. He ground his hips into her pelvis, demonstrating he was big and hard. "Let's have some fun."

"Now you're talking."

He grabbed the keys from her hand and opened the passenger side door. "Get in."

Chelsea wasn't going to complain. Trace raced to the driver's side. As she leaned her seat back, Trace started the engine and peeled backwards, flying dirt slamming into the undercarriage.

"Hey, what are you doing?" she asked.

"I want to see how much trouble this guy will get into before he arrives home—or should I say if he gets home."

Chelsea's body sagged. "Why would you want to do that?" Despite her effort, her voice came out as a whine.

"Oh, I don't know. With the way the second guy was tailgating that drunk, I'm betting some tempers might flare. I want to be there when the fireworks begin."

"Great." He'd rather chase a drunk around town than have hot, animalistic sex with her.

Trace peeled out of the lot, his grip on the wheel intense. Well, if he was more interested in a stupid fight than in having her, she needed to ratchet up the heat a notch.

It would be the supreme test of her sexuality if she could distract Trace enough to want to pull over and be with her.

Trace looked over at her for a second. "You okay, baby?"

"Peachy." Chelsea reached beneath Trace's seatbelt and rubbed her hand over his crotch.

"Not now, babe."

Chelsea withdrew her hand so fast it almost tangled with his seatbelt. "What's the matter? Did I say something wrong?" Why did incredible hunks want to dump her so fast?

Trace glanced over at her. "No, no. I want you real bad, but right now I've got this feeling something's about to go down."

"It's you and me that's supposed to be going down."

"Holy shit. Look, Chels."

CHAPTER NINE

"Need help with the combination?" Dom asked Tessa. She'd tried to lock several times and had failed to open the safe.

She looked up at him with a slightly creased brow. "When it says R-L-R, it means I'm supposed to go past the first right once, correct?"

"If it's like your standard lock, yes."

Dom's cell phone vibrated against his leg, and he stepped back and flicked a glance at the number. It wasn't the station. "Wrong number," he mumbled.

After closing the lid, he knelt beside Tessa to see if he could speed up the opening of the safe. A hint of fried chicken mixed with some scotch she must have spilled on her hand floated around her, and the cozy scene made his groin ache again. Why did his dick have to twitch every time he got near this woman? She was the victim here. Remember that.

"I got it!" Tessa announced with excitement.

He thrilled at the lightness of her tone. Dom couldn't recall the last time he'd heard her happy.

Tessa dumped the register money into the safe, pushed the door closed, and spun the dial. Dom stood, and when he held out his hand to help her up, her touch sent a violent need through him. Big mistake. He let go and planted his hands in his back pockets.

Tessa placed the paper with the locker combination in her desk drawer before locking it.

"Do you think it's a good idea to have the number written down?"

She bit her lower lip. "I just bought the safe and I haven't memorized it. As soon as I do, I'll toss the paper. I sure as heck will never leave the cash in the drawer again."

"If you don't learn the number soon, it will be the same as leaving the cash in the drawer," he warned.

"I hear you." She stood and turned to him. "Who was on the phone?"

"Wrong number."

She scrunched up her face. "Did they leave a message?"

"For a wrong number? I didn't look. I was busy watching you."

Her face held no reaction to his statement, as if she missed what he'd meant. "What if someone really needed to speak with you? You can't let him dangle."

He smiled at her concern for the unknown person and grabbed his phone. "If it'll make you happy, I'll check. Hmm. What do you know? The person left a message." He punched in his pin number and listened.

Static mixed with a huffed voice. "Dom, it's Trace. Send backup to Willow and Bayshore." Then Trace disconnected.

He knew his ex-partner. With such a short message, something bad was going down, and he needed help.

"Shit."

"What is it?"

"Trace is in trouble," he said as he dialed his office and relayed the information. "Listen, I need to go," he told her once he finished speaking to dispatch. "Will you be okay going home by yourself?"

"Of course. But if Trace is in trouble, and he's with Chelsea. I want to go with you."

In a flash, Dom grabbed her shoulders. "Listen to me. Trace is in trouble. Bad trouble. I can't have you there. There could be violence. Do you understand?"

"Fine."

She didn't sound happy about his following instructions, but from her slightly slumped shoulders he could tell she'd do as he asked.

"Thank you," he said, then expelled a long breath. Without a moment's thought, he drew Tessa close and kissed her forehead. Her eyes widened, but before she had a chance to respond, Dom dropped his arms and sprinted out the door to his car.

He couldn't imagine what he'd find when he met up with Trace. His good friend was on a date for God's sake, not assigned to some stakeout that had gone wrong. The intersection of Willow and Bayshore was a very ritzy area.

Dom replayed the message, listening for any signs of pain in Trace's voice, wondering if he'd been shot. Trace would have demanded an ambulance if that had been the case. Shit. Dom was so tired he had to blink to keep focused on the road.

With his light flashing on his roof but his siren off, he raced down Gandy Boulevard to Bayshore Boulevard. At this late hour, the traffic was thankfully light.

As he sped down the road that bordered the water, he normally would have marveled at the brightly lit Tampa skyline but not tonight. All he could think of was that Trace needed him.

For a split second, he considered his partner might be playing a practical joke on him, just like he'd done once or twice before, but with Chelsea in tow, he didn't think he would.

As Dom rounded a curve going north, he saw enough wattage to light half the city. The police had blocked off the entire southbound lane, forcing Dom to pull into the oncoming lane. He headed toward the wreck. Could Trace have called about the accident?

A civilian car headed the group, but he didn't recognize it as belonging to any of his men. Detective Fowler stepped in front of Dom's car and waved him away. He pulled over to the side of the road, shut off his lights and stepped out. Holding out his badge, he trotted toward Fowler.

"Pete, it's Dom. What happened?"

"Oh, hey, Dom. I couldn't tell it was you for a sec. We've got two dead bodies. The guy in the car has a hole in his head, and the other was shot in the chest."

Dom's heart raced. It couldn't be Trace. He pushed past Fowler and halted at the sight of his ex-partner lying sprawled on the ground, part on the sidewalk, part on the road.

"Noooo."

Dom dropped to his knees and gathered his bloodied friend into his arms. In a flash, two policemen pulled him away from Trace.

"Dom. Dom. Let go. Come on. You're contaminating the evidence."

It took a moment for reality to sink in. "He's dead."

Pete Fowler knelt down beside him. "Who was he?"

"My former partner, Trace. He was planning to move here."

"I'm sorry."

Dom lowered Trace to the ground and closed his partner's eyelids. Grief welled inside him, but he forced it down. Then raw anger consumed him. He stood and backed away, but the image of Trace's body would remain an unforgettable image.

"Dom, are you okay?" Fowler asked.

"What about the girl who was with him?" Dom asked, between gritted teeth.

"She's on her way to the hospital. Took two slugs to the chest. I don't think she'll make it."

His heart raced and his stomach soured. "I'm going to get this bastard."

As Dom tried to make his way toward the other men, Pete stepped in front of him. "We all want him, Dom. We all want him, but you know the drill. We have to wait for the ME and CSU before we can process the scene. When we do, we're bound to get enough evidence against him."

"I think it's the same bastard who killed Keri Wilkerson."

"You think so?"

"Who's lead on this one?"

"I am."

"Then I'll show you what I have on this guy."

Pete turned him toward his car. "Go home. We have everything under control. In the morning you can show me what you have."

Dom knew Pete was right. He headed back toward his car, but as he passed the civilian car, he looked in. Dear God. "Pete," Dom shouted.

Fowler rushed over. "You know this guy?"

"Kind of. He was just at the Blue Moon, as were Trace and Chelsea."

Pete took out his pad. "Your friend, Trace. He got a last name?"

"His real name is, or rather was, Harrison Lowell."

"And the girl?"

"I don't know her last name, but her first name is Chelsea. She works at the Blue Moon."

Pete placed a hand on Dom's shoulder. "Thanks. Now get some sleep."

Going home to an empty house held little appeal, but he wasn't fit for company. He'd get a few winks, and then work till he dropped.

The bastard would pay. Big time.

Turning his back to the horrific scene, he trudged to his car and took off. He dreaded having to tell Tessa another one of her people might die.

*　*　*

Morton couldn't believe he'd killed Chelsea. She was light and kind, never saying anything bad to him. Yet when he saw her running toward him, it was if someone else made him raise his arm and shoot her twice in the chest.

He knew she'd panic if she saw the policeman gurgle his last breath. What Morton couldn't figure out was how the cop had found him? Lowell had pestered him in Atlanta, hinting Morton had killed those three useless vermin. Because of that prick, Morton had to move away and change his name, for the second time in three years.

Too bad Chelsea hadn't been with Detective Rossi. Morton wouldn't have minded putting him out of his misery, since he didn't like how the guy was always sniffing about Tessa. With Rossi's friend dead, maybe he'd get the point and leave the Blue Moon—and him —alone.

Morton could protect Tessa and the baby. He didn't need no stinking police around to do the job. Fanatics like Detective Lowell and Rossi never gave up though. They were obsessed individuals, each and every one of 'em. If not for those jerks, he'd have been able to stay and take care of his Mama after Dad died, but the second he smashed the trophy on his father's head, Morton knew he'd have to leave Ohio.

It didn't matter it had been over eighteen years since his old man died, there were no statutes of limitation on murder. He could never go back and see his mom, and he never could send her a birthday card or Mother's day card.

If he let her knew he was alive, she might track him down, and that would lead to bad things. Sure she'd watched as Dad abused him, but some women were helpless against men like that.

Morton barreled down I-4 toward Polk City, far away from Tampa. No one knew of his hideaway in the swamp—except Audrey Mae. Not that she'd ever been there 'cause she was dead, but each time he wrote her, he explained how lovely and secluded his trailer was. He'd been honest about how he came to own the place. One minute this old, gray bearded guy was sitting out in front of his place rocking in his chair, and the next thing, he was dead. The old guy said life wasn't worth living anymore now that his eyesight was going, and Morton decided the only decent thing to do was help the old man out.

That's when he found Bruno, the alligator that lived in the lake. Boy did that gator like to eat fresh meat.

A car honked and whizzed by him, and he glanced at his speedometer. It read forty-eight miles per hour.

Concentrate, Morton, concentrate.

He slapped the steering wheel. Stupid, stupid. He should have grabbed a different gun from the one he'd used to kill that Wilkerson woman. He'd been about to toss the gun in the bay when Detective Lowell had to come along. Damn man. Now he'd have to lose it somewhere in the swamp.

Mrs. Wilkerson had been such a whiner. Her haughty attitude still pissed him off. That no-good bitch was so drunk she would have killed someone before she got home. That was why Morton had to kill her.

When that Doug fellow came into the bar, something inside him snapped too. Doug even had the nerve to send back the hamburger, saying it wasn't cooked right. If he'd shut up and not had so much to drink, he might be alive today, and Morton wouldn't have to worry about being caught for killing two innocent people. Well, one innocent person. The cop's friend had it comin' for snoopin' around.

Shit. The police would tie the Wilkerson woman's murder to Doug Walsh, Chelsea, and Detective Lowell since he'd used the same gun. Well, that couldn't be helped. Doug had to die. And if they never found the gun, he'd never be connected to their deaths.

Morton blew out a long breath, relieved he'd figured out how to avoid the police one more time. He checked his rear view mirror to make sure no one had followed him. He was pretty sure Rossi's friend hadn't thought to call anyone before he was gunned down. Lowell didn't identify him until he stepped in front of the truck.

Morton still questioned how those two had found him. At the bar, Chelsea was practically climbing all over Lowell. Maybe they just happened to be at the wrong place at the wrong time. Oh, well.

Then there was Tessa. Poor thing. She'd be so unhappy when she found out Chelsea was dead. The two of them seemed to have a special bond. But hey, at least Tessa and the baby were safe. That's all that really mattered.

Morton turned off I-4 to 98 North heading toward the entrance to Green Swamp. This early in the morning, the place was deserted. Good. He didn't need anyone to notice him.

He found his turnoff and after a short stretch came to the dirt road that led to his trailer. Except for his headlights, the place was completely black. Not even the moon was in the mood to shed its light in this jungle. His truck bumped over the potholes forcing him to slow down.

Ten minutes later, he pulled up to the front of his trailer. Home, sweet, home. He was really, really tired and just wanted to crash, but he had chores to do first.

Usually, he came here on his days off, but when Tessa's dad was murdered, Morton hadn't been able to make it here.

He pushed open the heavy wooden door and winced at the stench.

After opening the windows, he lit the propane lamps to lighten up the place. Good thing for his large gas tank. He hoped it would last him through the winter. Besides not having electricity, his primitive abode didn't have the luxury of running water either. That was the only bummer. It took a couple of long treks to the river to pump enough drinking water to last for the weekend, but washing up had to be done either in the streams or wait until he returned to his apartment in Tampa.

Once secure in his hideaway, Morton stripped off his blood-spattered clothes and dumped them into a trash bag. Such a waste, but he couldn't afford to leave a trace. Only thing he could do was burn the damn things.

He changed into another set of work clothes, pulled on his waders and headed outside. After throwing the bag in the metal bin, he doused it with lighter fluid and lit it.

The warm flames mesmerized him. As a kid, he loved setting pieces of old furniture on fire just to see them burn. By high school, he'd graduated to large wooden storage sheds, before moving on to houses. He still loved the crackling sound of fire and the intense heat, but killing gave him more satisfaction. Much more. That is, except for killing Chelsea. He hadn't wanted to hurt her. Morton had principles. He only killed people who deserved to die, and Chelsea hadn't deserved it. But he couldn't have let her live. She would have told on him, no matter how nice a girl she was.

Once he was satisfied the evidence of his crime was destroyed, he hustled back to the truck for the leftover meat. Tessa was nice enough to let him take home any meat that was past its expiration date. He told her the food was for his dog. She'd freak if she knew it was for Bruno.

Morton grabbed his gun, stuffed it in the waistband and picked up the soggy plastic bag full of meat. God it smelled bad, but Bruno would devour it in seconds. He and the alligator were pals.

He probably should wait until morning, but for some reason, the dark, wet swamp held a certain appeal tonight. It enveloped him in a womb-like cocoon. No one could see him and he could see no one. He liked being alone. Morton had never run into another person this far into the woods, and doubted he ever would. Sure, the ranger drove on the road to his house, but he'd never come all the way to the trailer.

Morton grabbed his flashlight and pulled on a pair of gloves. As he picked his way toward the lake, the croaking frogs quieted. Branches rustled as wild animals scurried away. Out here, he was king.

After a good ten to twelve minutes, the path turned to mush. The muddy morass seeped up from the lake, which meant he was getting close. With every step, his feet sunk into the mud, and a loud sucking noise popped up from the ground each time he lifted his leg. Kind of like gravity had doubled or something. Morton pretended he was on another planet, exploring the unknown. Morton the conqueror. Yes, it had a nice ring to it.

He stopped and shone his light around to make sure he was headed toward the right spot. It was real easy to get lost in the Green Swamp. He'd missed a landmark once or twice before, and it had taken him until morning to find his way back to the trailer. He didn't want to do that again.

There. His beacon lit the logs he'd placed on the ground that led to the lake and headed toward them. Once he stepped onto the planks, he had to pay attention to keep his balance. The rounded pieces of wood ran for maybe forty feet. He'd chopped the trees himself. And here his dad said he'd never make anything of himself.

At the end of the path, Morton had built what he liked to think of as a makeshift dock. It only extended about three feet into the water, but to him, it was elegant.

He stomped three times to call Bruno. The twelve-foot alligator was smart. He knew food was a swim away.

Morton turned off the flashlight and waited. Two eyes appeared from the murky depths of lake. They glowed a real cool green, kind of like the marbles he had as a kid.

Morton opened the food bag, reached in, and tossed the raw chicken and beef into the water one piece at a time. The loud splashes told him his friend had found the meal.

Pulling the gun from his waistband, he heaved it as far as he could into the lake. Sure hated to lose the weapon, but he couldn't afford to be caught with it. Good thing he had a stash of others. He really only needed one more. Then he'd have met his quota for the year.

Once he'd finished his chores, he headed back to the trailer. It was time to write Audrey Mae a letter.

***

At three in the morning, Ralph was pretty sure Tessa would be asleep. She'd arrived home late, much later than the other few nights he'd waited for her.

Through his binoculars, he'd seen her haul a baby out of her car. Never in a million years would he have thought she'd get knocked up. Sure they'd talked about getting pregnant, but Tessa claimed she was too stressed to conceive. Hell, if they'd had more sex, she would haven't have had a problem.

He grabbed his crotch and adjusted his pants. Just thinking about fucking his ex-wife got him hard. Maybe he'd kidnap her and do her over and over again until she conceived. Then she'd have a reminder of him every day of her life.

Yeah, he liked that idea. Liked it a whole lot. Mostly he liked the fucking part. Crap. Then he wouldn't have the pleasure of slowly killing her. The catch-22 sucked.

He could hear her now. She'd scream, and then cry every time he bit her tits. She'd call him all sorts of names when he shoved his cock in her. Hah. He'd have his way with her, all day, every day, whenever he wanted.

Enough of dreaming. Time to get back at her.

Ralph grabbed his duffel from the back seat of his rental and snuck down the road to her house. He'd practiced his plan a couple of times in the dark and could enter her house with his eyes closed.

His true stroke of genius had been stealing the kid's shoes. Two nights ago he'd followed one of the Blue Moon workers home. The stupid kid, who was a tad shorter than he was, left his shoes on the front stoop since they had mud on them. Ralph stole the sneakers and now wore them. The ends pinched his toes, but he'd deal. When he was done, he planned to return the shoes. A brilliant plan. Absolutely, fucking, brilliant. When they lifted a print of the shoe pattern, guess who'd be the number one suspect? Ha, not him.

Okay, time to do this. He pulled out the rubber suction cup and placed it on her back window. Wearing night vision goggles, it was a piece of cake to cut the glass with the knife. After he removed the six-inch pane, he reached in and unlocked the window. Now came the fun part.

So as not to make any noise, he raised the sash real slow, just enough to crawl in. He spotted the crib and the kid. He loved these infrared goggles. It was like friggin' daylight.

Ralph wasn't interested in a whiny baby—at least not yet. He walked slowly out of the baby's room and into Tessa's. He couldn't make out her features, but as she lay sprawled out in her bed, anger at her betrayal threatened to ruin his plan. His fingers clenched and itched to wrap them around her throat. He wanted to hit her right now, to hurt her, but her time would come.

After taking a few breaths, Ralph reached into his bag and withdrew the Polaroid camera he'd had to search far and wide for. He stood over Tessa's bed and took aim the best he could. Hoping the flash wouldn't wake her, he snapped the photo. Immediately, he wrapped the camera in a towel to lessen the noise as the motor ground out the picture.

Tessa moaned, and Ralph held his breath. When he was sure she hadn't awoken, he crept out of her room and closed the door. Removing a penlight, he examined the photo. Perfect. It was a little blurry, but she'd know someone was watching her.

Ralph propped up the picture on the living room coffee table. Wanting to spread out his surprises, he dropped a stack of photos on the kitchen counter. Ralph had fun capturing Tessa running from the restaurant to the store. His favorites were Tessa leaving in the morning, Tessa getting in her car looking all stressed, and Tessa schlepping the stupid baby around in the grocery store.

He was tempted to toss in the one of the cute babysitters, but he decided to hold onto that photo for later. He just might have to sample the young lady before he left town.

Ralph scribbled a note and left through the baby's window. Pride at his accomplishment raced through him. If only he could be a fly on the wall when she awoke.

Ralph grinned and sauntered back to his car, happy for the first time in years.

CHAPTER TEN

Mandy's small whimpers roused Tessa from a deep sleep, and she had to swallow to wet her mouth. "I'm coming, sweetheart."

Tessa sat up and stretched her arms over her head to get the circulation back into her body. Her lower back screamed from sitting so much yesterday, waiting for those damned policemen to fingerprint all the help. The long hours at work, not to mention the immense stress, were catching up to her.

She trudged out of her bedroom. Jeez. She'd walked through ocean waves faster.

The bedroom light illuminated a small object propped up on the living room coffee table. Tessa squinted to focus her weary eyes and stepped over to the square item that looked like one of those old-fashioned Polaroids.

At first she couldn't figure out how the picture had gotten there. Had Annie left it the other day? No, she'd cleaned since then and would have noticed.

Tessa carried the picture to the standing lamp next to the sofa and flicked on the light. It was a Polaroid, all right. Hell, she didn't realize they existed anymore. At first, she couldn't decide if the blurry photo with its too-light center rimmed by dark edges was a lumpy mound of fabric or a sheet covering some hidden cache.

After tilting the photo to cut the reflected light, she was able to make out a blue lamp with an anchor base in a shadowy region at the top of the photo. Hey, it looked just like the one in her bedroom. Her gaze dropped to the bright spot in the center. The cloth was a blue and white striped sheet, the same kind as on her bed.

Her heart nearly stopped. "Ohmigod."

Tessa sucked in a big breath. It was a photo of her bedroom, and she was in the bed facing away from the photographer. Her auburn hair looked dark brown, but Tessa had no doubt it was her.

Her fingers went limp, and the picture fluttered to the table as panic gripped her to the spot. When had someone taken this? She'd changed the sheets right before going to bed last night. No way someone could have broken into her house while she'd slept, could he have? Tessa didn't sleep through a sneeze let alone a break in.

She would have heard glass shatter or a lock turning. At the very least, she would have awoken when the flash went off—only she hadn't.

Dear God, he could have killed her. Or worse, he could have harmed Mandy.

Fear gushed through her veins. "Mandy!"

Her niece let out a cry.

Tessa raced to the baby's room fearing for the baby's life. Her stomach twisted into a knot. When she saw Mandy lying on her back, playing with her feet, Tessa nearly dropped to the ground with relief.

As she stood over Mandy's crib reveling in the child's healthy glow, the baby looked up and smiled. Tessa's heart swelled. She picked her up, kissed her dewy cheek and placed her over her shoulder.

"Good morning sunshine." Mandy smelled all powdery and clean. "You hungry?" She tried to sound upbeat, but her voice caught. Hopefully, the six-month old wouldn't notice. Of course, Tessa knew she couldn't answer, but it helped calm her to hear her own voice.

As she started back to the kitchen with Mandy clinging to her chest, she felt a rush of cool air coming from the window. She turned and strode across the room.

"What the..."

A large, neatly cut hole in the glass marred the pane. Clasping Mandy closer to her chest, Tessa whipped around half expecting the intruder to be pointing a gun at her.

In a shaky voice she called out, "Anyone there?"

It was a stupid thing to do, but if someone were in the house, he'd already know where to find her. Mandy kicked her feet, and Tessa let up on her death grip.

Where could someone hide in her two-bedroom house? Her mind flipped through the possibilities. The bathroom was the only space she hadn't checked, but she didn't dare test her theory and put Mandy in jeopardy. She needed help.

Trying not to act too nervous around her niece, Tessa jogged to the kitchen and picked up her cell phone. She dialed Dominic's number. Calling 9-1-1 wouldn't do. She didn't want a stranger coming to her house. For all she knew, her phone was tapped, and the intruder would show up as the policeman.

Dominic's cell rang and rang. "Answer, dammit," Tessa pleaded with the phone.

Mandy pulled on Tessa's hair. "Not now, sweetheart."

"Yeah?" he answered.

Finally. She sagged with relief. "It's Tessa. I'm sorry to wake you," she said in a whisper. "Someone broke into my house. I think he may still be here, but I don't want search for him."

"I'll be right there. Lock yourself in a room if you can," he responded. "I'll call for backup." Then he hung up.

Lock herself where? Mandy's room was easy to get into from the outside, and the lock on Mandy's side of the adjoining bath was broken.

She'd leave. Yes, that's it. She'd get in her car and wait at the end of the street for Dominic to arrive. Together they could search her place. Tessa refused to be a sitting duck.

Even though she was still in her nightgown, a rather see-through nightgown no less, modesty was the least of her worries. This early in the morning, the temperature often dipped to the low sixties, but she'd gladly suffer a little chill to keep Mandy from harm.

Tessa raced into Mandy's room and grabbed the crib's baby blanket.

As she wrapped the cover around the baby, a piece of paper floated to the ground, and Tessa bent down to picked it up.

THE BABY'S NEXT.

Tessa's knees collapsed, and she sank to the ground. "You won't get away with this you bastard," she shouted to the empty room. Blood pounded in her ears, preventing her from hearing a thing.

She had to get away from this maniac. Tessa scrambled to her feet and dashed once more to the kitchen, looking for her car keys. Where were they? "Damn."

She remembered that her keys were in her purse next to her bed—in her bedroom, where he might be hiding. So much for that plan. She thought about sneaking a peak in her bedroom from the bathroom, but if he knew she knew he was still there, he might attack. Damn. Her fuzzy thinking stamped out all logic.

She'd have to wait outside for Dominic. If Glenda was up, Tessa could seek haven there.

Tessa unlocked the front door and pulled it open, only to shut it quickly. The intruder could be lurking outside just as easily. She couldn't chance making a stupid mistake with Mandy's life at stake.

Her heart rattled her ribcage so hard, she couldn't think straight. There were too many unknowns.

What to do? What to do? Tessa peered out the living room window, looking for any kind of unfamiliar car the intruder might have used, but no strange vehicles were parked on the street. Good. Across the street, Glenda's house remained dark. That wasn't good.

"Damn, damn, double damn." Glenda said she'd be gone a few days to visit her daughter.

Tessa glanced at Mandy. "Sorry, sweetheart. Aunt Tessa has a potty mouth." Her brother would never let her visit again if Mandy's first words were cuss words.

Tessa glanced at the clock on the TV stand. It was only ten after six. How much longer would Dominic take? She paced the small living room wearing a path in the rug, planning her escape, all the while listening for any strange noises.

Decision time.

Given the boogieman hadn't jumped out since her phone call to

Dominic, he probably wasn't in her nine hundred square foot house. Okay. She'd stay by the front door with Mandy and await Dominic's arrival. With that plan, her pulse slowed.

She patted Mandy on the back to keep her from fussing. Too bad Tessa had no idea where the detective lived or how long it would take him to get here. Dominic claimed he'd call for backup.

Her shoulders slumped. How could she be so stupid? Ralph had to have been the intruder. Who else would pull a stunt like this? Was his goal to scare her to death? If so, he'd succeeded, but why threaten an innocent baby?

Oh, Jeez. Maybe he thought Mandy was hers. He'd always wanted a family, but Tessa wanted to wait until after she finished school to have a child. Her ex was the jealous type. He must think she'd remarried and become pregnant right away.

Now she understood what he planned to do: take away everything dear to her. He'd already killed her father and murdered her clients. That left Mandy.

How could she have married a man like that? She'd been such a fool.

Tessa glanced at her watch: 6:13 a.m. Pacing didn't expend enough energy. She needed to cook or clean, two acts that usually helped calm her. Her stomach grumbled, and only then did she realize she hadn't eaten since yesterday lunch. As if to join in, Mandy kicked and let out a wail.

"Oh, Mandy. I promised you something to eat. I'm sorry, sweetheart."

Tessa placed Mandy in her bouncy chair.

As she entered the kitchen, her gaze caught sight of a stack of photos on the counter. The top one was of her opening her car door. "What the…"

She picked them up, and as she leafed through them, a rumbling of fear traveled up her arms to her heart. Ralph must have followed her from work. He'd invaded her privacy—and now her home.

Mandy began to whimper. "Oh, I'm coming, sweetheart."

With trembling hands Tessa warmed some milk for her niece and fixed a cup of hot tea for herself, before grabbing a protein bar from the cabinet for nourishment. Her stomach couldn't handle a full-blown meal.

Fifteen minutes later, a sharp rap sounded at the door, and Tessa jumped, despite expecting the detective.

"It's me, Dominic," he called in a raspy voice.

Tessa peeked out the kitchen window and craned her neck to make sure the person standing at her front door wasn't Ralph. The tension poured from her body when she saw who it was.

She raced to the door and whipped it open. He ran his gaze from her head to her toes.

Tessa crossed her arms at the gush of cold. "I'm fine. Come in."

His shirt was buttoned wrong and his face looked like he'd sprinkled black lava bits on his face, but his mad dash to save her buoyed her spirits.

The stern set of Dominic's jaw and his strong shoulders spoke to her. The recent devastating events of the past few days had came crashing down on her, and she flung her arms around his neck and pressed against him. Her breasts molded against the hard planes of his chest and his warmth speared through her. She never wanted to let go.

"I'm so glad you're here," she half panted, half whispered.

"Are you sure you're okay?" The soft, tender voice melted her to the spot.

"Hmm-mm."

"And Mandy?"

"Yes, she's fine." A little sob escaped. If anything had happened to her niece, she'd never recover.

Dominic ran his long, strong fingers up and down her back, massaging away the tension, and the fear that had laced every nerve slowly dissipated. His arms brought such relief she never wanted to move.

What was she doing? Tessa stepped back and wiped the brimming tears from her eyes.

"Did you check out the rest of the house yet?" he asked, acting as if she hadn't just thrown herself at him.

"No, but the only place to look is my bedroom and the bathroom. I was too afraid to chance it."

"Smart thinking." Dom grabbed her hand and walked her over to the sofa, his strong clasp bringing her comfort. "Stay here. I want to check out the house."

She nodded, and his gaze shot to her chest. Tess dropped down onto the seat and grabbed a pillow to cover herself.

Dominic winked, then disappeared into her bedroom. Oh my. He'd looked at her as if she were a meal to a starving man. Why hadn't she thought to change? *Because the intruder could have been in my bedroom, dummy.*

Mandy banged her bottle against the bouncy chair, and Tessa rushed to the kitchen and lifted the baby out. "Have you finished?"

Tessa tried to concentrate on Mandy instead of what Dominic was doing, but she couldn't. First the closet door slammed, and then he tore back the shower curtain. She held her breath, waiting for a struggle, but none came.

Relieved, Tessa carried Mandy back to the sofa and sat down to burp her. Dominic stalked out of her bedroom a moment later. Not saying a word, he ripped opened the hall closet and poked his hand behind the clothes. Next, he marched into the kitchen. More doors opened and closed. Did he really think someone could hide in her crammed cabinets?

He returned to the living room. "The intruder's not in the house. I'll check out back, but with the small yard, I don't know where he could hide."

"Me neither, but if it's Ralph, he's very resourceful."

Dominic halted. "You think it's Ralph?"

"Who else would it be? Taking a photo of me while I was sleeping is personal. It's not something your ordinary thief would do."

"He did what?" His body stiffened as he advanced toward her.

"He took a photo of me while I was asleep." She leaned over to the coffee table and handed him the Polaroid.

Dominic studied the picture, his brows creasing his forehead. "When was this taken?"

"Last night." She explained about changing the sheets.

His lips pressed hard together. "This changes everything. Stay put.

I'll be right back." He withdrew his gun from his holster and headed out the front door.

She dreaded what he'd do when he saw the other photos.

The moment Dominic left, Tessa placed Mandy in her playpen and raced to her bedroom, confident her niece would be safe for the next few minutes.

Dear Lord. Two pairs of underpants, a bra, a dirty sweatshirt and a pair of socks lay scattered on the floor. Embarrassed, she gathered the dirty clothes and tossed them in her closet.

Tessa pulled on a pair of jeans and a sweater, not bothering with underwear. As she stepped from the bedroom, Dominic pushed open the front door. Now that was what she called good timing.

"Clear," he announced in an authoritative tone. "I'll call CSU and ask them to dust for prints. Beneath your window are some good tracks. If we find the guy, we might get a match."

Tessa's hand shook and her stomach suddenly threatened to revolt again. She didn't know how much more turmoil she could handle.

Dominic turned his back to her and punched in a phone number. He spoke for a few minutes, and then hung up.

"I called off the backup," he said. "I saw the hole in the glass. Did the intruder take anything?"

Dominic moved toward her and stopped inches from her. He must have splashed on aftershave for he smelled wonderful. She was surprised she hadn't noticed before.

"Not that I know of. In fact he left something."

"Besides the photo?"

"Yes. I'll get them."

Tessa hurried to the kitchen and grabbed the photos. She waited in silence as he perused them.

"The bastard is sick."

"He also left a note."

Dominic's gaze bored through her. "What else aren't you telling me?"

"That's it, I swear."

"What did the note say?"

"That Mandy was next."

"Jesus Christ." He raked a hand over his head. "Why is he doing this?"

Dominic didn't get it. "To scare me, of course. To let me know he could kill me at any moment. Don't you realize he could have kidnapped Mandy when he was in here?" Tessa knotted her hair behind her head. "I'm betting he thinks she's mine. That would really piss him off. Now that he knows where I live, he'll continue to mess with my head." Her breath came out faster and faster.

"He's doing a good job of it already."

The sympathy in his eyes stirred a deep yearning. None of the men she'd encountered ever tried to understand her. They expected her to understand their motivations. Where was the give and take in that? Dominic, a cop no less, listened.

"I'll handle it in my own way." Tessa wouldn't burden him with her fears. Instead, she studied his face, needing to focus on something other than her problem. "You look tired."

"Why don't you sit down?"

She'd rather stand. Actually, she'd rather pace to help rid her body of her nervous energy, but the seriousness with which he asked prompted her to step over to the sofa.

Dominic sat next to her and took her hand in his, and the tender act caught her off guard. Her mind told her to pull back, but her need for human contact let him hold on.

He rubbed her palm with his calloused thumb in slow, sensual circles, and the little pulses jumped between her legs. She squeezed her thighs tight. Tessa didn't need a reminder of what she didn't have in her life. Right now she needed to find Ralph before he came back, not have some hot affair with the sexy detective.

She shut her eyes to clear her head.

"If I look tired it's because I didn't sleep at all last night," he answered a full minute after she'd asked the question. "Do you remember I received a call from Trace around midnight?"

She clasped her free hand over her mouth. "I completely forgot about him." Sadness swept his features. "Did something happen?"

Dominic pressed his lips together and nodded. He took a deep breath. "Trace was murdered."

Her body quivered. "Ohmigod, no. How?"

Dominic's Adam's apple bobbed up and down. "When I got to the scene, Trace was dead and Chelsea had been taken to the hospital. Someone shot both of them."

Tessa's world spun out of control, and her heart raced so hard it almost burst. She pressed a hand to her chest. "Shot? Is she okay?"

"She took two bullets to the chest."

Tessa collapsed back onto the seat and withdrew her free hand from his clasp. The tears she'd expected to gush out had dried up.

She needed to see her friend, but when Tessa started to stand, her legs wouldn't hold her. Her hands trembled, and she collapsed back on the sofa unable to take a full breath. "I have to be there for her."

"I called the hospital on the way over. The surgeons were able to remove the bullets, but she hasn't regained consciousness."

"What are her chances?" Oh, God, please tell me she'll live. Deep in her heart, Tessa knew all of this tragedy was her fault somehow.

He looked away. "They aren't good."

First her father, then her friend—not to mention her two patrons. "Poor Chelsea. She didn't deserve this."

"I don't think Trace deserved it either."

She'd been insensitive. "I'm sorry. I didn't mean to imply—"

Dominic looked down at her. "I know. And I'm afraid there's more."

"What do you mean, more? Don't tell me someone else is dead."

"Remember the man at the bar who was drunk and stalked off right before Chelsea left?"

Tessa had to refocus on last night. Was it only seven short hours ago? "Doug. Doug Walsh. Yes. What about him?"

"He was murdered too. Someone put a bullet in his head."

Tessa's world went black.

"Tessa, Tessa, can you hear me?"

When she opened her eyes, Dominic was leaning over her, her head cradled in his hands. She jerked up but dropped back down into his caress. The rush of pain threatened to overwhelm her again. "What happened?"

"You fainted."

"I never faint. Fainting is for wimps." Tessa wanted to be strong.

Dominic helped her to a sitting position. "Let me bring you a glass of water."

Her mouth seemed to be filled with dried glue. "Okay." Tessa watched Mandy play with her mobile in the playpen. At least one of them was oblivious to the tragedy.

"Here." Dominic handed her a glass of cold water.

"Thanks." She shook her head. "My life is so out of control I don't know what to do. It's obvious someone wants to destroy me by destroying the business."

Dominic sat still and stared ahead as if he hadn't heard her. His face paled, and his lips pressed firmly together.

"You can't stay here any longer." His tone came out monotone, as if he were talking to himself. His gaze darted to the ceiling and then down to the floor.

Adrenaline shot through her heart. "I'm not going to let Ralph dictate what I can and can't do. I'll buy a dog or put in the alarm system. To hell with the landlord. No one's going to make me do anything I don't want to do."

He whipped back to her. "You don't understand. If Ralph was the intruder, or even if he wasn't, he'll return. I've been a detective for ten years. I know how these sickos think. If you don't care about yourself then think of Mandy."

Guilt swamped her. Mandy. Precious, innocent Mandy. "You're right."

"Okay, good." Dominic let out a long breath. "You'll have to move."

Was he talking to himself again? "Excuse me?"

He stood and surveyed the room before locking his gaze on her. "Everything that has happened in the last few weeks has been connected to the Blue Moon and its people, whether they work there or are patrons. I don't know what his game is, or what their game is, but you're smack dab in the middle."

That much she'd figured out. "I just remembered," Tessa exclaimed with a burst of energy. "I asked Mick to follow Doug Walsh for a few miles last night. Maybe he saw something."

Dominic grabbed his cell. "You have his number?"

"Not here. It's at work."

He swiped his cell. "It's Rossi. Can you get me a number for a Mick —" He cupped his hand over the phone and looked up at her.

"Stukes."

"For a Mick Stukes. Yes, I'll hold."

As he waited for the information, she wondered if he'd forgotten the bomb he'd dropped a moment ago. Not that she felt safe in her too-small apartment, but it was home. When Dominic said she'd have to move, she couldn't imagine where? To the women's shelter? A local hotel? Or did he mean out of town?

"Got it. Thanks." Dominic hung up and printed the number in his pad. Without saying anything to her, he placed a second call. "This is Detective Rossi. When you get a chance, could you call me on my cell. It's 813-555-1049."

He turned to her. "He's not home."

"Now what?"

Dominic stood up and squared his shoulders. "As I said, you can't stay here. I'll help you pack."

"I don't—"

"It's not negotiable, Tessa. You're in too much danger here. Besides, you have to think of your niece."

Of course Mandy took that moment to let out a shriek, confirming Dominic's suggestion.

"I'm not happy about this whole situation. Putting it bluntly, it sucks," she said.

"I'd rather have you unhappy than dead."

CHAPTER ELEVEN

Dominic was right. Tessa's situation was too serious to ignore. She couldn't afford to think only of herself. Mandy had to be protected at all costs.

"If I'm right about Ralph," she began, "he'll hurt Mandy for the sake of getting back at me. It would be better if I left her with my friend, Annie. She runs the women's shelter in town."

Dominic glanced over at her niece. After watching her play for a few seconds, his face softened. "Do you feel comfortable leaving her with her?"

Guilt spiked. "I don't have a choice. Besides, I trust Annie, and Mandy seems taken with her. If my friend can't personally keep her, Annie will find someplace where Ralph will never find her, and that's all that matters."

He slapped his knees and stood up. "Okay. Now that Mandy's destiny is settled, let's get you packed. The sooner we get you out of here the better."

The finality of his tone depressed her, but she understood leaving her home was best. "Do you think he'd dare come back?"

"Probably not right now, especially with my car parked out front, but there's nothing to prevent him from breaking in again, say in a few days."

Dominic always seemed to have the answers. "You're right." She couldn't stop saying that phrase.

Once Tessa plied Mandy with her favorite toys, she led Dominic into the small bedroom.

Her shoulders sagged at the onerous chore of figuring out what to bring. "My brother packed Mandy's clothes in the blue suitcase that's in the top shelf of the closet. Would you mind getting it down?"

"Not at all."

Tessa grabbed Mandy's belongings from the chest of drawers and laid them on the changing table. The closet door clicked open and then closed. With her back to him, the sliding of the suitcase zipper let her know he'd retrieved the case.

A moment later, he stepped next to Tessa, the slight hint of his menthol aftershave making her all too aware of his maleness. A longing to be held, to be told everything would be all right, blasted through her body so hard she shook.

"Are you okay?" he said, his voice laced with concern.

Tessa swallowed and turned toward him. As his gaze searched her face, heat raced up her body. When had the hardened detective turned so nice?

"Yes, I'm fine." If she allowed herself to open up, she'd be crying on his wonderfully supportive chest in no time. "If you wouldn't mind, you could help me pack."

"Tell me what I need to do."

"Help fold Mandy's clothes. I can fit more into her suitcase if everything's neat."

"I do neat quite well."

"I've noticed." Now why did she say that? She shouldn't be noticing anything about him, but she couldn't help it. She let out a long, controlled breath pleased he seemed unaware of her response.

Once she transferred half of the small outfits to the bed for Dominic to fold, she returned to her half of the packing. Even though he remained five feet from her, seemingly focused on preparing Mandy for her move, his presence unnerved her and confused her. Conflicting emotions continually assaulted her every time he neared.

Tessa finally admitted what was plaguing her.

She wanted him—in bed—badly.

Tessa needed to release of all the anger she'd stored up in the last month. The pure pleasure of being in his arms would make her feel like a woman again. Oh, how she needed a chance at normalcy.

Where she wanted the relationship to head, she didn't know—or if she even wanted a relationship. Heaven knows, she had enough turmoil in her life, and being involved with a man might send her over the edge, but the brief enjoyment could provide her with a lot of memories.

Out of the corner of her eye, she watched Dominic carefully stack Mandy's outfits in the suitcase as she'd asked. His sense of order appealed to her, and his control brought her peace.

"A baby sure has a lot of stuff," Dominic said shaking his head. He picked up Mandy's baby powder and lotion. "I guess she'll need all of this too."

"Yes. I have no way of knowing how long she'll need to be in the shelter. I didn't want Annie to have to purchase supplies."

"Good thinking."

His praise boosted her spirits. Tessa decided he'd make a great dad. When he wasn't asking Tessa questions or searching the house for an intruder, he'd glanced at her niece with longing. She wondered if Dominic dreamed of having a child, like she did.

"Have you ever been married?" she asked, trying to keep her tone light as if she were merely making idle conversation.

"No," he snapped.

Tessa stiffened and waited for an explanation but none came. Marriage must be a sore subject. His gaze looked distant, as if he were remembering a woman he'd wanted to marry, but never did. Or were his thoughts on his dead partner?

Trace seemed a safer topic. "I'm sorry about your friend. Losing someone important is difficult to handle." Thinking of friends, the image of her dad surfaced, and she tamped down a shudder.

"Oh, Trace. Yeah, sure. Thanks."

His mind must have been elsewhere, and an unwanted surge of jealousy coursed through her.

She waited a beat before continuing. "I'm a good listener, you know. Sometimes talking about a death can help."

"Some other time, maybe."

Tessa had the sense they were discussing two different topics. "Were you and Trace close?"

He shrugged. "Not really. We hadn't kept in touch after he moved to Atlanta. When he called a few days ago, I was surprised to say the least."

"I always thought when two people worked together night and day, they became part of each other's lives."

He took a moment before answering. "We never were tight. The guy was too reckless." Dominic stopped putting away Mandy's clothes and took a step toward her. "Trace drove too fast, jumped to too many conclusions, and rushed into dangerous situations. He and I were complete opposites. I like to analyze a situation before taking action."

So much for getting him in bed. "Couldn't you have asked for a new partner?"

His shoulders stiffened. "He had a good side. Trace was pure genius when it came to finding and identifying trace evidence. Hence the nickname."

Something didn't add up. "Why did he move away?"

Dominic turned back to the bed, shielding his face. "When he failed to follow procedure one time too many, I turned him in to the Captain." His hands fisted at his sides.

"Sounds like someone else I know." He turned around and a corner of his mouth turned up. Not quite a smile but not a frown either.

"There is a similarity," he answered.

"How did turning in your partner make you feel?" she asked.

"Like shit." He ran a hand over his stubble. "Sorry. I didn't mean to swear."

"That's all right, I felt the same way when I told on Ralph."

Dominic picked up one of Mandy's nighties he'd already folded and refolded it.

Tessa prodded some more. "Are you feeling guilty because you did what you believed was right?"

Dominic shut the baby's suitcase, picked it up, and walked out the door. He set the case down and turned around. "I guess I am. Let's get you packed too."

Tessa understood the topic still plagued him, and he wasn't in the mood to have an open discussion. With time, she bet she could get him to share—and not just about his former partner—but about the woman that had shut down his emotions.

Tessa followed Dominic into her bedroom, and the room seemed to shrink. Of course, he chose to stand next to her bed, and she couldn't help but picture him under the covers.

Naked.

Next to her.

In her.

"Where do you keep your suitcases?" he asked as he glanced around the room, looking as if he expected them to be in plain view.

"In the closet."

He pulled open her closet door. Standing on his toes, he reached the top shelf, tugged on the handle, and lowered the suitcase. When Tessa stared at his strong forearms and long, muscular legs, lustful thoughts filled her heart. Embarrassed he might catch her watching, she whipped around.

What she wouldn't give to let go of her inhibitions, to forget her problems, and indulge in an evening of mindless sex. Too bad a man like Dominic probably didn't do mindless anything. Everything about him seemed well planned. The notebook he carried around even had color-coded note pages. His neat handwriting and neat appearance were dead giveaways the man was a control freak. He even said he analyzed everything before taking action. Mr. Spontaneous, he was not.

Oh, well. She'd stick to fantasizing. It was a lot safer.

"You need both of these?" he asked.

"Yes." He must not understand how many clothes women needed for an extended stay—not to mention makeup and lotions. "You can set them on the bed." That way, she'd be forced to stand, hence avoiding the temptation to lie down.

"Now what?" he asked.

She didn't need him to help fold her underwear or handle her clothes. "Why don't you look in on Mandy while I pack." She didn't make eye contact.

"I'm sure the baby is fine. We can hear her fuss if she needs anything. She's less than ten feet from us." He paused a moment. "Do I make you nervous?"

Yes, she wanted to shout, but for all the wrong reasons. He was too sexy and too emotionally unavailable.

Tessa turned her back to him, trying to figure out how to reach her bras and panties into the case without his notice. "Of course not, why?" For almost being a psychologist, she should be better at expressing her feelings.

Without a sound, Dominic moved behind her and pressed his hands to her waist. "I think I have an antidote."

"Whoa." Her pulse sped up as excitement raced to her groin. She grabbed his hands and attempted to step out of his embrace, but he held on tight.

"What you do to me," he whispered against her ear.

Tessa whipped around in his arms, needing to see the expression on his face. His change of attitude had come out of the blue, and she wanted to make sure he wasn't imagining it.

His dreamy bedroom eyes and half-parted lips invited her to a place she wanted to go, but indecision took her breath away. He couldn't know she'd been contemplating this moment minutes ago.

"I'm not sure this is a good idea." Even to her, she sounded unconvincing. Her body wanted him—bad—but her mind told her she couldn't handle any more chaos.

He stepped back, and emptiness filled her. "I want you."

"Since when?" she asked. "I'm sorry," she immediately added. "You haven't exactly acted interested."

"Well, I am. Since the moment I saw you in fact." Dominic's gaze cut to her soul. "There's something tender and fragile about you, yet your inner strength shines through."

No one had said such kind words to her in her life. Certainly not her absentee mom, nor Ralph, for that matter. Her taciturn father might have believed what Dominic said, but he didn't use words to express his feelings.

"I don't know what to say."

Dominic dragged a finger down her cheek. "You don't have to say anything. Close your eyes," he commanded.

She knew he'd never hurt her. Tessa trusted him and did as he asked. Her senses sharpened from the loss of sight, and his masculine scent became more pronounced. Even Mandy's baby noises became more distinct.

His callused palms cupped her face. Tessa wanted to open her eyes, to see the yearning in Dominic's face, but she enjoyed the new sensations too much.

She raised her arms to latch onto his strong shoulders, but he said, "Not yet," in the softest voice she'd ever heard. His minty breath caressed her face, and the desire to kiss him overwhelmed her.

Suddenly Tessa's fears disappeared. Being with Dominic felt right. To hell with consequences. She'd deal with rejection, or whatever came her way, tomorrow. Right now, she wanted him. She deserved a little bit of happiness given all she'd been through.

Without waiting for his approval, she opened her eyes and drew his head downward. The moment their lips touched, energy surged through her. Dominic clasped her to his chest and drew her close, his strong pectorals pressing hard against the tips of her breasts. Tessa melted into him.

She opened her mouth, and his tongue darted in to capture hers. His rough beard scraped her skin, but his soft pliable lips encouraged her to explore. Her tongue mated with his—in and out, in and out. She wanted the parry never to stop.

Dominic pulled away and gulped in a breath. "Oh, God, I've wanted to kiss you for so long," he panted.

"Me too." At least since he'd come to her rescue this morning.

He stepped back to the bed, pulling her forward. Then like two dancers doing the waltz, he turned her around. Her knees hugged the comforter, and he pushed the suitcases to one side before gently laid her on her back. Thank goodness for a big bed.

The sight of his muscular chest hanging above her, coupled with his darkly, brooding face within inches of hers, began to cleanse the horrors of the past few weeks. Tessa shelved all the tragedy and allowed herself the freedom to drink in his magnificence.

"You are so beautiful," he said.

Tessa wanted to deny his statement but instead answered, "Thank you."

Dominic dropped on top of her, supporting himself on his elbows. "If I'm too heavy for—"

"No. Now shut up and kiss me again," she said half-giggling.

He smiled. "You got it."

Dominic descended upon her lips, nibbling, then kissing, and then nibbling and kissing again. She lifted her hips to meet his throbbing erection. My he was big.

Tessa wasn't satisfied with making out. Once she'd given into her urges, she wanted all of him. The need to feel his skin on her body overwhelmed her. "It's getting warm in here. Maybe we should—"

"—take off our clothes," he finished.

Tessa expected Dominic to unbutton his shirt and shuck off his pants. Instead he rolled to the side and pulled off her sweater in one quick movement.

His eyes widened. "Wow. I hadn't expected you to be the braless type."

Embarrassed, Tessa crossed her arms over her chest. "I usually wear one, but I was in a hurry to get dressed."

"I see."

He pulled her arms to her side and leaned over. When he sucked on her right nipple, a shiver of delight raced to her groin. He moved to the other side and laved her other nipple, and both her nubs hardened into tiny peaks.

"Let me say it again," Dominic whispered. "You are incredible."

"So are you." Well, she wasn't going to be the only one to enjoy all the touching and teasing. She wanted to drive him crazy too. "All's fair in love and war, you know."

Before he could rebut, Tessa reached over and unsnapped his jeans. His mouth dropped open. If her aggression took him by surprise, too damn bad. She yanked down the zipper, and his cock jutted out though the slit in his boxers.

"Whoa," she said. "Talk about being well-endowed." The man was amazing.

"I'm glad I please you. Two can play at this game, however," he said with lust pooling in his eyes.

"Oh, yeah?" Tessa couldn't believe how relaxed she'd become.

He reached over and with one pull, unzipped her jeans. Tessa lifted her hips, and he tugged them off. And then he smiled. A real, honest to goodness smile, complete with dimples. Her heart thudded in her chest.

"Very nice," he said, scanning her body.

Tessa drank in his appreciative look.

Dominic dove on top of her, and when he ran his callused palms down her sides, she shivered with delight. Tessa grabbed his shoulders, and when she massaged his tight muscles, it was if a starter gun had exploded. She raced to touch every inch of his sinuous body, almost expecting a referee to shout, "Time." Thank God, no one did.

Dominic closed his eyes and let out a moan that thrilled her to no end. His passion gave her the needed confidence to roll him over. "My turn."

He sprawled on his back. When she ran a nail down his hard length, he pulled her up to meet his lips. "I need you now, Tessa."

"I was wondering when you'd ask."

Dominic rolled them both over until he loomed above her, and then kissed her with what felt like years of pent up passion. She spread her legs, and he slid right into her. She gasped at his size.

He stopped. "Does it hurt?"

"No, but I wasn't expecting you to fill me so completely."

"Why don't you ride me instead? That way, you can move at your own speed."

She'd never straddled Ralph. He'd always wanted to have total control, so Dominic's willingness to relinquish the role of love leader sent her over the edge. "Okay."

He dropped back onto the mattress, and Tessa crawled on top on him. When she positioned herself over his jutting member, the power position enthralled her. "I'm going to like this," she said staring down at him. Her hair landed on his chest.

"I hope so. I certainly plan to."

Tessa slowly slid down his shaft him until he filled her completely. Dom closed his eyes and sucked in a breath, acting as if her deliberate approach was killing him. Good. She tested his fullness by rising up until she reached his tip, and then slid down on his thick shaft again inch by wonderful inch. A fresh flow of lubrication stopped all discomfort.

With the headiness of being in charge, she palmed his chest, and the soft down of his hair tickled her palm. As much as she wanted to take her time, her need overcame her. She rose up and down his tumescent cock, faster and faster, thrilling in her building climax. The scent of their sex filled the air.

Dominic grabbed her hips and held her still. Frantic from the loss of movement, Tessa tried to slip further down on him, but he held tight.

"Wait. I don't want to come too soon. You deserve to come first."

The absence of movement drove her crazy. Finally, he drove his hips upward, filling her with his being. Blood pounded in her ears as her heart threatened to burst. She let loose a primordial scream as Dominic's fluid exploded.

She clamped down on his sex, squeezing the last drop from him. Tessa had never reached the clouds—until now. When he let go of her hips, she dropped down on his chest, exhausted. She could lie there forever.

"I'm sorry," he whispered a moment later.

She bolted upright. "You're sorry? For what? For having sex with me?"

"No, no. What I meant was, I didn't use a condom. I didn't come prepared. I never dreamed I'd be with you like this. It happened all so fast."

The sincere look on his face made her laugh. "I forgive you. I think it's safe though."

Mandy began to cry and Dominic smiled. "Whoops. I guess we were a little loud."

"You mean I was a little loud." With care, Tessa rolled off him. "I'll get something to clean us up, and then check on her. I bet the noise did startle her."

"I imagine so."

Dominic's brow was smooth, and the smile on his face told her he'd needed their heady affair as much as she had. What a great way to start the day.

After she washed them off, she pulled on her clothes, this time making sure to put on underwear. Mandy had quieted, but she wanted to hold her niece.

Tessa shuffled back into the bedroom with the baby in her arms. "Do you know where I'll be staying while you try to find Ralph?"

He winked. "Yes. With me."

CHAPTER TWELVE

Ralph was still pissed. As soon as Tessa called the cops this morning, he figured it was time to get the hell away. Christ. He'd felt like a whipped dog skulking down the road, but he knew his day would come.

At least he'd heard his ex-wife's cries of distress when she found the photos. Her fear gave him great satisfaction. Boy did he love yanking her chain. The listening device he'd planted in the living room was worth its price. Her words came in loud and clear.

He'd thought about confronting her right away, but he then decided he'd derive more joy letting her stew before he showed his face.

Tessa's words kept echoing in his head. "I'm too afraid to look around the house," she'd whined to the cop. "Can you come over?" Jesus Christ. What had he ever seen in her?

Oh yeah, her hot bod—and those magnificent breasts. A guy needed a chick with great boobs.

Tessa would get her due if it were the last thing he did.

Right now he was on his way to the Blue Moon. She'd have to come to work sooner or later. He'd wait for her to arrive, and then follow her back to wherever she planned to hide. Tessa was such an easy read.

She'd do anything to keep the kid safe. And herself. She always was a coward.

**

Tessa called Annie to see if she could find a safe haven for Mandy. Twice during the conversation Tessa had to ask her friend to repeat the directions to the rendezvous spot. Remembrances of Dominic's naked chest and sexy body kept distracting her.

"She's welcome to stay with me," Annie offered. "I haven't had a baby in the house in five years."

Hope bubbled up. "Are you sure? I'd feel so much better if you'd watch her."

"Of course. I know how much Ralph's return scares you, and I promise I won't let her out of my sight."

"You're wonderful."

Annie laughed. "Just wait until you earn your PhD. I'll take my fee out in trade."

"You know I promised to help counsel the women for no charge."

"I know, but I'd feel better if I knew I'd be helping you out in the process."

"Well, you are."

Tessa hung up and wrapped her arms around her waist. The control she'd desperately sought, seeped in. Mandy would be safe—and so would she.

"It's all set, then?" Dominic asked, as he stepped behind her and pulled her hair behind her shoulders.

Oh, how his touch soothed her. "Yes." She turned to face him. Wow. Even with his rough beard, and her libido temporarily satisfied, he turned her on. "Here are the directions where we're supposed to drop off Mandy. I'm not very familiar with New Tampa."

He stepped back and studied the piece of paper. "I know the place. It's not more than thirty-five minutes from here. Once Mandy is in safe hands, you can follow me to my place."

"Okay."

Tessa wasn't sure why she wasn't more enthusiastic. Now that

Mandy would be safe, Tessa should be thrilled to be staying with the hot detective. Maybe with everything else hanging over her head, like her dad's funeral, Chelsea's life dangling by a thread, and her ex stalking her, joy eluded her.

She shivered.

"What's wrong?" Dominic asked.

She loved his solicitous attitude. "I feel like a damn puppet with Ralph pulling the strings. I'm so mad, I could scream."

He gathered her in his arms. "Don't worry. I'll find the bastard for you."

She reached up and kissed him. "I can hardly wait."

"We need to leave so I can do my job. Why don't you put Mandy in the car?"

"Sure." Tessa grabbed her sweater from the sofa and pulled it on. Next she gathered her niece and a few of her toys. "Are you ready for a little ride?" she asked Mandy.

Her adorable niece looked up and grabbed Tessa's thick sweater, apparently distracted by the little pearls sewn in circles on the front. She let Mandy tug away. Tessa didn't have the heart to deny the little girl anything.

Someday, when the danger had passed, they'd talk about how the two of them had run away from the bad man.

"Let's go," Dominic said, his hands and arms filled with suitcases.

Maybe she shouldn't have bothered with the cooler, but leaving food in the refrigerator to rot wasn't her style.

"I got it." Tessa pulled open the door. The depressing gray day greeted her. She needed sun. Sun and warmth were the eternal balm to one's soul.

While Dominic loaded her suitcases in the back of his trunk, she placed Mandy in the car seat. Tessa couldn't help but glance up and down the street searching for any strange vehicles. Even though Dominic was with her, she wouldn't put it past Ralph to be looming somewhere nearby. At that thought, goose bumps shimmied up her arms.

Pushing aside her fears, Tessa raced back to the refrigerator, stuffed as much as she could into the cooler, returned to the car, and climbed in. She took one last look at her dingy rental. It wasn't much, but she'd called it home for the last few years.

Dominic backed out her drive, and Tessa followed closely behind.

***

Tessa's silence worried him. Dom thought being in his house would have calmed her fears. Mandy was safe and sound with her friend Annie, and Tessa was hidden from her ex-husband.

"Is something wrong?" he asked.

Tessa stood in the foyer, glancing around. She looked up at him. "This place. It's so...grand."

He'd hardly label his twenty-five hundred square foot home, grand, but in comparison to her rental, he could understand. "And the problem is?"

She hugged her arms around her waist. Her security pose, he called it.

"Nothing. I'm surprised you could afford to live in such a nice place, that's all."

Dom considered telling her about his trust fund, but the last woman who'd learned of his wealth had become obsessed with spending his money. He'd loved her anyway. All his money couldn't cure Lisa of cancer so why not spend it?

"I've invested wisely and had a little luck." Tessa wasn't coming clean, so why should he?

"You invested in the stock market? I always thought that was akin to gambling. You don't seem the risk taker type."

"Ouch. Am I that stodgy?" A smile escaped. He placed his palm on the small of her back and didn't wait for her response. "Let me show you to the spare bedroom."

Her eyes widened for a moment before looking away. "Okay."

He would have asked her to put her things in his room, but he didn't want to rush her. Their one escapade would make his seven-wonders-of-the-world list, and he planned on having many repeat performances, but Dom wanted Tessa to set the pace. Anxious women held little appeal for him in bed.

"Here you go," he said as he pushed open the unused bedroom door. "You should find everything you need. I have to go to work. Will you be all right by yourself?"

She looked at her watch. "I'm not staying here. I do have a business to run, remember?"

He took hold of her shoulders. "I don't think you understand, Tessa. The only way I can keep you safe is if you stay put." He took a calming breath, not wanting to scare her. "I'm sure someone can run the business when you're not there."

"Yes, but—"

"But nothing." Dom stepped back and studied her. "What's the real reason you want to leave?" From the moment she'd walked in his house, Tessa's attitude had turned cold and suspicious.

She shrugged. Dom wanted to brush away the long reddish blond strand that fell across her eyes, but the fire that spat from her eyes made him beg off.

Tessa lifted her chin. "I refuse to let my life be ruled by a maniac."

Was that all? He admired her guts, but he didn't dare grant her wish. "Until I find him, you'll have to stay hidden, I'm afraid. End of discussion."

She grit her teeth. "I appreciate you letting me stay here, I really do, but..." She took two nose-widening breaths before relaxing her shoulders. "I'll be safe as long as I'm at work. Ralph wouldn't make a move with Charley, Mick, and Roger around, not to mention all the patrons swarming around on a Friday night."

She had a point. "I still don't like it."

"It's not your life, Dominic, it's mine."

Like a drop of water on a hot stove, her anger seemed to evaporate. She closed the gap between them, and when she ran a finger up his arm, his resolve softened, but he refused to bend. He recognized her ploy to use sex as a means to an end.

"I need to go to work," Tessa begged in the sexiest voice he'd ever heard. What a little siren.

"No." That one little word took all of his control.

She stepped into the small bedroom and plopped down on the bed. Her foot tapped some unknown rhythm on the hard wood floor.

"Okay. How about this?" she said, her face lighting up. "You drive me to work and escort me inside. Then you go to work. I'll call when I'm ready to come back here. I won't leave the restaurant for any reason."

Women. Tessa seemed determined to go to work no matter what he'd say. She'd probably call a damn cab the second he left. "Fine, but on one condition."

"What?"

"You temporarily shut down the Blue Moon until I find the creep who's killing your customers."

Her mouth opened then shut. He'd never seen her speechless before.

A full minute passed before she spoke. "I can't do that."

"Tessa, you have to or you aren't leaving this house. Think about it. If someone is picking off your customers one by one, you have to close down."

She bit her lower lip. "It'll kill Judd."

Her brows furrowed and her chin trembled. The urge to take her into her arms grabbed him, but he pushed it aside. Given her frame of mind, Tessa would no doubt push him away if he dared comfort her.

"He'll get over it." He failed to sound sympathetic.

"No, you don't understand. Without the income from the restaurant, he won't be able to afford his after treatment medications once he receives the transplant. The hospital told him his anti-rejection drugs will cost at least forty thousand a year."

Dom whistled. "Doesn't insurance cover the liver transplant?"

"Some of it, yes, but not all. Then he has to pay something like ten grand a year in insurance costs in addition to the medicine. That's a lot of extra money."

"I'm sorry, Tessa. Do you really think you can live with another death on your hands?"

She dropped her head into her hands, and her shaking body tore him up.

"Okay," she said. "We'll do it your way. I'll tell everyone I have to shut the doors indefinitely as soon as the lunch crowd leaves." Her response came out close to a whisper.

"It's for the best." Cop out answer.

"Easy for you to say."

"What do you want me to do?" he asked.

"Nothing."

Her trembling lip almost made him relent, but he held firm. She could do something. "Why don't you sell the bar?" He held up a hand. "And don't tell me Judd would have nothing to do with his life if you did."

She stood up and squared her shoulders. Her lips pinched. "I'll figure something out. Now, can we go?"

He couldn't stop the anger roiling in his gut. "Fine, but this is the last time I let you out of my sight."

She saluted and marched out the door.

**

Every time the restaurant door swung open, Tessa tensed, thinking Ralph might have somehow followed her. Exhausted, she slipped into her office to perform one of her final tasks.

She stared at the computer screen, trying to decide how to phrase her sign. Should she go with "Closed for renovations until further notice" or just plain "Closed. Will reopen soon." She figured, "Murderer on the loose—too dangerous to stay open," was a little over the top.

Once she opted for the first choice, Tessa hit print. Tears dribbled down her cheek as she withdrew the sheet from the printer. She swept a hand across her checks, grabbed the tape dispenser, and left her office.

A dull murmur permeated the restaurant. Only two tables remained occupied, and no one sat at the bar while her favorite Carole King oldie was playing on the jukebox. The upbeat tune should have buoyed her spirits, but the song had the opposite effect today.

An image surfaced of when she and Judd once sat up until dawn talking. He'd just come home after a six-month stint overseas. She'd played the Carole King's album over and over again, until he promised to buy her more music to add to her collection. Even though he was fifteen years her senior, he was the best older brother she could have hoped for.

Then Judd left the service, and his lack of focus caused him to take up drugs—at least that's what he'd said had happened. Maybe that was why she still could taste the anger from the day Judd had asked her to give up her life's dream and run the restaurant.

Funny, how things had change. Now, she didn't want to let go of their one connection.

Sucking up her courage, Tess stepped outside and taped the "Closed" sign to the door. As she returned to the dimly lit restaurant, the last of the customers swept past her.

"Good bye. Come again," she chirped in her usual refrain, forgetting there wouldn't be a chance for them to come back for a while.

Bottles clanked and chairs scraped the floor, drawing her back to her task. Charley was stacking the liquor along the back counter, and both Barb and Krystal were wiping down their tables.

Poor girls. Barb had come in on her day off to cover for Chelsea, and Tessa had hired Krystal only a few days ago. Tessa didn't know what was worse, telling the help they no longer had a job, or letting Judd know his prized possession no longer could remain open.

She stepped over to the bar. "Would you mind going in the kitchen, Charley, and asking Mick and Roger to come in here?"

"What's up?" His brows furrowed.

"I have an announcement to make."

"Okay."

Her expression must have let him know not to ask any questions.

The moment Charley disappeared into the back, Tessa called to the waitresses. "Hey, girls? Mind stepping over here?"

The next few minutes were the longest in her life. Mick came out of the back wiping his hands on his apron, followed by Roger and then Charley. They gathered around her.

"I have some bad news," she announced, barely able to keep her voice from trembling. "I'm afraid I have to close the Blue Moon."

A collective gasp went up.

Mick took a step forward. "Why? Because you were robbed?"

"No, but that's part of it. More like someone shot Chelsea and murdered Mr. Dirkman."

"Chelsea's gonna make it?" Charley asked, his face blank.

"I hope so."

Shock mixed with fear crossed their faces. "Look, I'm really sorry," Tessa explained. "No one wants to keep this place open more than I do, but I can't let anything else bad happen to my customers."

"It's not your fault all this shit has happened," Mick said. "Sorry."

Tessa ignored his slip. "I know, but I can't chance staying open."

Charley tossed a wet rag on the counter. "You gonna let that developer guy buy this place?"

Tessa couldn't tell if Charley was eager for the event, or angry.

"No. Mr. Jankowski knows I won't sell."

"You might have to if the killer fellow isn't found soon. This place might stay closed for years."

Her knees buckled, forcing Tessa to grab the edge of the counter for support. In a flash, Charley thrust out a hand to steady her. "You okay?"

"Yes." Tessa looked around. "I promise I'll let you know when I decide to open. I understand if you find other jobs." She blinked back tears. "If I don't see you again, it's been a real pleasure working with all of you."

As much as she tried to control her emotions, the dam of tears broke.

Heads down, her workers shuffled off. "Mick," Tessa called. "May I have a word with you?"

"Sure." He glanced around, as if checking if anyone could hear.

"The night Mr. Walsh was murdered, I asked you to follow him. Did you?"

Every muscle tensed in his sinewy body. "You think I had something to do with his death?"

Tessa jumped back. "No, no. I'm not accusing you of anything. I'm merely wondering if perhaps you saw something."

His shoulders relaxed. "No. I followed him like you asked, but only as far as Bayshore. He wasn't weaving or anything, so I figured the guy was okay. I split and went home."

"Okay, I believe you. You can go now."

He whipped around and mumbled, "Sure you do."

Being an ex-con must be hell.

***

The robbery at the Blue Moon still frustrated Dom. At first he thought it was an inside job. The person knew the location of the money and how to find it. Yet the thief hadn't known the alarm code, which dismissed Tessa and Charley. Dom discounted her brother from the get go.

Cantori tossed a folder on his desk. "Thought you'd want to see what we've come up with so far, seeing how the robbery might be tied to all your murders."

"That was fast."

"Yeah, well, we aim to please."

He was about to ask since when, but Dom thought better than to comment.

The folder contained a list of all the workers, their addresses and a brief history of their work experience. Mick Stukes had done time, Roger Denfield had dropped out of high school four years ago and had held more than a half dozen jobs. Charles Madsen had moved to Tampa close to a year ago and had been working at the Blue Moon ever since. Chelsea Andrews listed a local address but no previous work experience. Barb, the waitress, was a single mother of two. She too had flitted from job to job.

No one stood out as a sure fire bet or seemed to be a suspect in his murder investigations. "Thanks. Let me know what you find out."

"Will do."

"Hey, I'm guessing you haven't gotten anything back on the fingerprints, right?" Dom asked.

"You're dreaming right? I'm lucky if I get them back by Christmas, and I'm not exaggerating."

Damn.

***

After everyone left, Tessa made arrangements with the local shelter to come for the remaining food. She didn't want to waste what others could use. She then called Dominic, but he must have been on his cell, so she left a message for him to pick her up at 5:30.

Precisely at the pickup time, Tessa shut off the lights—maybe for the last time—and locked the door.

The cool salt breeze whipped her hair across her face as she stood outside, but Tessa didn't bother to brush it away. Her whole life had crumbled in such a short time she hadn't had time to process the changes. All she knew was that her life might turn worse before it became better.

She must have been staring off into space when headlights glared in her eyes, and she jumped at the intrusion. She hadn't even seen the car pull into the lot.

Tessa shielded her eyes against the glare, trying to figure out who drove a white sedan. Not Dominic.

The car door squeaked open, and Tessa froze.

CHAPTER THIRTEEN

"How did it go?" Dominic asked, as he stepped from the white car.

Heart pounding, Tessa took a few deep breaths. For a moment, she thought Ralph had found her. Maybe she'd been stupid to wait outside but remaining in the empty restaurant gave her the creeps.

"How did what go?" she asked, trying to keep her voice steady.

He looked at her as if she'd lost her mind. "Telling the employees you were shutting down the place."

"Oh. It was almost worse than finding out Judd needed a liver transplant," she said, keeping her head averted to prevent Dominic from seeing her tear strained cheeks. "It was like someone had ripped out my heart," Tessa blurted. Oh, God, why had she told him that? He'd never understand.

"I imagine it was." He glanced to the sky.

She couldn't tell how sincere he was. Gripping the car door handle, she pressed her lips together but failed to hold to tongue. "When was the last time your heart was torn apart?" Okay, so that came out a little bitter. She wasn't his therapist and didn't have to be politically correct.

He shrugged. "Let's just say it has been—more than once."

Whoa. His previous comment must not have been sarcastic. This time his tone came out distant as if he had lived through a lot of pain. If she could ever get him to talk to her, she might understand the man.

Tessa let the subject of broken hearts go. Now wasn't the time to prod him.

She cleared her throat. "I was expecting your red truck," she said, attempting to justify her anxiety.

The wind suddenly whipped her hair across her mouth, and she shivered at the cool breeze. With one hand, she wadded her hair behind her head. Needing the car's shelter, she scooted into the passenger's seat.

"This is my work vehicle. I didn't think to mention I'd changed cars. I'm sorry."

"Oh." She wrapped her arms around her shoulders and stared straight ahead trying to control the whirlwind of emotions.

Dominic slipped in the driver's seat. He glanced at her, and then leaned forward and pressed a display panel. Seconds later, much needed hot air shot through the vents.

"Thanks," she said.

Tessa concentrated on warming her hands and not on Dominic's physical presence. His cologne stirred images of their hot passionate foray. Sure, their one-night stand had driven away her temporary demons but lowering her defenses again scared her. She couldn't let her desires stand in the way of saving her brother's prized possession.

"I know it was hard for you to shut down the place, but I think it's for the best."

She'd begun to hate that platitude. "It's so unfair. A lot of good people are losing their jobs because of this maniac."

"Life's not always fair."

There, he did it again. His voice trailed off as if his mind went to a dark place. Anxiety, or was it raw anger, colored his words.

"Do you want to talk about it?"

Dom quirked a brow. "Talk about what?"

As if he didn't know. "What hurt you in the past to make you bitter."

"Bitter? I'm not bitter."

"Okay." Talk about denial.

Dominic glanced at his watch. "Look, it's close to dinner. How would you like it if we go to a nice restaurant?"

Slick. Really, slick. As if she couldn't see the dodge for what it was, but her stomach betrayed her and grumbled at the mention of food.

"We'll do it your way, but could we stop at the hospital first? With all that's happened, I haven't had a chance to visit Judd or Chelsea."

His clenched fists relaxed. "No problem. Just to let you know, I did call the hospital this afternoon and asked about Chelsea's condition. There's been no change."

"She's still in a coma?"

"Yes."

Tessa closed her eyes and leaned her head back against the seat. Life sucked sometimes—for Chelsea, for Judd, and for her workers.

The strain from the day had depleted what was left of her energy, so Tessa said nothing as they drove toward Tampa General. Only when Dominic pulled into the parking garage adjacent to the hospital did Tessa open her eyes.

He came around and opened her door. Good to know chivalry wasn't dead. Ralph never opened a door for her in the two years they were married.

Stop it.

Why did she insist on comparing the two men? Yes, both were cops, but the similarity ended there. One exhibited kindness, at times, and was generous in bed, while the other earned a big, fat *no* to both traits. One took bribes while the other was honest. True they were both as stubborn as a bad habit, but Tessa had figured out how to manipulate one of them—at least sometimes.

"Are you coming?" he asked.

"Sorry."

"You do realize that you can't visit Chelsea?" Dominic said as they headed to the main entrance.

A rush of disappointment whipped through her. "Why, not?"

"Only family's allowed in the ICU."

"I should have known, given Judd's been in and out of Intensive Care more times that I can count." Her legs lost some of their strength as she tried to keep up with Dom's long strides. "Poor Chelsea. Did you know she was a runaway?" He turned his head back toward her and quirked a brow. "At least that's what she told Annie at the shelter. I guess there won't be any family by her side when she wakes up."

"I never would have guessed she'd run from anything."

"I'll grant you Chelsea never needed assertiveness training, but as much as she chatted, she never spoke of her past." Tessa shook her head. "I bet her parents would be frantic if they knew what happened to their daughter."

Dominic waited for her to catch up, and then placed his palm on her back. His mere touch excited her. "I'll see what I can find out."

Tessa looked up at him. "You'd do that?"

"I'm not an ogre, Tessa. I do have feelings. Besides, if I had a kid, I'd want the same treatment if she ran away."

Dominic's impassioned speech surprised her. The man was always so in control—not counting, of course, their brief encounter in bed.

A nurse pushing an IV stand escorted an elderly gentleman down the hospital hall. Tessa dreaded aging and resolved to return to her regular exercise program, starting tomorrow.

"I just thought of something," Tessa said, coming to an abrupt stop. Dom turned toward her.

"What?"

"Chelsea might be able to identify Trace's and Doug Walsh's murderer. What if he tries to silence her?"

Dom lifted her chin, and his piercing blue eyes nearly melted her soul. "Don't worry. We've given her twenty-four protection for that exact reason."

Her smile faltered. "Thank you."

A group of giggling candy stripers whizzed down the hall, boosting her spirits. They arrive at the intensive care ward.

"I'll wait here," Dominic said. "I'm sure you want to be alone when you give him the bad news. Besides, they may not let me in."

"Thanks for driving me here."

As she reached Judd's room, dread replaced her worried thoughts about Chelsea. Tessa wiped her palms on her pants, knocked on the open door, and entered her stepbrother's room. His eyes were shut, his stomach was bloated, and his skin had a yellowish tinge. His condition looked worse than after last week's attack. Doctors and nurses who dealt with people this close to death deserved a medal.

Tessa pulled up a chair. "Judd?"

He opened his eyes and wet his lips. "Tessa." A small smile lit his lips.

"How are you feeling?" Dumb question, but she'd blurted out the question before she could censor it.

"Like shit." He held up two fingers. "And don't start again about how I ruined my life taking drugs. I know that, but twenty years ago things weren't so hot in my life."

This time she held her tongue and didn't comment his life wasn't so good now. Her frustration rose. Why did he have to bring up their one fight every time she visited?

"What did the doctors say about your transplant?"

"I'll be getting one soon." A small light flashed in his eyes.

"Really? That's fantastic." A sliver of hope edged its way in her heart.

"Yeah. Since this is the third time in six weeks I've been in here, they said I'm next in line for a transplant, but that I had to produce evidence I could pay for my meds afterwards. I said no problem. I was hoping you could talk with the hospital staff and show them my bank statement."

"Judd, I..."

He waved a hand. "Don't worry if the Blue Moon's not making a mint right now. Once I'm back on my feet, I'll bring in new business. I have lots of ideas."

His eyes closed again. Talking seemed to take such effort.

Tessa didn't know how to be subtle. "I had to close down the restaurant today."

Judd's eyes flew open. He coughed, sending specks of blood to his palm. He grabbed a tissue and wiped off the sputum, acting as if this were a common occurrence. Hell, maybe it was.

"I'm not in the mood for your jokes, Tess."

"I'm dead serious."

For the next fifteen minutes, Tessa told him about the series of events at the restaurant that led to her decision. She left out the part about Ralph's midnight visit.

"Well, don't tell anyone. As long as I can pay for my insurance, maybe I can get by. I know I need to come up with my co-pay, but I've saved over fifty thousand."

She'd researched the cost of the transplant. His out of pocket expenses would be over eighty thousand, and that didn't include the forty grand in follow-up meds. Besides, Tessa didn't lie, especially to insurance companies.

"Dad's house should bring in the needed money," Tessa suggested.

"The market's a little soft right now. I want to get the most we can. You know as well as I that it might take months to find the right buyer."

Tessa sat up straighter. "Then we'll have to sell the restaurant." Bile raced up to her mouth. "Mr. Jankowski said he'd give me some of the money up front to tide you over."

"No." Judd coughed again and grabbed his stomach, his face contorting in pain.

"Can I get you anything? Should I call the nurse?" Helplessness grabbed at her.

"I think you've done enough. Go home. I'm tired."

As if he'd slapped her in the face, Tessa slumped forward. "What about the restaurant? Jankowski's deal isn't bad."

"I said, no. In the open market we could get twice what he's offering. South Tampa is hot right now."

He was more stubborn than Daddy. "I'd pay for the medications myself if I could, but I've got over a hundred grand in student loans."

"It's not your place to come up with the money. I'll figure it out somehow, and if I have to sell then I'll sell—but only when I'm ready."

"Judd, you're too sick to hassle with the sale. You have Mandy to think about."

"Don't you think I know that?" His voice came out stronger. "I'm trying to live long enough to be a father. Now go." He rolled to one side and brought his legs up to a fetal position.

Hurt and devastated, Tessa rushed out, praying he'd reconsider.

Half way out the door, she turned. "You should be happy just to get the operation."

Judd didn't respond.

"Fine," she said. "I can be stubborn too. I'll think of some way to raise the funds."

Furious, Tessa stalked down the hall and ran right into Dominic's broad chest. Phones rang at the nurses' station, and two of the women laughed as if their own private world didn't include the ill.

"Hey, slow down. Things didn't go so well with your brother I take it?" Dom asked.

"Step-brother, thank you, and no. He was a real jerk. And stupid and stubborn."

"I thought you were supposed to be the psychiatrist."

"Psychologist," she amended.

Dominic waved a hand. "Whatever. Take it easy on the guy. He's probably not in his right mind. I was talking to one of the nurses while you were visiting, and she said liver patients can get crazy sometimes because of the poison in their system."

Tessa closed her eyes for a second to gain a smidgen of control. "I know. I keep forgetting he's so sick. I let my emotions get the best of me. I want Judd to be better so bad, I can't think straight. He's the only family I have."

Tessa couldn't deal with discussing Judd's failing health with everything else going on. She looked up at Dom. "Didn't someone offer me dinner?"

"You bet." He gave her shoulder a quick squeeze, which did more to bolster her spirits than if she'd won the lottery.

Despite the mixed emotions swirling inside, his smile made her heart flutter.

***

Dear Audrey Mae,

Hope all is well in heaven. There's a young woman with a child that reminds me so very much of you. I worry about her as much as I used to worry about you. That's why I had to kill her customers. How else would I get her to leave that awful place? Fortunately, she's seen the light and is closing the place down. The bar has caused her so much grief. Only her problems aren't over. She told me her crazed ex-husband is after her. I have no choice but to save her, just like I tried to save you. Only you wouldn't listen. I hope you agree that if you'd come with me that fateful night four years ago, you wouldn't be where you are today.

But what's done is done. Remember how much I love you, my dearest Audrey. Each night I picture your golden red hair wrapped around my fingers and I want to feast on you. I can still smell your spring-like perfume everywhere I go.

Tell me, does Bobby like heaven? I hope so. Keep an eye out for me when I come. Soon, my love, soon.

Sincerely yours,
Morton Richter

***

Dom probably shouldn't have brought work home, but he'd been distracted during the day worrying about Tessa. Her ex-husband was a clever man. He'd found out where she lived once before and had even managed to sneak into her house without notice. Dom wouldn't put it past the guy to find out she was staying at his house.

Tessa knocked on his study door.

"Come in."

She halted. "Oh, I didn't mean to interrupt."

Lust grabbed him so hard he had to shift in his chair. It didn't matter she was dressed in a nightgown up to her neck and wrapped in a terry cloth bathrobe.

Dom relaxed back in his chair. "You're not bothering me. Come in. Make yourself comfortable." He pointed to an overstuffed leather chair opposite his desk.

"I'm not staying. I just wanted to say goodnight."

He glanced at the gold clock on his desk. "It's a little early isn't it?"

"I'm tired."

The dark circles under her eyes implied she might be telling the truth. "Is something wrong?" he asked.

"I'm worried about Judd, that's all. I'm not sure where he's going to get the money for his operation. Regardless of what he thinks is best, I may have to take Mr. Jankowski up on his offer. Selling to him, though, makes me feel like I'm a failure, both to myself and to my brother."

When Dom had let the Social Worker take his brother away, he'd had the same reaction. With his father and mother dead, he should have protected Alex better. Only he hadn't. The horrible night the Social Worker escorted Alex to his new home still haunted him. Even the six different private investigators he'd hired over the years to find Alex had no luck. Damn it. His little brother couldn't have just disappeared.

He refocused on Tessa. "You aren't a failure. You have to do what's best for Judd."

"What were you working on?" she asked, acting as if he hadn't said a word.

She slipped into the big leather chair and clasped her arms around her drawn up legs. Her vulnerability made him want to wrap a protective arm around her, but he steeled his heart against her allure. Not picturing her naked took all his will power.

He remembered her question and debated whether he should tell her about Trace's file. He studied her eyes—deep blue and beautiful eyes. Her pinched brow spoke of much desperation. But about what? Her brother's condition? Losing the restaurant? Ralph? Or the serial killer who was taking out her clients?

Hell, anyone of those things was enough to bring anyone to his or her knees. She deserved to know the truth.

"Trace had his cold case files sent down from Atlanta."

"Why?"

"He thought there might be a connection between the serial killer up there and the person or persons responsible for the Blue Moon's deaths."

She let out a gasp. "Was there?"

Dom flipped through the pages again, forcing detachment from the horror. "The last three victims in Atlanta appeared to be related. All had gunshot wounds to the left side of their head and all three were found in their cars parked on the side of the road. This reminds me of the Keri Wilkerson case three times over."

She wrapped her arms around her shoulders and curled her feet underneath her. "Did the Atlanta police have any suspects?"

"No one for sure. The main problem, as I see it, is the calibers of the bullets were different in each of the three murders. That made it difficult to connect the cases."

She looked off to the side and then back at him. "Does that mean they think three different people committed the crimes?"

"I haven't had many dealings with serial killers, but I'd have to say, that's a definite possibility."

Tessa sat up straighter. "In one of my classes in school, we studied the criminal mind. Some of the killers are rather bright, some even brilliant. Maybe he, or she, switched guns with each crime. That would make sense if the crime was premeditated."

"Now you sound like a police detective." He had to chuckle.

A small smile formed on her lips. "Our lines of work, or rather what I hope mine will be in the future, aren't all that different. We both deal with individuals who have problems."

"You can say that again." Dom scanned more pages trying to find another similarity. "Hmm."

"What?"

Tessa leaned forward in the chair and dropped her bare feet to the floor.

"All three murders occurred in November."

"Really? All of ours happened in November too. Do you think it's a coincidence?"

"I don't know. It says here the Atlanta PD brought in several suspects. Trace made a handwritten note that said Morton Richter seemed the most likely candidate. His alibi checked out, but that Trace didn't believe him. Given time, he would get him.'"

"So what are you going to do?" she asked.

"I'll call Atlanta tomorrow to see where I might find this Morton guy. The only information Trace noted was an address in Ohio that belonged to the guy's parents."

Dom's phone rang. She half stood, looking as if she wanted to give him privacy. It was the station. "Tess, wait."

He swiped his phone. "Rossi."

"It's Fowler. The forensics came back on the bullets for Trace, Chelsea, and Doug Walsh. You won't believe it."

"Go ahead." Dom looked up at Tessa. She stood as still as a statue, her gaze fixed on him.

"All three bullets came from the same gun that killed the Wilkerson woman."

"Shit. I think we may need help on this one." Out of habit he straightened the files on his desk, helping him to think. "Listen, Trace said he worked on a serial killer case in Atlanta. While he never did find the guy, the MO is similar. Could you fax our information up to..." Dom picked up the top folder and noted the officer's name in charge. "To a Lieutenant Nauta, and ask if the ballistics match up."

"It's a long shot."

"It's all we've got."

"Okay. I, ah, thought you'd like to know we'll be sending Trace's body up to Atlanta tomorrow for burial."

Dom nearly crushed the phone. True his ex-partner had been undisciplined and didn't always use the best common sense, but he didn't deserve to die. "Thanks."

Tessa waited in silence while he finished reading the report. He jotted down a list of possible suspects for the Tampa crimes, starting with Grady Jankowski and ending with Mick Stukes. He leaned back in his chair and stared at the ceiling.

"Can you tell me what the call was about?" Tessa asked. "I'll understand if you can't."

He'd become so wrapped up in his thoughts he'd forgotten she was there. "I'm trying to sort out what's happened, that's all." No use going into the details until he had all his facts straight.

"Well, goodnight, then," she said.

"You don't have to go." Tessa's presence brought comfort.

"I'm really tired. It's been a long day." Tess turned and softly shut his door.

Damn it. Had he offended her in some way? She'd seemed perky enough and interested in being with him moments ago. Dom debated following her to her room, but he wasn't up for the rejection.

He stabbed a hand through his hair. Ever since Lisa had died, he'd not been able to be close to a woman. Then Tessa came along and wham. The emotional floodgates opened up, and he began to notice those elusive feelings like contentment, joy, and dare he say happiness?

His shoulders sagged. Fate sucked. If they'd met under different circumstances, they might have had a chance.

Not that he was in love with her, or anything—not at all. At best, he'd call it in lust.

Dom took a deep breath forcing his ardor to cool.

"Work, Dom, work," he mumbled.

He turned his focus back to the files and searched for a hint as to why Trace had been killed. Was his ex-partner in the wrong place at the wrong time, or had the murderer recognized him? Nah. Doug Walsh was the intended victim and Trace and Chelsea happened along.

Dom slapped closed the manila folder and glanced at the clock. It was eleven thirty already. He hadn't realized he'd been studying the files for close to two hours. It was time for bed.

As he pushed back his chair, his mind wandered back to Tessa. He would have thought she'd have been in a great mood tonight now that Judd would be receiving his needed operation. Or was she mad at Dom for some crime he'd unknowingly committed? Considering how great the sex had been between them, he wouldn't have been surprised if she'd seduced him again. So why hadn't she?

That wasn't his concern right now. His goal was to keep her safe. Nothing more. Nowhere in the safety manual did that include keeping up with her changing mental health—or sleeping with her.

***

"Tessa, wake up."

She moaned and cracked open an eye. Dominic had his hands on his hips and his feet planted.

"What's wrong?" She pulled the covers over her chest.

"We need to take a trip. Get dressed and pack."

"Huh? A trip? Where? What are you talking about?"

Tessa rubbed her eyes and focused on her tormentor. Despite the fact he'd practically ignored her last night studying his files, she couldn't help but admire how handsome he was dressed in a blue pinstriped suit. The silk tie alone must have cost thirty or forty bucks. The man knew quality, that was for sure.

"Pack a bag and meet me downstairs. Oh, and wear a skirt."

"Hold it. What's going on?" she asked to his retreating back. Damn him. "Why all the mystery?" she shouted after the disappearing man.

Damn. Tessa whipped off the covers and placed her bare feet on the cold floor. He needed one of his expensive carpets up here to warm up the place.

She shivered as she headed into the bathroom to wash up. In less than twenty minutes, she was dressed and packed. If she knew where they were going, she might have done a better packing job.

She hadn't brought anything dressy with her though. Dinner and dancing hadn't been on the agenda. The best she could come up with was a pair of black pants, a white blouse, and a black, kitschy jacket Annie had given her for her birthday.

She sighed. What was up with all the secrecy? The man would drive her crazy. Aargh.

Dominic was brewing a delicious smelling coffee when she entered the kitchen.

"Drink this," he said and handed her a cup. He eyed her from head to toe but said nothing. She guessed she passed inspection.

"Did you pack?" he asked.

"Yes, but I don't understand where we're going."

"I'll put your bag in the car."

Enough of the he-man attitude. "I'm not going anywhere until you give me some answers."

"We're flying to Ohio if you must know."

"Ohio? Are you crazy?" she asked.

"Probably." Dominic spun around and headed up the stairs.

Tessa plopped down at the counter determined to enjoy the heavenly smelling fresh brew. If she had her way, she'd stay here and enjoy the quiet morning, not traipse across the country for no good reason.

Besides, it was cold in Ohio. She had enough of dampness living in Colorado.

As she sipped her coffee, she had time to think. To be honest, she'd feel safer away from Tampa.

"Ready?" Dominic asked.

That was fast. "Can't a girl have breakfast first? It's still dark outside."

"We'll eat on the way to the airport."

She'd had enough. "Before I agree to uproot again, I want some answers. Why are we going?"

"To find a serial killer."

CHAPTER FOURTEEN

Tessa's hands wouldn't let go of the armrest. She hated flying. Big planes were bad enough, but ten-seater jets were nothing short of claustrophobic death traps. The sudden drops set her stomach into spasms.

And the noise. She was convinced she'd never hear again. The engine whined and whirred until she wanted to scream. Sure, the view out the window was nice, and even scenic, but some conversation would have helped passed the time. When she tried to ask Dominic a question, he pointed to his ears and shook his head. He either suffered from clogged Eustachian tubes, or he didn't want to discuss what they were doing a thousand miles from home.

Four endless, leg-cramping hours after taking off, he'd not said a word. She wanted to shake him and yell, but her throat had dried up. She needed something to drink. Tessa mimed drinking, but Dom shook his head. Stupid private plane.

Eventually, they landed, and Tessa couldn't wait to stand on terra firma again. She still couldn't believe Dominic had a friend who both owned a jet and was willing to transport him to God only knows where.

He and their pilot, John Hoffman, seemed to be best friends. They talked for at least an hour before taking off, laughing and slapping each other on the back, acting as if there wasn't a dangerous criminal on the loose. Okay, maybe it wasn't an hour, but it sure felt like it.

So why the hurry this morning if all they did was chat?

Maybe Dominic had been in the Air Force and looked forward to airplane talk. Who knows? There was no use asking him. He'd only clam up.

As she clambered down the metal stairs, her legs wobbled and the cold Ohio wind whipped across her face. Maybe the temperature technically wasn't freezing but coming from Florida, it sure felt arctic cold. If only she'd known they were going to Ohio when she packed the first time, she would have brought her winter parka.

Dominic followed behind. At the bottom of the steps, she turned around to await his instructions.

"John will show you where to go," Dom shouted, pointing to the terminal. "I'll grab the luggage."

For some strange reason, Tessa didn't want to be away from her protector even though no one could have followed them to the ends of the earth. "I'll wait."

He shrugged. "Suit yourself."

Tessa kept one hand on her hair to keep it out of her face and the other on her jacket lapels. Despite knowing Ohio would be cold this time of year, her three layers weren't enough to keep out the chill. Her nose began to run, and she questioned her choice of staying in the dampness instead of the warm terminal.

Dominic scurried to the luggage compartment and dragged out their bags while John put some wooden blocks under the wheels. It wasn't not as if the plane was going anywhere, so why bother?

Dom strode toward her from the plane with the luggage. "Let's get you inside the terminal before you freeze to death."

Now he noticed the cold?

Dragging both of their wheeled suitcases behind him, he walked ahead of her alongside John, who'd finished doing whatever pilots did once they landed. Their laughter trickled back to her. Apparently, she misjudged Dominic's chivalry quotient. She ducked her head against the wind and plowed forward.

The Parkersburg, West Virginia airport, though small, was blissfully warm inside. "Dominic," she whispered. "Are we in the right place? I thought you said we were going to Ohio."

He had the nerve to chuckle. "We are. Parkersburg is on the Ohio border. This is close to where we need to be."

"Oh. Well, I'm going to use the restroom."

"Sure."

Though there hadn't been anything to drink during the long flight, she had to go. When she returned to the airport's lobby, John and Dominic were shaking hands.

Dom's friend smiled. "Good luck with your search," he said to both of them. "I'm going to spend some time downtown, what there is of it. Call when you want to head back."

Dominic checked his watch. "Let's shoot for nine tomorrow morning."

"Sounds good to me." John faced her. "Take care," he said, and then winked.

What was that about? Had Dominic told him some tall tale about them being a couple?

"Okay, let's see if we can find our driver," Dominic said to no one in particular.

"We're getting a driver?"

"I called a private limo company. We'll need it for our cover."

"Cover?" Tessa put a hand on his arm. "What's going on?" He didn't answer. "Okay, then tell me who's paying for all this? Surely not the Tampa PD."

"No, not them."

Topic closed.

A uniformed man stepped into the lobby and looked around.

"This must be for us," Dom said with way too much cheer.

Once he confirmed that was their driver, they headed outside where Tessa once more shivered from the cold. To add to her discomfort, a shower burst from the dark gray clouds without warning. Great. Not waiting for the chauffeur to open the door, she slipped into the back seat. Seemingly oblivious to the foul conditions, Dominic waited until the driver put the luggage in the trunk before sliding into the seat next to her. He swiped a hand down his wet face.

The driver climbed in and turned around. "Where to?"

Dominic unfolded a piece of paper and rattled off the address.

"You sure you got that right? There's nothing out that way but a few old farmhouses. The roads are dirt for the most part."

"I'm sure."

Their driver shrugged and maneuvered out of the airport. The shower dissipated as quickly as it had appeared, and Tessa busied herself watching the scenery. She didn't need to think about Dominic and what he did to her. If they were here to find a serial killer, she needed to keep her wits about her.

Stark rolling hills accentuated the poverty that abounded in the Appalachian area. All the while, Dominic looked lost in thought as they rode in silence.

Finally, curiosity got the best of her. "If you know where this man lives, why couldn't the police bring him in for questioning?" she whispered not wanting the driver to hear.

"Oh, he's not there. His parents live here. I'm hoping they'll tell me where I can find him."

"Now why would they do that?"

"Because I'm going to tell them their son has won a Florida drawing for a new car, and I need to give him, and only him, the keys."

Tessa's jaw dropped. "That's preposterous. You think they'll fall for such a ploy?"

"People have in the past. Money is a powerful aphrodisiac."

"And you have no qualms lying to people?"

"To find a killer, I'd do anything."

Tessa asked no more questions. Dom reached into his pocket and pulled out a handful of balloons and some string. "Help me blow these up."

"You're kidding. Why?"

"Don't you watch TV? Sweepstakes people always have balloons."

"Okay." Tessa held out her hand for her share and blew up the balloons.

Just as they finished, an unpainted wooden house came into view.

Needing a few boards on its east side, it sat at the end of a long dirt drive. Tessa shivered just thinking how cold the place must be inside. After mile upon mile of vast farms, the limousine finally slowed and pulled down a long, bumpy drive. The slight rain had created puddles in the dirt, adding to the already uneven terrain.

Pigs scurried across the front yard and mixed with the roaming chickens.

"How are you going to explain my presence?" she asked as the driver came to a stop.

"Clearing houses send more than one person to deliver good news. That's why I had you dress up. Just follow my lead," Dominic said as the limo driver pulled open the door. Dominic hopped out and extended her a hand.

"Why say we're from a Clearing House? I thought you said you were pretending to give him a car."

"We are. Morton entered his name in a drawing on our website, and he has to pick up his car in the next seven days or forfeit the prize."

"Oh." His poise and confidence convinced her he'd given his plan quite a lot of thought. "Have you ever done something like this before?"

"A few times. Worked like a charm," Dom said as helped her out and then led her to the house.

He didn't have to act so cocky. She looked down at her feet. Mud oozed up the sides of her shoes. Oh, well. If it would help find the murderer, she'd sacrifice her well-worn black pumps.

Dominic held her elbow as they marched up the three steps to the front porch.

"Smile and act as if we're really excited about our news," he said.

"I'll try."

Dominic's shoulders relaxed for a second as he smiled down at her, and her traitorous heart skipped a beat. She didn't want to like this man. He had too many flaws, too many hang-ups, but damn, he was good in bed and easy on the eyes.

Stop it, Tessa Jean. Now act happy.

With no doorbell, Dominic knocked. A moment later a small, gray-haired woman peeked her head out from behind the door. "Yes?"

"Mrs. Richter?"

"Yes." She clung to the doorframe as if she couldn't stand up on her own.

"Hello, ma'am. We're here to see Mr. Richter. We have some good news for him," Dominic said handing the woman the bouquet of balloons.

Mrs. Richter turned her head and shouted behind her, "Someone says they have good news, Pa." She pulled open the door. "Come in." Her eyes sparkled.

No surprise, the inside held little in the way of niceties, but the close placement of the sofa, coffee table, and chairs gave the place a welcoming look.

An elderly gentleman remained in a wheelchair, bundled in a navy blanket from his feet to his waist. His mouth moved, but no sound came out. His gnarled hands grabbed the blanket, acting as if they'd come to take his one prized possession.

Mrs. Richter tied the balloons to the back of a desk chair. "Have a seat," she said, pointing to the sofa covered in a stained beige sheet.

Tessa gritted her teeth, smiled, and dropped down on the sofa's edge. Dominic had the nerve to plunk down right next to her, his thigh plastered against hers. Her thoughts immediately shot to the heated sensation and what he did to her insides.

"...or something, Miss?" said Mrs. Richter.

Tessa had no idea what the woman had asked her. Focus. "No, thank you." She hoped her response was appropriate.

"You, mister?"

"No, thank you. We don't want to keep you." Dominic pulled a piece of paper from his pocket, nodded, and stuffed it back in his pocket. "A Morton Richter won a drawing from Synergy Corporation. Is he here?"

The elderly man squirmed in his seat. His mouth opened, and then he grunted. Tessa was unable to make out what he was saying. Perhaps he'd suffered a stroke.

"Don't worry about him, dear," Mrs. Richter said. "Pa hasn't spoken since the accident."

Tessa wisely decided not to ask about it.

"Morton's our son, but he doesn't live here," she explained. "Hasn't for close to eighteen years. What's this about a drawing?"

Dominic sat up straighter. "Well, he placed his name in a drawing, and he won a new car."

Mr. Richter slapped the arm of his wheelchair, drawing Tessa's gaze.

"Now, Pa. It's all right," Mrs. Richter said. She turned back to Tessa and Dominic. "You see, we're not allowed to speak of Morton."

"Your son put this as his address."

Mrs. Richter shook her head. "There's been a mistake." Her calm delivery surprised Tessa. It was as if her son not coming home for such a long time was a common occurrence.

"You haven't tried to find him in eighteen years?" Tessa asked not believing anyone could not forgive a relative. Dominic nudged her knee.

"Pa wouldn't let me. Morton tried to kill his daddy, you see. That's why my husband can't talk. Morton hit him over the head with a bat and left him for dead." No outward sign of distress showed on her lined face.

"The police never found your son?" Tessa found this story hard to believe.

"We told them a robber came in and beat Pa up."

"And Morton never contacted you in all those years?" Dominic asked.

"No. I don't blame my boy. You see, Pa hurt him bad when he was growing up, and I wasn't strong enough to stop the abuse." Finally, her face clouded over. She glanced down at her hands. "It was all my fault I didn't stop it. I shoulda stopped it, but I couldn't. I wasn't strong for Morton. I failed him."

"I'm sure you did your best," Tessa said, her voice cracking. She wouldn't be surprised if the father abused Mrs. Richter too. Poor woman was a co-dependent enabler.

Before Mrs. Richter could answer, Dominic stood. Was the interview over? They'd learned nothing.

"Do you have a photo of your son?" he asked.

Morton's mom stood and hobbled over to a side table and pulled out the top drawer. "Pa doesn't like to be reminded of him, so I keep his picture hidden. Mort was a good boy, though. He never hurt anyone, except Pa here."

She handed the photo to Dominic. He stood so still, Tessa moved beside him to look at the picture. The round face in the faded photo appeared familiar, but the graininess prevented her from making a positive identification.

"Would it be possible," Dominic asked, "to keep this for a little while. I want to make a copy. I'll be sure to send this back to you, with a little payment for keeping it."

She shrugged. "I hate to give it up, but if it's important, go ahead. What good would it do though?"

"We're going to put ads out asking Morton to claim the car. When he shows up, we'll know it's really him."

Tessa watched Mrs. Richter. The woman couldn't possibly fall for the lame story.

"I would a thought a driver's license would be good enough, but if you promise to tell my son to write me when you find him, you can take it. And tell him his Pa ain't dead. I know he thinks he killed him, but he didn't. And tell him I forgive him." She looked over at her husband, whose lips were pulled back, exposing blackened teeth. "We don't have a phone, you know, otherwise Mort could call."

"I promise."

She smiled, but Mr. Richter slapped his armchair and grunted, his face turning red. Poor man. Tessa bet he'd turn the law on his son if he could.

Dominic grabbed Tessa's hand and led her out the door. This time the cold air felt good on her face.

As soon as they were inside the limo, Dominic leaned his head back and closed his eyes. "I feel like a cad that I lied to them."

She grabbed his hand. "You did what you had to. I guess we're lucky Morton wasn't there."

Dominic turned to her and smiled. "Maybe you're right."

***

"May I have another look at the picture?" Tessa asked as she finished putting her clothes in the hotel room dresser. "There was something about him that looks familiar."

"I thought you said you didn't want to think about the case for one night."

"I know, but I can't help it."

Dom was pretty sure he knew the man's identity, but he wanted Tessa to confirm his thoughts. He pulled the photo from his suit jacket pocket. "Here."

While she studied the photo, he placed his unopened suitcases on the small table in the hotel room, wondering if she'd recognize the man who worked at the Blue Moon.

"This photo is so cracked and faded, it's hard to tell much," she said.

"Why don't you mentally go through all your employees and customers, focusing on those who'd be in their late thirties or early forties now. Also consider they probably have gained some weight in the last eighteen years. Some might have grown a beard or shaved their head."

Tess shook her head. "Oh, no, it couldn't be."

Dom sat on the bed next to her. "What couldn't be?"

"This looks like Charley."

That's exactly what he'd thought. "How so?"

"If you take away his hair, like this," she said, placing her palm across the top of the photo, "and you get rid of the mustache, I think it's him. What do you think?"

Dom dreaded confirming her suspicions. He understood she'd trusted her bartender and had even allowed him to help care for the baby. How would she feel if she knew her ability to read people was so off?

"Come on. Don't clam up on me now," she said. "What do you think?"

"It's him all right."

"You say that as if there's no doubt."

"Once I have our crime lab cross reference Charley's prints with those of Morton Richter, I'll know for sure."

"You think Charley is Morton? I can't believe it."

"I'm sorry, Tessa. If Charley is our serial killer, this has nothing to do with you. The guy has avoided capture not only in his home state, but also in Atlanta and Tampa as well. Until now."

She placed the photo face down on the bed. "I've read that many criminals were abused as children. The pattern fits. But if his mother stood by doing nothing while his father abused him, I'm surprised he doesn't hate women."

"We don't know he doesn't," Dom said softening his voice.

"No, we don't. So now what?"

Her doe-like eyes tore into his soul. "I'll call Phil and have him put out an APB. I'm betting Charley doesn't have a clue we've connected him to the murders."

Dom drew her close and kissed her before she had a chance to pull away, and his heart thudded at her sweetness. She leaned into him for a moment but then withdrew. Saddened, he let her go.

"Dominic, we can't."

"I know, but I want to."

She scooted off the bed and his erection strained against his zipper.

"I'm going to take a shower and then try to sleep." She avoided his gaze.

For her sake, he was sorry there hadn't been another vacancy at the hotel. As it was, only a last minute cancellation yielded this tiny room with a queen sized bed. He wasn't enough of a gentleman to suggest he sleep on the floor. Tessa would have to deal.

**

As the hot water poured over her body, Tessa ran through her interactions with her bartender over the last month. Nothing pointed to him being a killer. In fact, he'd treated her with more care than Dominic had recently.

Charley went out of his way to protect her against any angry customer. How could he have murdered anyone? And why would he kill?

Certain the young man in the photo was merely a look-alike, and not related to Charley at all, she let herself enjoy the warmth of the shower. When her fingers pruned, she shut off the tap. The steamy bathroom would make changing into her nightgown a sticky affair, but she couldn't change in front of Dominic. Just because they'd made love didn't mean she felt comfortable prancing around the room naked.

Tessa took as long as possible in the bathroom, hoping Dominic would be asleep by the time she finished. His every touch excited her, yet something about him caused her to distrust him. Was it his apparent wealth or the way he withheld information from her?

She toweled off, slipped into her nightgown, and headed to bed, hoping against hope she could keep her hands to herself.

CHAPTER FIFTEEN

Dom was thankful for the aisle between Tessa and himself. The last thing he needed was to sit next to her and smell her perfume for five hours on the flight back to Tampa. He'd not had a wink of sleep last night, in part because her cute little ass kept rubbing up against his crotch. He'd flip over only to find Tessa snuggled against his back. Ass to crotch or breast to back—both resulted in a ragging hard-on all night.

He'd have initiated the love making, but Tessa had barely looked at him after her shower. He could only imagine what demons she was fighting after learning one of her employees might be a serial killer.

During the whole flight, Tessa didn't attempt to speak with him. In fact, she kept her eyes closed for the most part. Had it not been for her clenched fists, he would have assumed she'd been asleep.

Only when the wheels slammed down on the runway did she awake. She looked over at him and gave him a half smile, but he bet she was none too happy to return to the land of Ralph and Charley. Given his house had a state-of-the-art alarm system, he didn't worry about anyone breaking in.

The seventy-five degree temperature was a nice change from Ohio. As Tessa exited the plane, Dom slipped John a few hundred more to cover the cost of the flight. His friend objected, but Dom insisted. Learning who'd killed Trace was worth ten times the amount.

"I hate to do this to you, Tessa," Dom said, "but I've have to see about getting the lab to hurry up the fingerprints on Charley. I'll call Dean to make sure he stands guard at the house while I'm at work."

"Can't your partner call the lab?"

He grabbed hold of her shoulders. "He's out looking for our man now. I promise nothing will happen to you."

"Okay, but don't leave me alone too long." Her bottom lip jutted out, but he doubted she was trying to be coy.

"I promise. Besides, I want to find Chelsea's parents."

She brightened. "That would be great. I know she'd love to see them when she wakes up. At least I think she'll be happy."

***

The cool, damp night air crawled down Ralph's back as he stared up at the second floor of the detective's house. He wet his cracked lips, angry he'd forgotten his lip balm. At least he'd figured out which was Tessa's bedroom.

Two days ago he'd hidden behind the warehouse a hundred feet from the restaurant waiting for Tessa to emerge from the Blue Moon. When she'd come out, he couldn't believe how pathetic she looked standing by the dilapidated bar awaiting her white knight to pick her up. As if having a bodyguard would stop him from doing what he wanted with Tessa. Please.

Dumb cop couldn't even spot a tail. What a loser. Ralph had followed them from the restaurant to the hospital, then to dinner, and then to the cop's mansion. Ralph thought about letting Tessa know he knew where she was staying, but when it started to rain, Ralph decided he'd come back the next day.

Okay. He admitted it. For a split second he thought they'd gotten a jump on him. The cop's car was gone all day. Royally pissed, Ralph had driven around the neighborhood in an old truck with a landscape sign attached to its side awaiting their arrival. If they hadn't shown up today, Ralph might have burned the place down just to teach them both a lesson.

Ralph had studied the property. The detective left the blinds open to his study, making him an easy target should Ralph want to execute the guy. The detective's turn would come later. Who in this day and age left their blinds open at night? Like a reality TV show, Ralph watched Tessa stop in the office once, but she didn't stay long. Maybe they weren't doing each other. If they were, it might be interesting to see how she'd react to seeing her lover lose a few body parts one piece at a time.

Once Tessa left the detective's office, Ralph only had to wait thirty seconds before a light flicked on in an upstairs window. Bingo. He'd found his sweet little bird. Her shadow appeared through the sheer curtains on the second floor and must have thought no one could see her.

Ralph shook his head. He still couldn't believe Tessa was staying with a cop—and a rich one at that. Women sure were a strange breed of animal. The guy probably took bribes right and left given his one-acre estate was so near to the city. The other houses on the street were crammed together, but not his. No, the guy had money that was for sure.

Wouldn't the schlep be in for a surprise once Tessa caught him doing something illegal? And she'd find out, all right. The woman was a born snoop. She never could keep her damn nose outta other people's businesses.

Ralph stepped next to one of the downstairs windows on the other end of the house from the office and checked for wires along the edge of the window. Yep, just as he suspected. The place was alarmed all right. Sure he could disarm it, but the time it would take and the noise he'd make wouldn't be worth it.

Had the place not been so well alarmed he might have climbed up the oak tree near Tessa's bedroom window and greeted the little bitch with a quick hello. Kind of a I'm-going-to-get-you-when-you-least-expect-it kind of hello. Maybe another time.

Not that anyone could catch him if the alarms did sound. No. He was too smart for that. He'd be long gone before any security arrived.

The detective would probably race upstairs to check on Tessa before he stole outside. Ralph decided it would be best to have a more precise plan to scare the crap out of her.

As he turned to leave, Ralph reached into his pocket. He wanted Tessa to know he was watching—always watching. That way when he did show up, she'd be prepared for what he had in store for her.

He couldn't wait until he and Tessa were alone, and he could do things to her she never could imagine. The only perk of doing time was learning every conceivable way to fuck and torture a woman.

Three years was a long time to wait for revenge, which was why he had to make it worth his while.

After he deposited his little surprise, the urge to brag bested him.

***

Tessa awoke to a strange noise. Sweat had bathed her sheets. Maybe it was her recurring nightmare of gunshots that made her think she'd heard a noise.

Ping, ping.

She bolted upright in bed, her pulse skyrocketing.

The noise was not her imagination. It had come from something hitting the window. Was someone tossing pebbles at the glass, or had a woodpecker mistaken the pane for wood?

She glanced at the glowing clock. It was in the middle of the frigging night. Who'd be outside at this hour?

Oh, God, no. Ralph? Or Charley? Dread sparked a chain reaction that sent pain first to her eyes, then squeezed her chest, and finally, dropped straight to her stomach. Rationally, she knew he couldn't have found her. Not this fast. She was safe here. Dominic had assured her.

"Tes-sa," came the voice from outside.

She froze. Her breath whooshed out of her lungs, and her muscles wouldn't move. Tessa concentrated on the timbre and tried to remember if Ralph's voice was that deep. She couldn't recall. How could she not recognize the voice of the man she'd been married to? Good Lord. His courtroom threat was never far from her mind. Could it be him?

Maybe she'd imagined the eerie call.

"Dominic?" she called. Fear had dried up her throat so much that her voice floated no further than a few feet.

Tessa swallowed and tried again. "Dominic?"

Her weak voice would never reach his bedroom.

Move, Tessa, move.

Perhaps Dominic had gone out to investigate, found no one, and locked himself out of the house. Yes, that could be it. Her muscles relaxed, and she was able to crawl out of bed.

On tiptoe, she padded over to the window. Not wanting to be seen from the outside, she stood to the side and pulled back the sheers.

As if she were standing under Niagara Falls, her pounding blood blocked all sound. *Calm down.* Tessa tried to take a deep breath to slow her heart, but her life force pumped to its own rapid rhythm.

No more stones hit the window, and no more voices sounded from below.

Tessa reached across the window to unclasp the sash. If she could open the window, maybe she'd be able to hear better.

Jittery, she clamped down on her jaw to prevent her roiling stomach from erupting like Mount St. Helens. Sweat dribbled down her back despite the chill in the room, and her fingers slipped on the lock. After three futile attempts to open the damn thing, she wiped her hands on her gown and tried again. This time the window budged. The second she threw up the sash, an ear shattering alarm sounded.

As if electrified, Tessa scurried back from the window, her heart ready to burst. She raced toward the bedroom door holding her hands over her ears.

Guilt and fear collided. She'd only been trying to see who was out there calling her name.

She reached the door just as it swung open. The hall light illuminated a big hulking body, and Tessa screamed.

***

Relief shot through Dom upon seeing Tessa was safe. He flipped on the light switch, and her eyes widened. A split second later she was plastered to his chest, but he didn't recall who'd moved first. He pressed his face to her hair. She smelled sweet, like strawberries and sunshine.

"Are you okay?" he asked, shouting above the alarm.

She nodded. "I'm sorry. I opened the window and the alarm went off."

"That's it?" He'd feared an intruder had tried to get in.

"Yes."

Dom held her away at arm's length and checked her over. She appeared fine. "Wait here. I'm going to turn off the alarm."

Tessa looked up at him with tear stained cheeks, which did nothing to calm his racing heart. He released his grip on her shoulders and sprinted down the hall. He punched in his security code and the screeching stopped. He let out a deep breath, reveling in the ensuing silence.

His phone rang. Damn. It must be the alarm company checking to see if he was safe.

"I'll be right back," he yelled to Tessa as he raced to his bedroom to grab his cell.

After giving the security team his code and password, he returned to her. She hadn't moved. "Why did you open the window? It's cold outside," he said.

"Someone was throwing rocks at my window and then called my...my name," she choked out.

Dom studied her face. "Are you sure you weren't dreaming?"

"No. I swear to you, someone was outside. I went to the window to check if maybe you were stuck outside and forgot your key."

"Oh, Tessa, I'm so sorry. Crawl back into bed, and I'll have a look to make sure no one's out there. Okay?"

Her smile faltered. "Okay."

Dom closed the window and locked the sash. "Let's leave this closed. I'll be back as soon as I've checked the perimeter."

He didn't want to leave her alone in her fragile state, but he certainly couldn't take her outside with him.

Dom dashed to his bedroom, threw on a pair of jeans, a shirt, shoes, and a warm jacket. He grabbed the flashlight he kept by his nightstand, and then stuffed his revolver in his waistband. He didn't want to chance Ralph had found Tessa. The guy had located her once. It was possible he could do it again.

The crisp November air held a damp chill, but Dom ignored the cold. Sweeping the area with his light, he proceeded to scope out the section under Tessa's bedroom.

Dom halted halfway to her window. The dewy grass was matted down in several spots. And the matted prints weren't caused by animals either. Damn. Tessa hadn't been dreaming.

A pyramid of stones drew his attention. Light from his flashlight caught an object resting on top of the pile. He pulled a handkerchief from his pocket, bent down, and picked up a ring.

"Christ."

Tessa's nickel ring. He'd seen her wear it on numerous occasions. Had Charley found her? Was she his next victim? Or had he ex left it?

With his revolver drawn, Dom scoured his backyard. Depression colored his steps as he did a sweep. Tessa had done nothing to deserve this treatment. He checked behind the bushes and canvassed the whole property but found no other incriminating evidence.

Convinced the intruder was gone, he slipped back into the house. Running up the steps to the second floor, he eased into Tessa's room in case she'd fallen asleep.

Tessa was standing near the window, still as an angel with the lights off. She must not have heard him enter.

"Tessa?" He used his softest voice before turning on the light by her bed.

She whipped around, her face frozen in fear. "I found no one," he said.

"No one?"

"Whoever was here is gone. You can go back to sleep."

She inched her way toward him. "Okay, but I don't know if I can sleep."

"He won't be coming back. The house is a fortress."

He tamped down the urge to hold her, caress her, and then make love to her. The timing sucked. Her frame of mind was still too fragile.

When they did make love again, he didn't want her to worry her life was in jeopardy.

Besides, he couldn't chance losing his focus. Tessa had the ability to make him forget everything about the do's and don'ts of protection.

Before Tessa could convince him to stay, Dom left. Once he reset the alarm, he trudged back to bed. He knew he wouldn't sleep, but he certainly didn't want to be near temptation. Tomorrow he'd tell her about the nickel ring he'd found.

***

Tess had watched every soap opera and design show possible during the day. As far as she was concerned, Dominic had basically abandoned her again. All the man did was work, work, work. Yes, he had a killer to find as well as her ex-husband, but he wasn't the only one employed by the precinct. He could have asked for some time off.

The worst part of her exile was in not being able to leave the house. Dominic had actually forbidden her to go out for any reason. Jeez, he acted as if she were a recalcitrant child who'd been grounded. Although, truth be known, she was afraid to leave the premises.

To make sure she followed his orders, Dominic had hired a uniformed policeman to sit outside in his squad car. Oh, sure, he'd said it was to keep the riff raff out—read Ralph—but from his tone, it was more to keep her under house arrest.

She'd asked if the policeman could escort her to the mall, but Dominic said someone might spot her. Didn't her ex already know where she was holed up? Of course, that was assuming the footprints Dominic had found in the grass belonged to Ralph. They could have been Charley's, but her money was on her ex.

Bored out of her mind, Tessa called Annie.

"Hello?" said the comforting voice.

"Hi, Annie, it's Tessa. How's my adorable niece?" she asked with false happiness.

"Tessa, I've been worried about you. Are you okay? I called your house a few times and left messages, but you never called back."

"I fine. I'm staying with...a friend. Call me on my cell next time."

For some reason, Tessa didn't want to say she'd agreed to stay with the terminally attractive detective when only a few days ago she'd told Annie she didn't trust the man.

Muffled screams of joy emanated from Annie's end.

"Jeremy, don't hit your sister, please. Sorry about that," Annie said. "Please don't worry about Mandy, she's fine, but you're the one I'm concerned about. How are you, really?"

"Good, I guess." Tessa didn't want to burden Annie with what had happened last night, and she didn't want to spread the word that Charley was a serial killer until Dominic had absolute proof the man was a murderer.

"I'd really love to I see Mandy. I miss her so much."

"Tessa, I don't think it's such a good idea. What if Ralph is watching you? You can't take any chances."

Now her friend sounded like Dominic. Ralph already knew where Tessa lived, but he didn't know where Annie lived.

"You're right. I know Judd would love to see the baby too, but I realize this stalker might already know Judd's in the hospital and wait for me or you there."

"This mess will be over soon," Annie said with reassurance. "Judd will be healthy in no time, and Mandy will be reunited with her father."

Annie's cheeriness lifted her spirits. "Thanks, Annie. I owe you a big one."

Tessa swiped her cell closed and slumped down in front of the television. Why hadn't she asked Annie if she could stay with her? Because Tessa didn't like the general shelter or trust the place could keep her safe.

She wrapped an arm over her face, upset that she had no one else to call. The police had yet to release her father's body, so making funeral arrangements had to wait. And being confined to the house meant she couldn't visit Judd either, not that he wanted to see her anyway.

Dominic wouldn't be home for another few hours, and she was plain bored. If he hadn't taken his laptop with him to work, she'd have played on the Internet.

With little to do, she turned her concentration to the type of man

Dominic appeared to be on the surface. The fact his floors were hardwood and covered with oriental carpets, and his counters were granite, did not bode well for him being a straight arrow cop.

The only way to find out would be to look in his office. Yes, it would be snooping, but a girl had a right to learn what kind of man lived in such an expensive home.

She'd taken art history in school and recognized the Marc Chagall painting above the fireplace that had to be worth a mint. Even if a few of the other masterpieces were replicas, the frames alone were worth several hundred dollars, far more than your average cop could afford.

Tessa knew the signs of a man on the take. First came the nice truck, and then the toys for him and the presents for her. She'd even believed Ralph when he'd told her his aunt had died and left him money.

Before she knew it, Tessa ended up in Dom's study. The thick, Damask drapes, leather high-backed chair and mahogany desk indicated the man had expensive tastes. But then, she already knew that about him.

Pulling out Dom's top drawer, she found a pay stub and studied it. Her shoulders sagged. He didn't make much more than Ralph had. So where had he the money to decorate his house come from?

Now that she'd crossed the ethical line, she might as well be thorough. The file cabinet in the corner contained his bills, organized alphabetically from Automobile to Water Company. No surprise there. Nothing, however, suggested any kind of illegal activity. Not that she expected to find a file labeled, "Bribes."

"Hello?" came the familiar voice from the front of the house.

Her pulse sped up. Dominic was home early. Tessa closed the file drawer, raced from his office, and ducked into the half bath. Heart pounding, she flushed the toilet and ran the tap, hoping he wouldn't notice her blotchy face.

Tessa strolled to the foyer. "Hi," she said, straining to keep the guilt from her voice.

"I'm glad you behaved yourself. Ron said you didn't step outside."

Hello to you too. His chilly attitude had intensified since she'd set off the stupid alarm. It wasn't as if he'd warned her or anything about his high tech system.

He waved the two bags in his hand. "Dinner. Would you mind heating up the food? I have an important call to make."

Dom brushed past her, strode into the kitchen, and set the bags on the counter. She followed behind.

Oh, God. Maybe he'd found something out about Ralph. "Is there something you aren't you telling me?"

He whipped around, and his gaze seared right through her. "No. Don't worry. Everything will be okay."

He patted his pockets, jammed his hands in, and drew out a handful of change. An object dropped from his fingers and pinged and rolled on the floor. His eyes widened for a split second. Simultaneously, they squatted to pick up the fallen item, but Dominic beat her to it.

As he slipped the object in his pant pocket, she recognized the ring.

"Dominic. That's the ring my mother gave me. Where did you get that?"

He pulled it out and blew out a breath. "I'm sorry. I found it outside last night, but knowing you'd be upset, I wanted to wait before I told you."

"Damn right, I'm upset. How could you keep this from me?" Tessa's heart sped up. "You know what this means? Ralph wants me to know he knows I'm here. Now that I have proof he was the intruder, I can't stay here."

He stabbed a hand over his short hair and took a step toward her. "Tessa, I understand how frightened you must be, but you'll be safe here. I promise. I'll hire someone twenty-four seven if that's what it takes to make you feel secure."

"You'd do that?"

"Of course."

"And I'm to trust you? One well-placed bullet to the head of the hired man would put all of us in jeopardy." Tessa's gaze darted around the kitchen. "How could Ralph have found me?"

He placed his warm palms on her shoulders. "I don't know, but that's all the more reason why you can't leave."

Tessa wasn't convinced. She stepped out of his grasp and held out her hand. Dominic withdrew the ring from his pocket and placed it in her palm.

"My mom gave me this ring for my tenth birthday. The nickel in the ring turns my finger green, but I've never had the heart to throw it away."

The fact he'd hidden evidence of Ralph's presence ticked her off. She took a step back.

"Listen, I need to make that phone call," he said. "Are you going to be okay?"

"I'm fine. I'll start dinner. You go do your thing."

Dominic's face hardened, and he stalked off.

What did he expect? Gratitude he'd found her ring? If he wanted to protect her as he claimed, he should have stayed home and not left her with a rent-a-cop.

The wonderful aroma of chicken permeated the bags and halted her musings. Her stomach grumbled. Tessa read the store name on the side. Ooh, Wright's Gourmet. How fancy.

She unwrapped the meal. The instructions said to warm the casserole in a 325-degree oven for twenty minutes. Easy enough. She'd eat first and then figure out what she wanted to do.

While she was waiting for the oven to warm, she wanted to know if Dominic had been in contact with the hospital today. Good news might help keep her mind off the maniac who was after her. Tessa prayed Chelsea would pull through.

As she neared his office, Dominic's deep voice filtered through the slightly open door. She stopped and was about to turn around when Dominic said the word *bank account*. She stilled, and then crept closer.

"Deposit the eighty grand in account number 46209845... And remember, don't use my name. Got it? I don't want to get caught by you know who."

Tessa fell against the wall. Eighty thousand dollars? He had that much money from a cop's salary? Her heart beat so fast, she thought it would jump out of her chest. She didn't want to listen to another word. Her nightmare awoke all over again. What was he into—drugs, extortion, or was he taking bribes, like Ralph?

She rushed back to the kitchen for a much needed glass of wine when her cell rang.

Caller ID told her it was Annie. "What's up?"

Annie whimpered. "Tessa, I'm so sorry."

"What are you talking about? Calm down, I can hardly understand you."

"Ralph has Mandy."

Tessa grabbed the countertop for support and slid into the seat next to the counter. "How? When?"

"Just a few minutes ago. He said he'll kill her if you don't meet him at the Blue Moon by 5 p.m."

She checked the time. "Annie, it's 4:40 already." A sob escaped. "What else did he say?"

"He said if you tell the detective, he'll know, and he'll kill my two kids. He bugged the detective's house while you two were away yesterday."

Oh, God. He knew they'd been gone? Was he still watching her every move? The image of the photographs flashed in her mind.

But hadn't Dom alarmed the house when they left for Ohio? Maybe Ralph was lying, even though her ex was quite the expert at electronics.

"If you call the police," Annie added, her voice trembling, "He'll kill my kids." Her strong friend started to cry.

Tessa hyperventilated. This couldn't be happening. If she went to the Blue Moon, Ralph would kill her for sure. But could she sit by and do nothing? She couldn't notify the police or Annie's children would be endangered.

"Annie, I'm so sorry." Tessa wanted to console her friend, but she didn't have time. "I have to go." Tessa hung up before her friend could convince her to abandon her niece.

Tessa raced up to her bedroom and grabbed her keys. She fumbled in her purse for a piece of paper.

Sitting on the bed, she wrote a short note to Dominic. Her hand shook, creating wavy letters, and her sweat and tears left big blobs on the paper. Her sheers were open. No! Bile raced to her mouth. Surely

Ralph hadn't been able to install a hidden camera inside the house. Could he?

The paper crunched on her lap, and Tessa finished writing.

Place bugged.

Ralph has Mandy.

Gone to Blue Moon.

Don't involve police.

Please let him understand everything she meant to write. She didn't have time to explain.

She hurried into Dominic's room and grabbed the small gun she'd found in the table next to his bed while looking for incriminating evidence. He'd be pissed when he found she'd taken his weapon, but too damn bad.

Armed with the revolver, she tiptoed down the squeaky wooden stairs and left the note on the kitchen counter where he'd be sure to find it.

Thankful Dominic's office was at the other end of the house, she ran to the front door and looked out. The security cop was gone. She guessed he planned to hire the second cop for tomorrow night. Little good it would do her now.

Careful not to alert Dominic to her departure, she eased out the front door. Once clear of the house, she sprinted to her car, her feet pounding on the pavement. Tessa jumped in the driver's side and started the engine. It backfired. Dammit. She didn't need Dominic rushing after her.

Fifteen minutes until Ralph killed Mandy. Oh, God. *Please let me be on time.*

Her sweating palms slipped on the wheel as she peeled out of the driveway. People were pouring into the neighborhood. Damn. The rush hour traffic would be hell. Tears streamed down her cheeks and blurred her vision.

A car pulled around the corner and honked when she nearly rammed into him. Tessa swerved back to her side of the road as adrenaline raced through her system.

Concentrate, concentrate, concentrate.

Her wheels squealed as she pressed her foot on the accelerator. She shivered and flipped on the heat lever. Tessa took three wrong turns before she made it to the main road.

Eight minutes to go. *Please let my baby be safe.*

Before she realized it, the restaurant's glowing sign appeared and Tessa's trembling hands stopped shaking.

The parking lot was empty. Where was Ralph? Had she mistaken the location? No. Annie had positively stated to meet him here.

Tessa checked her watch for the hundredth time. One minute before five. Surely, he hadn't come and gone.

No. Ralph was clever. He liked playing mind games, always had. He was here someplace hidden. He wanted to scare her. While he'd succeeded on that account, he wouldn't win the game. She hadn't taken all those self-defense classes for nothing.

Tessa parked, gripped the handle of the gun, and shoved the weapon into the back of her waistband like she'd seen Dominic do too many times to count in the last month.

Taking a deep breath, she pushed open her door and eased out.

CHAPTER SIXTEEN

Tessa stepped from her car, and had to wipe her sweaty palms on her pants. She refused to look around for Ralph. Doing so would give him power. She needed to act in control—for Mandy's sake. The moment Ralph spotted weakness he'd use it to his advantage.

Head held high, Tessa strode to the front of the restaurant acting as if she were in control, pretending it was just an ordinary day.

Don't hesitate, and don't act nervous. *Confidence, girl, confidence.*

Her promise to her brother that she'd look after his daughter rang in her head. Mandy needed her and nothing was going to stop Tessa from finding her niece.

Behind her restaurant, a construction crane swung a large piece of cement, accurately placing the long beam on top of the eight-story building, and a jackhammer pummeled the earth, making the ground shake. Each day, the dreaded Jankowski project crept closer to Judd's property.

Tessa's phone vibrated against her thigh and she jumped. Her fingers twitched as she started to grab the phone.

Don't answer it.

What if it was Dominic calling? She still shouldn't answer it. Ralph might be watching, or worse, listening with some high tech device.

Could he bug a cell phone? With him, anything was possible. Even if it wasn't Dominic, Ralph might believe she was speaking with the police.

The phone stopped, and her last lifeline for help was gone.

She prayed Dominic had found her note and was at this very moment formulating some clever plan to save both her and Mandy.

Tessa reached out and tested the front door handle. It was locked. Maybe Ralph had gained access in the back through the kitchen. She pulled out her key, took a deep breath, and let herself in.

The stale smell of beer assaulted her senses, and the dark interior made her question if anyone was even here. Once more she wondered if Annie had mistaken the location? Tessa flicked on the overhead lights and glanced around.

Her underarms moistened and her stomach wouldn't stop doing summersaults. No one was here. As she ducked behind the bar, a few peanut shells crunched under her feet. The big wooden structure would give her some protection against her maniac ex-husband, and having a few bottles to throw at him might come in handy too.

She stilled, straining to hear Mandy's cries, but only the clicking of the clock behind the bar sent out any noise. Tic...toc...tic. Shades of Alfred Hitchcock assaulted her, and she shivered.

Tessa's jaw clamped together, as her resolve strengthened. The no good bastard wouldn't live long enough to regret messing with her niece.

As much as she wanted to, Tessa couldn't bring herself to shoot Ralph in cold blood, but she would kill him if he laid a hand on her or harmed the baby. In her heart, she hoped when the time came, she'd be able to pull the trigger.

"Ralph, you here?" Her voice cracked. Damn.

Her heart thudded as she awaited his response.

None came.

Damn it. Did he want her to search for him? Of course he did. When she least expected it, he'd grab her from behind. No. She'd wait for him to come to her. She could play the waiting game too.

No way would she let him control the situation. She scooted back against the wall.

"Hello, Tessa."

Her heart skipped a beat. She whipped around and watched Ralph as he sauntered out of the kitchen, gun raised, pointed right at her heart. The door swung back into place.

She grabbed the counter to keep from collapsing. Ralph looked ten years older. His eyes were unfocused, and his unkempt beard indicated he'd let himself go.

"Ralph."

"Is that anyway to greet the love of your life?"

Don't answer that. "Where's Mandy?" There, she'd kept her voice even.

"Wouldn't you like to know?"

"Yes, I would. It's why I've come, Ralph." Not to see you, that was for sure.

"Come out from behind the bar," he said, waving his gun. "I want to look at you. It's been a long time since I've seen you up close and personal." The leer in his eye sickened her.

"You can see me perfectly well where I am."

Ralph's eyes narrowed as he stepped toward her. "Do as I say, bitch, or you'll be sorry." His insecurity shone like a bright light. Too bad, she hadn't seen his flaws before she married him.

She raised her hands in surrender. "I'll do as you ask."

Tessa took one step at a time as she moved backwards the entire length of the bar toward the door. Her gaze caught the clock. Six minutes past five. Had Dominic left the house? Please hurry.

"You were wrong to turn me in, you know." His lip curled.

"You're right. I never should have ratted you out."

His brows rose in surprise. "So now you're playing the devoted wife?"

"No. I've had a lot of time to think. I realize I never gave you a chance to explain yourself before I called the station that night."

"You got that right, bitch. Your one phone call cost me three of the most miserable years of my life." His shoulders relaxed. "However, I too had a lot of time to think about what I wanted do to you once I had you alone."

"Listen, Ralph. You had a gambling problem. Stopping you before you hurt anyone else might have saved your life. I'm truly sorry for all the trouble I've caused you."

"Are you saying I was better off in jail because I would have ended up dead if I hadn't stopped gambling?"

"Maybe."

"Oh, that's rich, Tess."

"You're right to be angry. I betrayed your trust. I should have tried to help you instead of turning you in." She prayed the techniques for diffusing a situation like this worked—or were they just textbook examples written by shrinks with no practical experience? God help her.

"Damn right you betrayed me. And for that you'll pay."

Tessa's hands turned cold and her muscles wouldn't move. "I want to see Mandy." She tried to keep her tone soft.

"Mandy. What a nice name." He slid his hand up and down the barrel of the gun. "Speaking of which, who knocked you up?"

He never used to be so crass. "No one. She's not mine. She's Judd's daughter. He's sick and asked me to look after her."

His face contorted in anger, as if his leverage had suddenly evaporated. He slapped the gun in the palm of his hand. "It doesn't matter. I'll kill her anyway."

A door slammed shut in the kitchen area, and Ralph turned. He glanced back to her. "Who'd you tell?"

"I didn't tell anyone. You told me not to. You've got to believe me." She let her voice rise, hoping whoever had arrived would hear the panic in her voice and come to her rescue. Surely Dominic wouldn't make such a racket.

"Since when did you ever do as I asked?" Ralph spit back as he stepped toward the kitchen.

Before she had a chance to answer, Charley came crashing through the swinging door, and her rapid-fire heart threatened to burst. She didn't care if her former bartender had killed ten people, she felt safer with him than with Ralph.

Ralph raised his gun and pointed it at the bigger man, and a scream lodged in her throat. Charley ducked and rammed his head into

Ralph's midsection, knocking him to the ground. When a gun blast shattered the air, Tessa's legs turned to mush.

On his way down, Ralph's leg kicked the bar stool and the wooden chair clattered to the floor. Tessa clasped a hand over her mouth, frozen from the horror.

As the two men rolled around, struggling to gain control of the gun, every instinct told her to run, but there was no way she'd leave the Blue Moon without her precious Mandy.

Her niece had to be in her office. As the men punched and kicked each other, Tessa made a wide sweep past them, hoping they were too focused on each other to notice her.

She ran passed the kitchen door and was halfway down the hall when a loud report startled her, and the doorframe next to her head splintered. She grabbed her head and ducked. When she realized she hadn't been hurt, she chanced a look back at the two men. Charley was pummeling Ralph's face. Her ex struggled to rise, and the gun went off again. Tessa couldn't afford to gawk or see if either had been hit.

Desperate to find her niece, Tessa rushed into her office and flipped the light switch. Damn. The place was empty. A hoarse cry tore from her throat. The only other viable place to stash a child would be the kitchen.

As she rushed back down the hall, Charley stepped in front of her and blocked her path.

"I killed him for you," he said with a look of grim satisfaction.

Ralph's dead? Part of her wanted to rejoice, and the other part cry. Tessa despised the loss of life, even Ralph's life. "You shouldn't have done that."

Cold eyes stared back at her. Gone was the warmth that often colored his face.

"I had no choice. Come on," he stated. "I want to find a safe place for you."

"The danger's passed, Charley. With Ralph gone, you don't have to protect me any longer, don't you see?"

He looked confused. "What about the serial killer your detective friend is trying to find?"

You mean, you, she wanted to say. "I don't know what that has to do with anything."

"You could still be in danger. He's already killed three people. You could be next."

She swallowed hard. How could Charley have learned of Doug Walsh's death unless he was the one who'd killed him? "I'll take my chances."

Tessa pulled her cell phone from her belt loop.

"What are you doing?" Charley grabbed her wrist in a hard clench.

"I'm calling the police to report Ralph's death."

"I can't let you do that."

A nervous laugh escaped. "Come on, Charley. I know it was self-defense. You won't get in trouble. I'll testify for you."

"I don't care about whether I'll get in trouble or not. I care about you and the baby."

Tessa jerked her hand away from his grasp and took a step backwards. "Ralph kidnapped Mandy. I have to find her."

Charley raised his gun and swung it around, as if a phantom kidnapper might appear. "Mandy's here?"

"Yes. I bet you could find her. Why don't you look in the back storage room while I search the kitchen?"

He hesitated for a second too long. "I'll help look for her, but we'll look together."

"Fine."

Hurry, Dominic, hurry.

Charley shadowed her as she slowly opened every door in the restaurant, constantly calling Mandy's name.

"Where could she be?" Tessa asked more to herself than to Charley.

"I don't know, but we gotta get outta here."

"Charley, I can't leave. Not with Ralph dead and Mandy all alone. If you had a daughter, would you leave her?"

Once again, his face contorted, and his eyes darted everywhere. "No. I'd want protect her like I want to protect you."

"But to do that, we have to find my niece." She snapped her fingers as if a bright idea suddenly came to her. "I'll call Annie. She was caring for Mandy when Ralph came and took the baby. Maybe he told her something."

"No. I gotta protect you."

"Protect me from whom?" Charley clearly was not rational.

Unless... he wasn't the killer.

"From the man who killed the lady, Mr. Dirkman, and Mr. Walsh."

But you're the man, she wanted to shout. Wasn't he? He had to be if he knew Doug Walsh was dead.

"You're right. I do need to be protected, but I need to tell my friend, Annie, to look for Mandy, all right? You know how helpless a six month old is. She'll starve to death if we don't find her soon."

His lips firmed. "Okay, but don't tell her you're with me."

"No, I won't, I promise. I'll tell her when I arrived to the Blue Moon, I found Ralph dead."

"Okay." He lowered his gun hand.

Charley didn't seem bright enough to be a serial killer, yet the photo Mrs. Richter had given them looked remarkably like her bartender. She couldn't chance bringing up the Richter's name since it might be the trigger to set him off.

Tessa pressed Dominic's preprogrammed number. If Charley asked to speak with Annie, he'd know she was lying. He'd kill Tessa as surely as he'd killed the others.

She paced but never turned her back to the man. Charley didn't say a word, but his gaze never left her.

"Tessa, my God. I've—"

"Annie, thank goodness I got a hold of you. Listen, Ralph is dead. He can't harm you and the kids anymore, but I couldn't find Mandy. You've got to—"

Shit. She banged the side of the phone and replaced it next to her ear. Dead. Crap. She'd forgotten to recharge her batteries.

"Phone's dead," Tessa said holding it in front of him. "I need to use the bar phone."

"No." His compliant demeanor disappeared. "Come on. I want to take you someplace safe." He waved the gun at her.

She wished he'd stop saying that. "Charley, really, it isn't necessary. And please put down the gun. You're making me nervous."

His eyes clouded over as if a demon had jumped inside his skin. She'd never seen such a transformation before. She'd only read about split personalities in her psych books.

He stepped toward her and yanked her arm, and the force of the pull caused her to drop the phone. It bounced and clanked at her feet. Charley tugged her away from her lifeline and Tessa resisted.

"You're coming with me. Now," he growled.

"Charley, you're hurting me. Please stop it."

He hesitated for a moment, then half-pulled, half-dragged her through the kitchen to the back entrance. Charley bulldozed through the back door with Tessa in tow.

In the moments since she'd arrived, dusk had darkened the sky. Frantically, Tessa looked around for someone to help her, but no one was near. All the construction workers from Mr. Jankowski's project had evaporated. Even the jack hammering had stopped, and the crane was swinging empty in the air.

She spotted two boats tethered in their boat slips, but Tessa couldn't remember if the boats had been docked when she'd arrived.

"Help," she screamed, hoping someone could hear her.

Charley shoved his gun in the back of his pants, turned, and grabbed hold of both of her arms. He shook her hard. "Don't... ever... scream... like that again, do you hear me?"

His severe tone forced her to blink.

Be reaffirming. Be solicitous. Be careful.

"I'm sorry. You're right. It was stupid of me to yell. You're too kind to hurt me. You want to protect me and help me find Mandy."

He relaxed the grip from fifty pounds of pressure to maybe thirty, but her arms still throbbed. For a split second she considered kicking him in the balls and running to the road five hundred feet away, but he'd angled his body in such a way that she knew her plan would be futile.

"I'm glad you understand. After that little tantrum of yours, I'll have to tie you up and put you in the back of the truck." He acted as if she were ten.

Was that what his father had done to him? "Please, don't. I'll be good, I promise."

Charley smiled. "You should have thought about your actions before you screamed. I hate people who scream, and I hate people who make a fuss." His voice sounded different now, very authoritative, like his father probably had sounded.

Out of desperation, Tessa pulled away one last time, but she was no match against the large man.

The handle of the Dominic's gun scraped against her back. If she could just get a few feet of separation between them, she'd shoot him.

Certain he planned to kill her, Tessa realized she could kill him.

As Charley propelled her toward his truck, her feet windmilled backwards. She tripped and nearly fell, but Charley lifted her off the ground like a case of liquor.

She struggled with all her strength, despite knowing the more she tried to get away, the harder he'd hold on. The self-defense class she'd taken did nothing to help her now. Charley was too strong.

He pinned her back against the van with one arm and one leg, and then leaned over the back of the truck to pull down the tailgate. He lifted the hatch. Jostling her closer to the back, he suddenly let go and reached in.

"Turn around and face the truck."

Her gaze fixated on duct tape. "What are you going to do?"

"Do as I say."

"Charley, please. I promise I won't yell or say a word," Tessa said, trying with all her might to keep from whining, but her breaths came out in rapid puffs. Charley said he hated people who whined. "You don't have to tie me up. I'll be good. You'll see."

Dominic, where are you?

Charley turned her back to him. "What's this?" He pulled the gun from her waistband. Her last chance of escape evaporated and bile raced up to her mouth.

She swallowed. "I wanted to protect Mandy."

"Well, you won't be needing it anymore."

Faced away from him, she couldn't tell where he stashed the weapon. Both of his hands must have been freed since he was able to tear off a piece of duct tape. The ripping sound sent a shiver to her gut.

He turned her around and slapped the tape over her mouth,

catching part of her hair in the process. The sticky back prevented her from moving her mouth, causing her heart to pound harder in her chest.

When he pulled on her shoulder to turn her around, her forehead banged into the raised window, and blood trickled down her face. He yanked her hands behind her.

"Keep them there," he commanded.

What choice did she have?

Don't whimper, don't cry, stay calm. Dominic will come.

More ripping of duct tape. Tears streamed down her cheeks. She couldn't help herself. Her nose started to clog forcing her to swallow.

Charley wrapped several rotations of tape around her wrists. She strained to keep her palms as far apart as possible in the hopes she'd have a little leeway to loosen them.

He grabbed her by the neck and shoved her face down onto the tailgate. Her eyes widened. A filthy looking mattress lay in the bed.

"Get in," Charley demanded. "It will be a lot less painful if you do it yourself." He let go of her.

Tessa realized the moment she crawled into the back, she'd be dead. And what would happen to poor Mandy?

She had to make him see reason, but with her mouth taped shut, she'd lost the leverage. As she turned toward her attacker, Charley pressed a smelly cloth to her face. She fell backwards from the pressure, and her back slammed into the hard metal floor.

Even with blurry vision, she attempted to lift her legs to push away her attacker, but her body wouldn't move. It was if someone had poured cement in her veins. Her eyelids fluttered.

"Don't bother fighting it, Tessa." His voice wavered like an underwater diver's.

She held her breath for as long as she could, but the ether fumes overtook her.

***

Dominic slapped the phone closed. Tessa was in trouble—serious trouble. Ralph was dead. That part was good. But the anxiety in her voice implied something else had gone wrong.

He let her note flutter to the floor.

Christ. Dom stabbed a hand over his head. He'd only been on the phone in his office for a few minutes. How had she escaped without his notice?

Tessa's situation required more help than he could handle. Dom called the station. Screw the *no police* part in her note. He was going after her with an arsenal of backup if he could get the Captain to okay it.

"Tampa Police Department," the dispatcher answered.

"This is Detective Rossi. Let me speak with Captain Leffers."

While he waited to be connected, he jogged to his bedroom to retrieve his spare gun. He pulled open the drawer only to find it was empty.

"Damn it, Tessa."

Crazy woman would get herself killed if she wasn't careful. Good thing she didn't know where he kept his 357.

"Leffers."

"Rossi here." Dominic explained Tessa's note and panicked phone call.

"She say anything else?" his captain asked.

"No. Given she called me Annie, I'm assuming she's with someone and didn't want him to know she was speaking with me. Then her phone went dead or else someone took the cell from her. I'm sure she would have called me back on the landline if she could have."

Dominic held his cell between his cheek and neck as he checked to see the gun was loaded. As a precaution, he stuffed an extra clip in his pocket.

"I'll send a team in," his Captain said. "Don't worry. They'll keep a low profile."

"Thanks. Is Phil there?"

"No, but I'll give him a call. He'll want to help."

"I appreciate the fast response."

Dominic disconnected and raced outside. He would have suggested a team watch Annie, wherever she lived, but with Ralph dead, the threat to her children was gone.

Dom decided not to turn on his siren since sound traveled far near the water. He headed down West Shore Drive toward Gandy Boulevard. By his calculations, the team would take a good half hour to get to the Blue Moon, whereas he'd make it in under ten.

"Come on, come on. Move it, people." He had to bite his tongue to keep from honking at the slow rush-hour drivers.

Finally, the turn off to the Blue Moon appeared. Even though the restaurant set back from the road, Dom parked down the street. He couldn't chance running into whoever was with Tessa—assuming she was still inside.

He jumped out of his car. Gun hanging by his side, he crept along the perimeter, ducking between one construction storage unit and the next. The cool salt air slapped against his face as his gaze darted behind every dumpster and crane, looking for some sign of a struggle.

The parking lot came into view. Tessa's car sat in front of the restaurant. Alone. Relief rushed through him, but he realized he couldn't let down his guard.

Dom checked his watch. It had been fifteen minutes since he'd spoken with her. He didn't want to think what she might be going through.

Please let her and Mandy be alive.

Heart racing, he moved closer to the side of the building, praying like hell the backup would arrive soon.

Two large boats creaked against the dock that ran along the waterside of the bar, and seagulls squawked, masking his pounding feet on the dirt lot.

Dominic couldn't wait for the rest of the team to arrive. He had to go in and find Tessa—independent, lovely, pain-in-the-ass, Tessa.

Not wanting to use the front door, he circled around to the side and spotted the door leading to the kitchen. As quickly as he could, he pulled it open, jumped in, and closed it behind him. His heart beat loudly in his chest.

When no sounds emanated from inside, he didn't know whether to rejoice or be scared.

Except for the lights on the stoves and the dials on the freezer, the nearly pitch-black kitchen was a veritable cave.

His key chain held a small penlight. Taking a chance he wouldn't give away his position, Dominic pressed the button. The red light provided enough illumination for him to make his way to the other side. Holding his breath, he pushed open the swinging door to the restaurant.

Dom squinted at the bright lights. He ducked down next to the cash register and scoped out the place. No one jumped out at him or shoved a gun in his face. Except for the ticking of the clock above the bar, the place was eerily silent.

He chanced a search. He tiptoed toward Tessa's office and pressed an ear to the door. Again, he was met by silence. Twisting the knob, he rushed in and swung his gun around in anticipation. Finding it empty, he flicked off the light.

Where was she?

As he returned to the seating area, he nearly stepped on a cell phone leaning against the baseboard. Tessa's cell phone. The multi-colored cover was a dead giveaway.

He pressed the On button, but the phone failed to chime. That explained the dropped call. He pocketed her cell and walked towards the bar.

Dark marks stained the floor. Dom knelt down and withdrew a handkerchief from his pocket. He dabbed an end into the dark liquid. It was blood, and his gut soured. Had Ralph cut Tessa? The overturned barstool let him know she hadn't gone quietly.

Wait. Tessa said Ralph was dead. He shook his head. Ralph must have forced her to lie. Bastard.

Before Dom called off the rest of the team, he wanted to check the storage room and freezer in case Ralph had tied up Tessa or Mandy and left them to die. Nothing would surprise him about that ass.

"Tessa? Can you hear me?"

He waited. No answer. Dom then jogged to the kitchen, flipped on the lights, and looked around. The walk-in freezer was smaller than he expected. The overhead light came on when he opened the door, and sat close to empty. Relief shot through him.

As he turned to finish his search, the side door burst open.

CHAPTER SEVENTEEN

Mandy whimpered and Annie rocked the baby. "Shh."

Her husband walked into their bedroom. He was finally home. Thank God.

Annie rushed into her husband's arms. "I'm so glad you're here." Her voice trembled.

He wrapped his strong arms around her and the baby. "What's wrong?"

"I tried to call you on your cell. Where have you been?"

"I'm sorry. I left my phone at work by mistake." He gently held her at arm's length. "You've been crying. What's happened?"

In spurts and starts, she told him about Ralph's visit and his horrifying threats.

"My God, Annie. Did he hurt you or the children?"

"No." Tears streamed down her face.

"I'll call the police." He stepped over to the phone and picked up the receiver.

Annie rushed over to him. "We can't. He said he'd hurt the other children."

"And if we don't, Tessa could be in a lot of trouble."

"I know, but..."

"Did you try reaching Tessa to see if she's okay?"

"Yes, but her cell's not on. Something bad must have happened or she would have called back. I feel so bad."

"All the more reason to call the police."

Annie rocked Mandy. "I know, but if we violate any of the bastard's rules, he'll come back and harm us. The man holds a grudge like no other. He still hasn't forgiven Tessa after three years."

"Sweetheart," Tony said. "That's why I have to call the police."

"The police won't be able to do anything. I've seen too many women get restraining orders and end up on the wrong end of a fist, or in this case, the wrong end of a gun. The police can't shadow us twenty-four seven."

"That may be, but if you don't call, you'll be an accessory—to murder possibly. I can't let that happen to you, to us, to the kids." He waved the phone.

"But Ralph—"

"You think this Ralph fellow has an honor code? Just because you uphold your end of the bargain doesn't mean he will. He could be doing despicable things to Tessa right now, then harm you and the kids."

Annie placed Mandy in her crib and shook the rattle over her head. The baby reached up to grab the plastic ring, and Annie let her have it.

She turned and nodded her assent, knowing they couldn't sit by and do nothing. She prayed the police would find the bastard soon and the nightmare would end.

***

Tessa cracked open her eyes. Her head throbbed the moment she moved, and a slightly sweet taste tinged her tongue. The horrible experience came rushing back to her.

Charley had turned into a monster right before her eyes. And here she'd trusted him—until Dom made her meet Charley's parents in Ohio. What if Charley wasn't Morton Richter, but some look alike? Did it matter?

Her vision blurred for a moment, and then cleared. What had Charley used to drug her? The rag smelled like ether, but it must have been chloroform. Was he always prepared to drug a person? How could he have known she and Ralph would be at the restaurant? Or was it pure coincidence? Maybe he'd followed her. But why?

When the pain lessened, she tried to crawl to the end of the mattress to see out the back of the camper window, but a rope tied around her waist and attached to a hook on the inside of the truck prevented her from moving. Oh God. He'd even taped her feet together too. A mummy had more freedom.

Without the gun, she couldn't surprise him when he stopped, and a huge wave of depression struck her at her helpless situation.

The truck jerked to the left as if he was passing someone. If only there was some way to signal the cars behind them. She'd seen TV shows where the kidnapped person punched out the rear taillights and waved to the car in the rear. Only this stupid truck didn't have any visible taillights in the back.

The streetlights shone through the camper's back window, but she had no view through the side windows. She should have wondered why Charley painted the windows black, but it never occurred to her he might have less than honorable intentions. Dumb, dumb, dumb.

Tessa needed to know where he was taking her. She tried the judge the speed with which the streetlights flashed. They came fast, and the pavement underneath the truck clicked every few seconds, sounding like the expansion joints in the concrete. They never came to a stop or slowed due to traffic, implying they were on I-4 or I-275. That meant they were going someplace far from Tampa. But where?

A loud truck rumbled up right behind them and flashed his brights. Had he spotted her inside? Hope surged until his headlights veered off the left. Damn it.

Tessa closed her eyes for a moment and took a deep breath in an effort to control the pain that stabbed behind her eyes. Her head continued to pulsate with pain from the after effects of the drug. The enormous stress didn't help matters either.

The truck's vibration, coupled with the chloroform, eventually lulled her body into a relaxed state. Somehow she must have fallen asleep, for when she awoke, the truck was moving slower and only periodic light flashed through the back window. Fewer cars sounded in the distance.

Charley must have turned off the highway for the constant thrumming of the tires on the pavement wasn't as loud. Then the truck slowed to a crawl, and her body tensed.

The truck jerked to the left, and then accelerated. Her muscles relaxed. As long as he kept driving, he couldn't harm her. Tessa needed to free herself, and her time was running out.

For starters, she needed to be able to breathe better. The tape over her mouth prevented her from taking in a full breath. Placing her face on the mattress, she dragged her cheek across the canvas in an attempt to loosen the duct tape. Over and over again, she dragged, lifted, and then dragged again. Eventually, an end lifted up and some relief came. Thank goodness he'd only slapped the tape over her mouth and hadn't wrapped it around her head.

After a few more swipes, she managed to tear off the suffocating binding and gulped down mouthfuls of stuffy air. Hurray!

Panting from the exertion, she focused on her next maneuver. She lay on her side and curled her legs back until her fingertips touched her feet. The stupid rope around her waist was in the way, but she pushed it aside. With her muscles straining, she managed to peel the tape back about an inch before her thighs cramped. Stretching them out, she rested, and then renewed her attack.

The truck made a sharp right turn, throwing Tessa off the mattress, and she landed on the ridged metal. "Damn it," she shouted, but then realized if Charley heard her, he'd know was awake and trying to free herself. Stupid security rope did nothing other than to tangle her up.

After two failed attempts, she succeeded in getting onto the mattress, only this time with multiple bruises for her effort. Next, Tessa busied herself freeing her legs.

When the last piece of tape came off, she sagged and wiggled her feet, reveling in the freedom.

What was her next move now? When Charley opened the back, he'd be royally pissed she'd undone his bindings. Since she'd failed to loosen the tape on her wrists, a surprise attack was quite impossible.

Hold on a minute. She could replace the leg tape, only this time not as tight in order to give herself some slack. When the opportunity presented itself, escaping again might be easier.

Buoyed by her new plan, she curled up again and rewrapped the tape. This time she let part of the tape overlap her jeans instead of cover her delicate skin to give her a better chance at freedom.

Using her teeth, she dragged the tape he'd used to cover her mouth next to her. When he stopped, she would roll on top of the tape to replace it. Maybe he wouldn't notice she'd tampered with his work of art.

The truck hit a pothole and she bounced off the mattress again. Dammit! Her elbow smashed into the hard metal, and pain shot up her hip. Then he hit another hole and another. Shit, shit, shit. Tessa bit her lip to keep from crying out. The truck made another turn onto a dirt road, and she prayed they weren't going to his trailer—his all-too-hidden trailer where no one would ever find her.

Think, Tessa, think. She'd let him take any out-of-date food to feed his animals in his hunting trailer. Where did he say it was? Crap. She couldn't recall.

Then the engine died, and her heart sank to her stomach.

* * *

Dominic paced Captain Leffer's office floor. "I can't sit here any longer. I've got to look for Tessa."

"Calm down. We're doing everything we can to find the girl."

Her name was Tessa, but Dom held his tongue. "You know the statistics as well as I do. It's been over three hours since she disappeared. If she isn't found soon…"

The Captain's phone rang and held up a hand. "Leffers…There was? Who?…Did you get a statement?…You're sure?…If he's willing, absolutely…Thanks."

Leffers looked up, and his pinched brows relaxed. "We have a lead."

"Tell me." Dom dropped down to the seat.

"Apparently, there was a twelve year old kid who was on one of the boats at the dock behind the Blue Moon. He said his folks had gone for food after they found the restaurant closed and told him to stay with the boat. Bored out of his skull, as he put it, he was watching out one of the portholes when he saw a woman being dragged outside by a large, bald man. He shoved her into the back of his camper."

Dom's hands gripped the chair and his legs flexed, ready to spring. "I'll speak with the kid."

Leffers waved a dismissive hand. "His parents are bringing him in now." The Captain stroked his mustache. "But you're not on the case anymore."

Dom shot up. "The hell I'm not." Tessa had called him and asked him to save her. He needed to be there for her.

His captain raised one brow. "Sit down, Dom."

Dom's fists balled at his sides. "You can't take me off the case."

"You almost killed Frank as he came through the door at the Blue Moon."

True, but he pulled back in time when he realized it wasn't Ralph. "I wasn't expecting the team to barge in."

"Did you expect them to knock?"

He didn't answer the rhetorical question. "Fine."

He had other clues to follow—like finding Annie and seeing what she had to say. Dom pushed back his chair and almost knocked it over.

"Go home. Get some sleep, and forget about the girl. We'll find her," Leffers said. "Besides, you've got lots of other murders that need your attention."

Dom understood the threat in his tone, though he didn't plan to heed the warning. His job meant everything to him, but so did Tessa.

Before he left the station, Dom grabbed the file folders and waved them across the room at Leffers. He wanted to appear as if he was following orders.

Dom patted his pocket to be sure Tessa's cell phone was secure. Once he charged it, he'd find Annie.

**

"You said you called 9-1-1 after Ralph left?" Dom asked Annie as he paced his home office, cell phone in hand. Why hadn't Leffers mentioned Mandy was safe with Annie, which would have spared him a lot of anguish?"

"Yes, but I waited until Tony came home. I'm sorry I didn't call earlier. I wanted to help Tessa, but I couldn't put my family in jeopardy. It was Tony who made me see reason."

"Tell him thank you."

"And thank your captain for sending a man over to keep watch over our house."

Dom ground his teeth. "I will." *Assuming I talk to the man again.* "Did you ask this person for identification?" he asked, worried the supposed cop outside her house might be impersonating an officer.

"Yes, Detective. I even verified his identity with your captain. Running the women's shelter has taught me a thing or two about deceit. Now find Tessa, please."

"I'll do my best." Dom disconnected.

Royally pissed Leffers conveniently forgot to mention Mandy was safe and that he'd stationed a man at Annie's house, Dom's conscience eased. Orders or no orders, he wasn't going to sit back and let the bastard take Tessa without a fight. To hell with his job.

Every crime scene held clues. Even crime scene units overlooked some obvious pieces of evidence once in a while. Dom hoped he might spot an item out of place since he'd been there before the crime. When he first checked out the Blue Moon, he'd been too distraught over losing Tessa to thoroughly check the place.

He grabbed his gun and dashed to his car. On his way to the restaurant, he called the hospital for an update on Chelsea. The nurse told him Chelsea had awoken briefly but had slipped back into a coma. She was hopeful Chelsea would wake up again soon.

He hoped so. Possibly she knew something that would help him find Tessa.

Hoping Leffers hadn't told Phil about him being taken off the case, he called his partner.

"Phil Orloff."

"Phil, it's Dom. What do you have?"

"Nada. I searched the bartender's apartment but come up empty-handed. Sorry. You learn anything?"

"There was an eye witness, a kid, who saw some big bald guy drag Tessa into a truck with a camper top. Sounds like the bartender's our man. I'm on my way to the restaurant now. I'm thinking I must have missed something."

"I'll join you."

Dom hesitated for a moment. "Just so you know, Leffers took me off the case. I don't want you to get into hot water by joining forces with me."

"I'm just meeting you for a drink, I'll say."

His partner was A-Okay. "At a closed bar?"

"Why not? See ya soon."

Dom disconnected the call as he pulled into the parking lot. His lights illuminated a red sports car, and the backs of two women stood at the front.

They turned. Dom's spirits lifted immediately when he recognized them. He cut the engine and slipped out, keeping on his headlights to further illuminate the darkened restaurant parking lot.

"Ladies, what a pleasure to see you again."

Madge and Eleanor shielded their eyes. "That you, Dominic?" Eleanor asked as they headed toward him.

"Yes. What are you two doing here?"

"What we always do. We came for a drink, but obviously the place is closed. We're in shock. What's going on?"

"Like the sign says. The Blue Moon is temporarily closed. With three of her patrons dead, Tessa thought it wise to close the place until the criminal or criminals could be brought to justice."

"Poor Tessa. She must be beside herself," Madge said grabbing her chest.

Eleanor took a step toward him and planted her hands on her hips. "Spill it, Detective. We want to help, and we can't if we don't know the details."

Ethically, he shouldn't disclose any information, but if these two ladies could shed light on where Tessa might be, he was willing the bend the law.

He told them about the trip to Ohio, the subsequent kidnapping threat, Tessa's frantic phone call, and the boy's observation.

"You think it was Charley who took Tessa? That's ridiculous. Charley's not the only bald man in Tampa," Eleanor said. "Why he was always so nice. He gave me extra gin all the time. Besides, he adored Tessa." Madge nodded her agreement. "Why would he kidnap her?"

"I wish I knew. I can't think of a motive."

The women stood there, Eleanor wringing her hands and Madge searching her purse for something. A moment later, she pulled out a tube of lipstick.

Eleanor perked up. "I bet he was trying to save Tessa from her horrible ex-husband. She told us the jerk was out to kill her. If the husband met her at the restaurant, as you claimed, and Charley saw them together, he'd fight to save her. And given how big and strong Charley is, I bet he won."

"When Tessa called me, she said her husband was dead."

Eleanor clapped her hands. "You see? I was right. Charley is a hero, not a villain."

Dom shook his head. "If he killed Ralph, where's the body? I've been inside, and the place was empty."

"Detective." Her patronizing tone surprised him.

"Yes?"

"Maybe he took the body with him."

"I thought the same thing until the boy claimed to have seen Charley only dragging Tessa to his camper. I didn't speak with him, but there was no mention of a dead body."

"I know where the docks are," Eleanor said. "The boy wouldn't have been able to see if Charley left by the front door and dragged the body somewhere. There are lots of construction dumpsters around here."

She had a point. "Okay, let's suppose Charley did kill Ralph, and then moved the body out of sight. Bottom line is, Charley has Tessa."

The two women looked at each other in horror. "We don't know what to say," Madge said.

"Would either of you sleuths know where your prince charming might have taken her? Such as a favorite haunt?"

They seemed to need confirmation from each other before talking.

"I bet he took her to his trailer," Eleanor announced with amazing confidence.

Dom's heart sped up. "Where's this trailer?"

"Well, I don't know exactly, but he told me about a pet alligator he had. He mentioned he had a small trailer outside of Lakeland in the Green Swamp. He likes to hunt."

"The Green Swamp?" He'd never heard of the area.

"Yes. It was a Wednesday night, I believe. Oh, about a month or two ago. Hardly anyone was sitting at the bar and we got Charley to open up a little."

Madge finished putting on her lipstick. "I remember that conversation. It was rather gruesome if you ask me. Charley has a pet alligator he feeds with the leftover food from the restaurant."

Dom tamped down his impatience. The ladies tended to ramble. "Did he give you a specific location for this trailer?" Dom withdrew his note pad from his front pocket ready to write down the information.

A gust of wind blew Eleanor's hair across her face, and she brushed it away. "No, but I think Judd's been there. The hunting is quite good in the area or so I've been told, and Judd loves to hunt. Why, he once—"

"Eleanor," Madge chastised. "Don't wander."

"Sorry."

Excitement raced through him. "Ladies, you've both been very helpful."

They beamed. "We have?"

"Absolutely. If you leave me your number, I'll be sure to call the moment I find Tessa."

"I'm so glad we ran into you then, Dominic," Eleanor said with more perkiness than at first.

"When all this is done, I'd like to buy you two a drink."

Eleanor beamed. "We accept." She turned to Madge. "Don't we, Madge."

"Absolutely."

"Now if you'll excuse me, I need to check out the crime scene."

"Oh, of course," Eleanor said. "Come on, Madge."

Dom waited until the ladies were safely in their car before he jogged to the back of the restaurant. He'd made it as far as the back door when the sound of an engine halted him. It must be Phil. Instead of having Phil struggle to open the door, Dom headed out front to greet his partner.

CHAPTER EIGHTEEN

Ralph's head throbbed like a bitch. He'd stumbled out of his car about ten miles after leaving the Blue Moon and puked on the side of the road. He still couldn't figure out where that hulking monster had come from? One minute he was about to have his way with Tessa, and the next a linebacker with whirling fists came flying out of the kitchen and attacked him.

Playing dead had been his only hope of getting out of the bar alive. By the time he crawled outside, Tessa and the giant had vanished.

He was too late to follow them, but he knew who might know where baldy had taken Tessa—the detective. With the way Rossi seemed to be keeping close tabs on his ex-wife, Ralph was pretty sure the detective would be out looking for her right now. Why should he expend all the energy when Tampa's finest would find her for him?

He'd parked across the street from the detective's house. The cop arrived home around midnight and stayed home until he left at seven.

Looked like the guy was headed out of town. Dumb detective couldn't spot a tail if Ralph bumped into him. Ralph had already decided he was finished fucking with Tessa's head. He wanted her dead —right after he tortured her.

***

Tessa's brother looked bad, wincing every few minutes. The bloating would make anyone want to give up, but Judd seemed to have this will to live. He probably wanted to be a father to Mandy.

Dominic held up his badge and introduced himself and his partner. "We won't keep you, but we have a few questions."

"What about?"

"Your bartender, Charley Madsen."

Judd coughed and spit up blood. "Is he in trouble?"

"Should he be?"

A wave of pity assaulted him. Tessa would be so distressed to see her brother so ill. He tried to blank his mind to Judd's bad situation.

"I dunno, you tell me."

Dom had been practicing how he'd break the news to Judd. He'd settled on the direct approach, although it bothered him to burden Judd any more than he had to.

"We have an eye witness who saw Charley kidnap your sister."

Judd's eyes widened and he grabbed his stomach. "She all right?"

"We don't know. We believe he took her to his trailer in the Green Swamp." Dom still couldn't get over the name of the area. "Do you have any idea where his place might be?"

Judd closed his eyes for a moment. "I've been there only once. Charley drove. It was one big blur."

A nurse whizzed in behind Dominic and Phil carrying a clipboard. "Gentlemen, you'll have to excuse us. I have to take care of Mr. Redman."

"Of course." He flashed her his badge, but she showed no reaction. "Can we ask one more question, please?"

"Make it fast. Mr. Redman tires easily."

Dom turned to Judd. "Do you remember any landmarks or the condition of the roads or anything about where his place might be? We need something to narrow the location."

Judd rubbed his abdomen and sucked in a breath. "I'm trying to remember. His trailer was near one of those bike paths. You know, where you can ride your bike for thirty or so miles. We almost ran some guy off the road as he was crossing from one side of the path to the other."

"Sure, like our Pinellas Trail." Dom had ridden his bike for hours without encountering bothersome traffic. "Anything else?"

"I remember driving down a long dirt road to get to his place. I couldn't believe anyone would put a trailer in the middle of nowhere. There was nothing but swamp, mud, and dense foliage everywhere."

Dom's heart sank. He'd never find Tessa in time. Even if he could requisition a helicopter, he couldn't do a wide enough search in time to find her.

"Your time's up," the nurse said as she placed her hands on her hips.

"If you think of anything else, Judd, let us know."

Dom pulled out his card, printed his cell on the back and placed it on Judd's nightstand. Nurse Ratchet tapped her clipboard.

"We're going," Dom said.

"Find Tessa for me," Judd pleaded.

"I'll do my best."

"Officer?" Judd's voice sounded weaker.

"Yes?"

"How's Mandy?" Judd had the same look in his eyes as Alex had when the two of them were separated by the horrible Social Service woman.

"She's fine. Don't worry about her. I'll let you know the minute we find your sister."

Judd's smile barely lifted his lips. He closed his eye and the nurse moved in front of him.

"Now what?" Phil asked once they were out of Judd's earshot.

"Hell, if I know."

"There has to be a tax record of Charley owning the property," Phil offered. "It'll have his address."

"Good thinking. Too bad the Green Swamp encompasses five counties."

"I'm betting each of the county courthouses will have the information."

"Let's hope. Lead the way."

"If we do find something," Phil said, "we'll be all the closer to Tessa."

Her name evoked a rush of desire, fear, and intense anger. He needed to find her.

As they exited the hospital, Dom's phone rang. "Hello?"

"Mr. Rossi, this is Smithers Watkins."

The name wasn't familiar. "Yes?"

"I've located your brother."

Dom stopped in mid step. "Alex? Where?" His heart pounded. He'd waited nearly twenty-five years for this moment. Watkins. Of course. He was probably the tenth investigator he'd hired over the years. Dom had all but given up hope of ever finding his brother.

"Alex is in California."

"California?"

Phil motioned he keep walking.

"Yes, but I'm afraid there's bad news. Your brother was in a car accident a few days ago and is in the hospital. That's how I found him."

Dom's head spun. "Is he going to be all right?"

"Ah... The doctors give him a one out of ten chance he'll survive. If you want to see him, you'll have to fly there, ASAP."

"Are you sure it's him?"

"Yes. I'm sure. He was adopted by David and Madge Sheffield and took their last name. That's what made the trace so hard."

"How did you find—never mind. Give me the information." The hows weren't important."

Dom pulled a pad out of his top pocket and scribbled the information along with the name of the hospital and its location. "Thanks. Send me your bill."

"Good luck, Mr. Rossi. I wish my call would have been under better circumstances."

"Yeah, me too."

Phil jumped in the passenger side. "Come on. Every minute we waste could mean Tessa's life."

Alex. Tessa. Dom needed to be in two places at once.

He couldn't believe he'd found his brother. Dom had spent his whole life looking for a family connection and now he'd found one. If he didn't rush to see Alex now, he might never get to talk to his brother—ever again.

Dom slipped into the passenger seat. "I found my brother."

"That's great, man. Once we get Tessa back, you can have that family reunion you've wanted."

Dom peeled out of hospital and slipped onto Bayshore toward downtown Tampa, his mind reeling. "He's dying."

Phil glanced at him. "I'm sorry."

"He was in a car accident and might not live. I really need to see him," Dom mumbled more to himself than to Phil. Dom slipped through downtown toward the Interstate, his mind reeling.

"So what are you going to do? You planning of leaving now or are we going after Tessa?"

Dom swallowed and let his gut decide, or was it his heart? Tessa was now. Alex was from the past. He loved Alex, but he also... Dom didn't want to finish the thought.

"Find Tessa."

"Good."

As Dom drove, Phil tried to narrow down his search on his laptop. God praise Bluetooth's wireless network. Being able to surf while on the move made their job easier.

"I found the Green Swamp, but nothing else." Phil said.

Dom pressed his foot to the floor and passed five cars. "We've got to find him. Look for a bike trail."

Phil tapped away on the keys. He couldn't get his mind off poor Tessa. If Charley so much as touched her, he'd pummel the guy till his brains fell out.

"Hey, turn here."

Dom jerked the wheel and exited I-4. "You find the path?"

"I found the path, but unless we get an address, we'll never find her. The record's department at the courthouse is our only hope."

Phil directed him to the government building where they parked and then raced up to the property appraiser's office.

"Hi, Fran," Dom said to the clerk behind the desk whose nametag sat prominently on her chest.

FROM TERROR TO TEMPTATION

"What can I do for you?"

He explained the urgency of finding Charley Madsen's place.

"Give me a minute." She clicked away on her computer. "I have no listing for a Charles Madsen."

"Try Morton Richter." He carefully spelled the last name.

Fran's search took longer. "Nothing."

"Damn. Thanks." Dom turned, stopped, then turned back. "I have an idea. Could you print out the owners' names of those who own land in the Green Swamp?"

"Sure, but it would be a long list."

"That's fine."

Dom paced while Fran created the list. "What do you hope to find?" Phil whispered.

"I don't know, but I'm thinking Charley only moved here a year ago. I'm going to check which properties were sold in the last year."

"Good thinking, but serial killers usually don't go through proper channels to obtain property."

Dom snapped his fingers. "You're brilliant."

"I am?"

"Fran, get me a list of all the properties with taxes in arrears."

Phil nudged him. "What are you thinking?"

"If my hunch pans out, I'll let you know."

***

Dear Audrey Mae,

This may be my last letter. Soon we will be together. I'll be bringing someone with me to meet you. You two are so alike I almost think she is you sometimes. She has a little girl too, a little younger than Bobby, but her ex-husband stole her. I'm gonna have to look for the baby before we come.

I know we'll all be so happy together. The police are closing in, and I've failed to keep my promise of silencing four drunks this November. I hope you'll forgive me.

Sincerely,

Morton Richter

Morton put down the pen and glanced over at Tessa. She appeared asleep. As Tessa lay on the cot, all bound up, he lit the candles on his altar. He'd dedicated his place to sweet Audrey Mae. The smoke rose to the ceiling looking like heavenly clouds.

Tessa moaned and Charley rushed to her side and loomed over her. Her eyes popped open and widened in fear. She whimpered.

"I guess I can take the tape off your mouth. No one can hear you this far in the woods. It's just you, me, and the animals." Morton didn't mention Bruno by name. Knowing an alligator roamed the lake might scare her too much.

He had no idea how long they'd be out here and eventually she'd want to take a walk in the woods. The path led to the lake and right to Bruno. If she was good, he'd take her to his special place, and they could feed the alligator together.

Right now, he had to find the baby, which could take him a while. Maybe he shouldn't have killed her ex-husband. Only he knew where he put Mandy. Shit. Maybe his Papa was right. He never thought through things good enough.

Morton took a deep breath. The trailer smelled musty. A pretty woman like Tessa shouldn't have to suffer in a stale place, so he cracked open a window to air it out and to let the candle smoke escape.

"Charley?" Her voice caught, and she wet her lips.

"You want some water?" He never wanted Tessa to suffer.

"That would be nice."

Excitement raced through him. Soon he'd be able to see his sweetheart and have Tessa at the same time.

He grabbed a glass from the cabinet and polished it real good with the cloth. Tessa was fussy when it came to cleanliness. She was always using bleach to disinfect the bar. Maybe he should buy some bleach for her, so she'd feel more comfortable staying here.

Good thing he had a stash of bottled water. Otherwise, he'd have to go to the lake and pump some.

"Here ya go," he said, as he handed her the glass. "Oh, sorry about having to tie you up like that. I'd like to oblige and take off your bindings, but I can't chance you'd run away."

She shook her head. "Where would I run to? You said we're in the middle of nowhere."

Charley scratched his chin. She made sense. "I know, but... I don't know."

Tessa struggled to sit up but then fell back down on the cot. "Please, Charley. Can you at least tie my hands in front of me? My arms are asleep and my wrists are raw from the tape. Then I can eat and drink by myself."

"Okay." He snipped the tape between her wrists. "There."

The tape popped. She drew her arms to the front and rubbed her wrists.

"Thank you." She looked around the place. "Do you have a bathroom?"

He didn't like the way she asked the question. Did she think he did his business in the woods or something?

"Of course. It's outside. You got a problem with that?"

Her face softened. "No, no, not at all. Just cut me loose. I promise I'll be good."

She pleaded the way he used to when his father hurt him. How could he not help her? "Okay."

He'd let her loose when he was home, he decided, but when he went out, he'd tie her back up. Good. He liked that he had a plan. Successful people always had plans, and he wanted to be successful.

She stretched out her legs, giving him access to her pretty little ankles. Morton slipped a knife from his back pocket and cut off the duct tape.

Once free, she looked up at him with worship in her eyes. He liked that. She appreciated him and didn't get mad at him for bringing her here. He'd made the right choice.

"Thank you again. Could you show me where the outhouse is? I really need to go."

He figured she was telling the truth. If he'd taken anyone else, he might have thought they just wanted to get outside and try to escape. What was he thinking? Tessa always told the truth. She was practically a doctor. "Okay."

Morton helped her to her feet, but when she took one step, her knees collapsed. He caught her before she hit the floor.

"Careful now. You still have a lot of drugs in your system. It'll take a while before you're back to normal."

He was fine with her not being able to move too good. Less chance she'd escape. Morton swooped her up into his arms, and she stiffened, but he guessed it was because Tessa never was close to anyone.

"I won't hurt you," he said, remembering this time to lower his voice and talk soft, like women liked.

She pressed her lips together. At least she didn't yell at him like Audrey Mae had right before she was killed. His true love's threats still stung.

Morton carried Tessa outside and set her down next to the wooden structure. "I'll wait out here."

She looked at the outhouse, and then back at him but didn't comment. She opened the door and slipped inside. He moved away to give her privacy, but not so far that she could run from him.

Thinking about her naked, jump-started his dormant desires. Ever since Audrey Mae had come into his life, Morton hadn't been interested in another woman, until Tessa.

He imagined Tessa naked, but only for a moment. He forcibly blocked his mind from those dirty thoughts. He'd brought her here to protect her, not have sex with her. Tessa wasn't the kind of woman who went for a guy like him. She was educated, and he wasn't.

He couldn't even enjoy the tranquility of the swamp like he used to while Tessa was out of sight. He checked his watch several times. "You okay in there?" he asked.

"Yes."

She sounded fine. Eventually, she came out, and her walking appeared better. Tessa looked around as if judging her chances of escaping.

"You'll never find your way out of here, you know."

She jumped. "Oh, no, I wasn't thinking about trying to get away. I was admiring the beauty of the place."

Her tone sounded sincere, but he bet she was just saying that to make him let down his guard. He knew first hand how shrinks tried to get him comfortable only to end up tricking him into saying something he didn't want to.

"Come on. I bet you're hungry," he said.

***

Tessa had felt safe inside the outhouse. It stunk, yes, but Charley didn't seem willing to intrude on her privacy. She'd tested the strength of the wall behind the seat, but it seemed too sturdy to break from the inside.

The longer she could keep Charley talking, the better chance she'd have of convincing him to let her go. He didn't seem to have a grudge against her personally. In fact, he appeared protective, almost as if he didn't want any harm to come to her.

Charley followed her into the trailer. The makeshift altar on the kitchen counter creeped her out.

"Is there any significance to the lighted candles? And to the plastic pink carnation and the baby toy?"

"Yes. I wore the carnation the day I was going to get married, but my fiancé was killed in a car wreck. A drunk driver slammed into her and killed her and our baby."

"Oh, Charley, I'm so sorry. When was this?"

"Four years ago, November 4th at 10:37 p.m." His gaze focused on the flickering candles.

Tessa stumbled backwards. She grabbed a chair to steady herself. November. Oh my God. Keri Wilkerson had been drunk—real drunk—when she left the bar a few weeks ago. As had Bob Dirkman and Doug Walsh. It was true, then. Charley must have killed them out of revenge.

Her mind spun as she tried to figure out how to deal with him. Sympathy? Validation? Did it matter when the person she was dealing with was crazy? Why hadn't she noticed his behavior before? The man didn't talk much, which had seemed odd for a bartender, but Judd had sworn by him. Tessa had too many other items to deal with than wonder about Charley.

"Do you have a picture of her?" Knowing something about his fiancée might help her deal with the man better.

"Yes. It's in the bedroom. Come with me."

Tessa backed up and waved him on. "I'll wait here."

Charley's eyes narrowed, and his fists clenched at his side. He took a step toward her. "Are you defying me?"

The sudden change in character scared her. "No. Never. You're right. I should come with you. I'd like to see the rest of the place too." All one other room of it.

His hands relaxed, and the tightness around his eyes disappeared. The soft approach seemed to work with him. Taking a deep breath, Tessa stepped toward him, half expecting Charley to grab her. She needed to pay more attention to his mercurial personality.

He turned and disappeared into the bedroom. She followed. The bed was made and covered with a worn comforter. The small room contained a wooden chair and a scarred dresser whose knobs didn't match.

With his back to her, he riffled through the bottom drawer. A second later he stood and held up a photo. He glanced down at the picture and ran his hand lovingly across the glass. "She was all I had."

Tessa waited for him to present the picture to her. His lips first smiled, and then frowned as if he were reliving her last moments.

Charley looked up and handed her the frame. Tessa grabbed the edge, careful not to touch his fingers. She glanced down and stilled.

The woman with the strawberry blond hair, slightly curled to her shoulders, could have been Tessa's double.

CHAPTER NINETEEN

"This is bullshit. We've been driving aimlessly for a couple of hours and getting nowhere," Dom said.

"Hey. There. Stop," Phil shouted, pointing to an official looking cruiser parked off to the side with a uniformed officer inside. "Rangers know everyone, or at least they should."

Dom did a U-turn and pulled behind the SUV. The logo on the side read, "Florida, Fish and Game."

"Let's go." They both jumped out.

The middle-aged officer eased out of his car and stepped toward Dom and Phil. Dom flashed his badge and the officer nodded. His nametag read, "Officer Mark Federer."

"Howdy, fellows. What can I do for you?"

Dom and Phil filled him in on their dilemma.

"Well, let me see. About a mile down the road is the Van Fleet Trail. It's probably the bike path your friend was telling you about. But thirty miles of trail covers a lot of territory." He shook his head.

"How about roads near the trail? Any old hunting trailers or cabins, stuff like that?"

The officer laughed. "Now you're asking for the proverbial needle in a haystack. All we have is hunting trails, old trailers, and cabins."

Frustrated, Dom whipped out the list of owners who hadn't paid their taxes. He spread the paper out on the hood of his car. "I was thinking the kidnapper might be living out here illegally. I'm taking a stab in the dark that he somehow moved into a place without the owner's permission. I wouldn't be surprised if he killed the occupant, which would account for the owner not paying his back taxes."

"That's a good thought, but the folks around here are quite poor. Not paying taxes is nothing out of the ordinary." He touched the tip of his nose. "I have an idea. Just a sec." The officer jogged back to his SUV and reached into his glove compartment. He came back a moment later.

"Here were go." He spread out a large map. "We are here." He tapped a spot in the southwest corner.

Dom's heart sank at the size of the shaded green area. He studied the map for a second. "This the Van Fleet Trail?"

"Yup. I don't know all the names of the owners, mind you, but I do know some. I live a few miles down this road." With Dom's list in his hand, he marked on his map the location of those who hadn't paid their taxes. "I'll star the ones owned by some loners, someone a less reputable person might take advantage of. I wish you fellows lots of luck finding that young woman." He folded up the map and handed it to Dom. "And here's my number in case you need to contact me. I'll stop by a few places on my way home and let you know if something comes up."

Dom scribbled his cell on his card and handed it to the officer. "Thanks. We'll need it."

***

"Where would your ex-husband take Mandy?" Charley asked as he paced in front of her.

He'd become more agitated as evening fell. Tessa couldn't figure out if he was worried she'd escape if he went to look for Mandy, or the fact Mandy was missing.

"I don't know. He doesn't know anyone in town, so I couldn't tell you his habits. Maybe he contacted Judd."

Charley stopped. "Or he brought her back to your house to lure you back there."

"Yes, that's brilliant."

His eyes focused on a distant object for a moment as if he reveled in her praise.

"We should go back there," Tessa suggested.

"No," he practically shouted.

"Why not? Ralph is dead. He can't hurt me now. He could have dropped Mandy back off at the house before heading to the Blue Moon. It makes sense now." Please let him go along with this.

He looked at her. Had she sounded too enthusiastic?

"No. You can't leave here."

As if she'd jumped out of a plane with no parachute, her stomach roiled and bile shot to her mouth.

"Why not? Surely you don't plan to keep me here forever."

The glazed look in his eyes told her he had no intention of ever letting her go. "What are you going to do with me?" There. She'd finally asked.

"Take you with me when I go to Audrey Mae and the baby."

"But I thought you said they were dead." Or had she misunderstood?

"She is."

His jaw tightened, and she recognized that if she didn't get out of his trailer tonight, she would soon die. She had no idea how she'd escape or which direction to take, but somehow she'd needed to escape.

A car rumbled outside the trailer and headlights shot through the window. Hope surged. Was it Dominic? Could it be him?

In a flash, Charley placed his hand over her mouth as he lifted her up. "Say one word and I'll kill you right here."

Tessa's heart beat so fast, she couldn't scream even if she'd tried. He dragged her to the bedroom and threw her on the bed. Grabbing a roll of duct tape, he slapped the tape over her mouth before she had the chance to protest.

A loud rapping on the front door gave her hope. Charley grabbed both of her wrists and tied them to the bedpost in less than five seconds. Then he wrapped her legs together and tied them to the other bedpost. Tessa didn't try to struggle, wanting to appear cooperative.

"Don't make a sound," he warned.

She nodded. She closed her eyes, praying Dominic was at the front door.

"I'm comin'," Charley shouted, acting bored.

Did he have neighbors who visited him? He claimed he didn't come to the trailer often.

Tessa strained to hear the conversation through the closed bedroom door.

"Howdy, Officer. What can I do for you?" Charley said in a tone more friendly than she'd ever heard.

An officer? As in the police? Had Dom contacted the locals to check the area? The newcomer's boots sounded on the floor as he headed toward the back of the trailer. He must be checking out the living room. Would he think all the lighted candles an odd touch for a rundown trailer and a bald, taciturn man?

"Is Carmen around?"

Carmen?

"He's in Ohio visiting his nephew," Charley answered.

"That so? Did he say how long he was going to be gone?"

Tessa couldn't detect any suspicion in the man's voice.

"For another few weeks, I think. I promised I'd stay here and keep the vandals away."

The man chuckled. "Yeah, the four legged type."

For the next minute, neither man spoke.

"Who do these belong to?" the officer asked.

What had she left out there? Her shoes! She'd slipped them off when Charley had placed her on the sofa.

Tessa banged her feet on the mattress, but she was unable to produce enough sound to be heard through the closed door.

"My girlfriend," Charley announced with enough pride one would have thought he'd won the Nobel Peace Prize.

"Where is she?"

"Gone."

No I'm not. I'm in here. Look in here, she screamed in her head.

"She left without her shoes?"

Good, the ranger was sharp.

"She wore her boots out. She always keeps a pair here in case it gets muddy. Guess she forgot to take the sandals with her this time."

The officer laughed. "Yeah, the Green Swamp is no place for a woman in sandals. Didn't you tell her about the snakes?"

"I will when she stops by tomorrow. Say, when Carmen comes back, you want me to tell him to give you a ring?"

"Sure, that would be great."

Tessa held her breath, waiting for the Deputy to see through Charley's lies. A moment later, the front door slammed shut, and she sagged into the mattress, letting the tears stream down her cheeks. Her one hope of being saved just disappeared.

She believed the officer's car or truck turned right after he drove down the drive, but Charley took that moment to burst into the room, interfering with her ability to listen.

"Damn nosey ranger. He'd come looking for Van Witt."

Tessa moaned in an attempt to convince Charley to untie her, or at the very least, take the suffocating tape from her mouth. She needed to be able to reason with him, assuming one could reason with the insane.

"Stay here. I don't trust that guy. He might be back."

Like she had a choice? Surely, he wouldn't leave her there all night.

***

Charley had taken his sweet time before he took off her duct tape gag and untied her.

"Thank you."

Her lack of negative response seemed to surprise him. One thing she had learned after working with him for a month was that he didn't take criticism well. Once she learned his father had abused him, she could understand his poor self-esteem.

After he cut off the tape, her arms ached when she lowered them.

Her hands had fallen asleep, and painful pinpricks of blood pulsated down her arms.

Charley was none too careful when he ripped the tape off her ankles however, but at least she was free. Red welts marred both her legs and arms, but Tessa didn't dare complain.

"You want to use the outhouse before you go to bed?" he asked.

"I'd like that. Thank you for being so considerate."

"Consideration has nothing to do with it. I don't need you peeing in my bed."

Oh God. Did he expect her to sleep in the same bed as him? If he touched her, she didn't know if she'd survive. She needed to take one minute at a time. She would get through this, just as long as she thought about being in Dominic's arms.

Once more, Charley followed her out to the outhouse. The sliver of moonlight lit the path, and the chill in the air bit into her skin. Her teeth chattered even though she doubted the temperature was much below sixty degrees. Perhaps it was the humidity and brisk wind that made the air feel colder.

The small wooden structure gave her a few minutes of peace away from the monster. How could she not have seen his demented personality? Hadn't Judd done a background check on him? Maybe her brother had been as desperate as she when she'd hired Mick. For all she knew, her short order cook killed and maimed too.

Tessa rubbed her raw wrists as she took care of business. Charley pounded on the door what seemed like seconds after she'd entered.

"Your time's up."

"Coming."

Fearing he'd bust down the door, Tessa dressed and stepped outside. Her eyes had grown more accustomed to the dark, but the overhanging trees added to the ominous atmosphere. They had to walk around the trailer to reach the front entrance.

Even though the inside smelled musty, its walls protected her from the elements.

Tessa flapped her arms around her shoulders. "It's cold out, and I didn't bring a sweater," she said. "Do you have something I could borrow?" The thought of putting on something Charley owned grossed her out, but she had to concentrate on getting out of this hellhole.

Charley grumbled and muttered something about women and their delicateness.

She wasn't cold inside the trailer, but if she had any hope of escaping, she'd need warmer clothes. Thank goodness she'd worn jeans. Her sandals weren't ideal, but they were better than nothing.

Charley huffed off into the bedroom. For a split second, Tessa contemplated sprinting out the door, but she knew she wouldn't get far. Instead, she took a different plan. She removed the nickel ring her mother had given her and placed it on the small wooden table next to the sofa.

Tessa rubbed away the green deposit around her finger.

Charley held out a ratty sweatshirt. "Here. It's the best I could do."

She tried to smile, but her lips quivered. "Thank you. You're very kind."

"You better believe it."

What did that mean? Tessa didn't dare ask.

"Are you hungry?" Charley asked.

"A little."

"I got some eggs. You could make us an omelet."

"Sure."

Moving about and doing something would help reduce her anxiety and give her time to think. If she could convince him she wasn't an escape threat, he might let down his guard.

Tessa spent the next fifteen minutes searching through the drawers as she prepared the food, pretending she was trying to find a spatula or some spice. She made a note where he kept his knives. No other kitchen appliance appeared to be weapon grade. Even the frying pan was made out of lightweight aluminum and wouldn't hurt Charley even if she managed to smash him in the face. The matches to light the propane stove might come in handy if she ever managed to escape.

After she'd stalled for as long as she could, Tessa placed the meal on the small table. "You want a beer?" she asked. His mostly empty fridge did contain that staple.

"Why not."

Tessa didn't know if Charley would be easier to handle if he drank, or if it would make her plight worse.

"If you don't have electricity, how do you power the refrigerator?"

"Propane. The whole house is on it."

"Oh."

Charley scarfed down his meal and chugged his drink in record time. He burped, pushed back his chair and grabbed his plate.

"Oh, I'll get that," Tessa offered. "Why don't you relax, and I'll clean up."

He stopped in mid stride. "You trying to soften me up or something, Audrey Mae?"

Her correction to the misnomer was on the tip of her tongue, but she decided to let the slip pass. If he confused her with the woman he loved, perhaps he wouldn't harm her. Maybe he had brought her to his place to keep her from Ralph, even though her ex-husband was dead. Charley did seem to confuse the two states of existence.

If only she could contact Dominic. Once again she scoured the trailer, hoping for a phone. Even though there wasn't electricity, she thought the phone company might have hooked up a line, but he had nothing.

"Answer me." Charley's sharp comment made her jump.

"Ah, no. I'm just trying to be helpful. In all the time we've worked together was I ever anything but honest and helpful?"

He scrubbed a hand over his chin. "I guess not." He extinguished one of the two lamps in the main room. "Leave the dishes until morning. I'm beat. Let's go to bed."

He acted like they were some old married couple. Did he truly believe she was his wife? Her heart sped up thinking maybe he wouldn't tie her up.

"Coming."

Charley picked up her discarded sandals and disappeared into the bedroom. Tessa followed behind. He pulled back the shabby comforter on the double bed and shoved the shoes under the mattress. Her heart sank. She swallowed hard, not wanting to crawl into bed with him. Images of bedbugs surfaced, and her muscles froze.

He stepped over to the small dresser and picked up the duct tape.

Her first instinct was to beg him not to tie her up, but she couldn't think of a good reason to give him.

"You know it's for your own good."

"Why?"

"Because I can't chance you'll leave me again." Again? "And there's no telling what's outside. We got black bears and panthers roaming around ready to pounce. A hungry mama bear might do unspeakable things to you."

If his intent was to scare her, he'd succeeded, but Charley posed a bigger threat than any animal.

"I'm afraid of the dark. I'd never leave at night."

"Still, I gotta do it."

Tessa sat down on the bed and held out her hands. She'd never free herself if he tied her hands behind her back. Charley didn't blink as he wrapped her hands together. He taped her ankles together under her jeans. Damn.

"I'm a real light sleeper, so don't try anything," he warned. "If you really gotta go, let me know."

Charley blew out the lamp and crawled into bed. How was she ever going to escape?

CHAPTER TWENTY

Tessa listened to every one of Charley's breaths until they evened out. Convinced he was finally asleep, she eased back the covers. Shoes or no shoes, she had to escape. Now.

Ripping the duct tape from her ankles would wake him, which meant she needed to crawl outside before she could fully free herself. Tessa slithered out of the bed, letting her feet drop to the cold floor. Unable to take a step with her ankles bound, she lowered herself to her knees, and then onto her stomach. Face down, she wiggled toward his dresser propelling herself with her toes and elbows, stopping every few inches to check the rhythm of his breaths. If there'd been more room, she would have rolled to a stand.

Even though she'd memorized the position of the dresser, she was thankful the slivers of moonlight lit the way. She didn't need to bump into the bed and wake him. That would suck big time.

Once she reached her destination, she rose to her knees and grabbed the prized duct tape—her secret weapon.

As silent as a snake through grass, she crawled back to the door he'd left open a crack. Maybe her luck was changing. His over confidence in believing he'd secured her would be his last big mistake. She'd make sure of it.

Carrying the duct tape in her mouth, Tessa managed to leave the bedroom without disturbing him, and then nudged close the door. The exertion, however, threatened to undermine her attempt. Man, or rather woman, was not meant to slither. Oh how she appreciated propulsion by foot.

Her rapid heartbeat forced her to breathe quickly, and the duct tape made it impossible to open her mouth.

Don't stop, don't stop, don't rest. Go.

She was thankful the generous moon helped guide her toward the kitchen. Every few seconds, she stilled to listen for Charley. If he awoke, she didn't know what she'd do other than beg forgiveness.

Enough resting. Move.

Once in the kitchen area, she rolled onto her butt and sat up. Inch by inch, she peeled off the tape around her ankles, careful not to make noise.

Now free, she stood and stepped to the cabinets that lined one wall. She slid her hands along the row of knobs, stopping at the third drawer on the right—the silverware and knife drawer.

After an agonizingly slow pull, she extracted a knife and began to saw her way through the duct tape around her wrists by holding the knife between her knees.

Tessa sucked in a breath, when the knife nicked the side of her off hand and warm blood trickled down her palm. She raised her arms to prevent the blood from landing on the floor and creating a trail. Pain shot up her arm when she touched the sensitive spot again. Suck it up, Tessa.

A few seconds later, the tape split open, and her heart beat faster. Freedom was near. Not wasting any time, she grabbed the duct tape, along with the knife and let herself out, praying Charley wouldn't hear the latch on the door open or close.

Her first step landed on a sharp-edged rock.

"Shit," she said, and immediately clasped a hand over her mouth. She couldn't worry about the pain on her feet until she was far away from the trailer. She blew out a breath to test the coldness of the air. The overhanging trees blocked the moon, preventing her from seeing the frosted air, but she could tell it was frigging cold. She never remembered November being this frosty before. Then again, she didn't make a habit of being barefoot outside in the middle of the night either. At least she had on Charley's ratty sweatshirt.

On tiptoe, she scurried behind his van. She didn't dare open the driver side door as she remembered it squeaked. Damn, she should have thought to notice where he'd placed his keys. Knowing Charley, his set was safely by his side.

She tore off a long piece of duct tape and wrapped it around her tender feet. One strip at a time, she made duct tape boots. She tested her handiwork and smiled.

One last glance at the trailer convinced her Charley hadn't noticed her defection. Treading softly, she hurried to the end of the drive, wearing the roll of duct tape as a bracelet in case she needed more later.

If the sound of the officer's tires could be trusted, he'd turned right. Was he going back to the road or did he live in that direction?

Not having any idea of the correct direction, Tessa chanced the right. If only she'd found a flashlight, she could make better time but having the light might guide Charley to her when he woke and found her missing. A light in the dark woods would travel far.

Tessa kept on the road, what there was of it. Large puddles periodically swamped the path and mud oozed in between her toes. She'd forgotten to cover them when she'd taped her heels and soles.

Tessa bent on one knee, ripped off another piece of tape and attempted to cover the rest of her foot, but the tape wouldn't stick to the old, wet tape. Aargh. She wanted to yell and scream her frustration, but she didn't dare. She tried again, but the tape ran out.

Not wanting to leave anything behind for Charley to find, she hurled the cardboard center into the woods. A noise sounded off to her left, and she stilled. From the soft rustling, it wasn't human. A bear would make more noise. Was it a squirrel perhaps? Or an alligator? She shivered. Oh, how she did not like the dark, especially the swampy dark with unknown creatures, like spiders and snakes crawling about.

Tessa stomped her feet hoping to scare off the animal. Good. Her plan worked. The retreating footsteps, or paws, raced away from her.

She'd rested enough. If for no other reason than to keep warm, she had to keep going. After a half hour, exhaustion set in. Her legs turned heavier with each step. As much as she wanted to rest she didn't dare. Charley could be right behind her, and right now, her only hope was to find the officer.

Tessa repeated her goal over and over again as she plodded forward on the muddy road. She rarely looked up, careful to watch her footing in an attempt to avoid the large holes and branches that crossed the roadway. For the times the moon dipped behind the clouds or was obscured by the trees, she slowed and shuffled her feet, making her progress painstakingly slow.

When she did rush, she often slipped on the wet ground, once landing on her tush. While she wanted to cut through the swampy woods to make it harder for Charley to find her, the dense trees and vines made it impossible to move more than a foot in either direction.

After what seemed like miles, the road forked. She stopped and listened for some sign of life—human life, that is. No lights peeked through any of the branches. Damn. It was as if both roads led to nowhere. But the officer had to live somewhere.

Returning to the trailer was not an option. As soon as the sun came up, Charley would be out looking for her. Tessa closed her eyes and prayed for guidance. As if an invisible hand guided her, she chose the road to the right.

She hadn't gone more than a hundred feet when a small echo filtered toward her. Was it her name? Oh God. The sun hadn't risen yet. Charley couldn't have found her so soon. The trees let in some moonlight and illuminated a footpath to the right.

Dredging up all her reserve energy, she sped down the new route, running as fast as she could. Branches and spider webs slapped her in the face while her feet slipped on the muck. She nearly fell again, but a nearby bush stopped her fall. She gulped down mouthfuls of air.

"Tes-sa," came a voice not far behind her.

Oh, God. She stopped and looked around for a place to hide. Tangled vines blocked her way to the left and swampy water sat off to her right. She grabbed the knife tight in her hand and pushed onward, aware her pounding feet echoed in the darkness.

"I can hear you," Charley called.

He was getting closer. Tessa rounded a bend and the path ended. Oh, God. Please help me. She stepped to the side and her foot sank into the earth, and cold water pooled around her ankle. She plucked it from the morass, sending out a loud sucking noise like that of a gunshot in the still night.

She had to find a way out. Her breaths came in short puffs. Arms flaying, she stepped backwards, and her foot landed on a log. Finally, solid ground, or so she thought until she looked down and made out what appeared to a dock leading to a small lake. For a second she was tempted to jump in the water and swim away, but she had no idea how shallow it was or who lived in it.

"There you are," Charley said stepping from behind a tree. "Why did you run away?" He acted as if her leaving was a common occurrence. He didn't seem angry. Could she hope he'd do her no harm?

Tessa froze. "I, ah—"

"Don't be afraid. I want to take you away from here—to a nicer place."

Charley sounded insane. She assumed *here* meant someplace other than Earth. "I like it here. I don't want to go anywhere." Especially with you. Tessa edged closer to the water and gripped the knife behind her back.

"This is my favorite place, you know. I built the dock myself," he said waving his hand in the air. "I like to get away here. It's so peaceful."

He clicked on a flashlight and pointed it at her face.

She squinted and held up her hand to shield her eyes. "It's, it's very nice. You're a talented man to be able to build a dock."

"Aren't you cold?" he asked in a voice devoid of all emotion. "Look at your feet. Tsk, tsk. You don't have any shoes. Wouldn't you like to go back? The van is just down the road."

So that's how he'd arrived so fast. Why hadn't she'd heard the engine? Her heavy breathing, coupled with fear, probably had blocked the sound. If only she'd succeeded in clawing her way through the swamp, she might have hidden until morning.

"I'm fine. Please let me go. I haven't done anything to you." Her mouth turned dry.

He pressed his hand to his chest as he advanced. "I don't want to hurt you. I want to help you."

As he reached out to grab her, Tessa took a step toward him and thrust out her arm. The knife sank into his gut. Horrified, she let go of the blade and circled to his other side, closer to the road.

Charley's eyes widened, and he teetered toward the lake, grabbing the knife and pulling it out. He dropped the flashlight, and its ray shot out over the water, and then sunk into the murky lake.

As if he realized what had happened, he lunged toward her, brandishing the knife. Tessa turned to run, and he grabbed her arm from behind.

"Charley, let me go!" Tessa yanked her arm, but he held on tight.

Grabbing her fist with her other free, but injured hand, she brought her arm forward, and then slammed her elbow back, connecting with his chest. Charley grunted. A hot, piercing blow to her back made her stumble forward.

The next thing Tessa knew, she was free and Charley was yelping like a hurt dog. She turned. He'd fallen in the lake and was flaying his arms, trying to get up, his white face glowing against the black water. She stared as the apparition attempted to stand.

A loud splash made her jump back, and the horrible sight paralyzed her. The tail of an alligator bobbed in the water. Charley windmilled his arms, and then slid face down into the water. A second later, he surfaced and reached toward her.

"Help me," he cried. "Bruno will kill me."

Seeing a person in need catapulted her into action. As Tessa stepped forward and reached out to give him a hand, a searing pain in her back shocked her into reality.

"I can't, Charley. I can't."

"Audrey, please help..."

The alligator dragged Charley under the water. Horrified, Tessa watched as two other predators joined the foray and tore him apart. To see another human suffer sickened her, but she needed to flee. There was nothing she could do for him. And more of the alligator's friends might come after her.

Charley was a big bull of a man, so maybe he could wrestle the alligator and free himself. Water splashed, and the full moon caught the scene in black and white. The noise stopped and the ripples diminished.

She had to move—only she couldn't.

After a full minute, reality sunk in. Charley was gone, but the backs of the alligators remained shimmering above the surface.

She pivoted and raced along the path, praying the monster beasts wouldn't come after her.

Tessa's breath came in rapid succession as she raced away from the scene. The turn off to the road shouldn't be far ahead. Damn, her bad sense of direction had completely turned her around.

The dark sky was turning a paler shade of gray signaling day would soon be upon her. Her feet were no doubt bleeding as was her back, but she couldn't take the time to do anything about them now.

The cold, damp air had chilled her to the bone, and blood was trickling below her shoulder blade and pooling along her waist. She ran a hand along her waistline and contacted the sticky goo. Her stomach clenched. Numbness raced down her arm on the side of the injury. She tried to lift her hand, but her muscles refused to cooperate. Fear at her potentially paralyzed arm shook her.

She needed help—fast. If she could just find the van, she could drive to a hospital and be warm and safe.

Keep going, Tessa. The turn off can't be far.

Through the thick swampy brush, she thought she could make out a light colored van. She was almost there. She could make it.

One moment she was focused on the van, the next her foot landed in a deep, watery hole.

"Ow," she screeched.

Her momentum catapulted her forward, and a second later she landed on her face into cold water. An unbearable pain speared her ankle and shook her knee.

"Damn it to hell. Shit, shit, shit. It hurts." Tessa didn't care if the world could hear her. No one seemed to be within a hundred miles, anyway. The pain swallowed her up.

Tessa pushed up from the ground, but with her right arm limp, she only managed to roll over. Panting heavily, she gritted her teeth and sat up. Her butt sat in waist deep water and her foot was stuck in the mud.

Drenched, in pain, and terribly cold, Tessa grabbed her knee to free her foot. The tugging motion sent nail-like spikes through her ankle and caused her back to scream in protest, forcing her to stop to catch her breath. When the wave of nausea passed, Tessa tugged again, this time succeeding in retrieving her foot from the ground's muddy grip.

"It hurts, it hurts," she moaned. Tessa wanted to touch the ankle to test the severity of her injury, but she didn't want to cause any more pain.

Exhausted, she rolled to her side, and crawled out of her wet hole, keeping her ankle above the ground and had to clench her jaw to keep from crying.

Her body screamed for rest, but she had enough sanity left to understand she couldn't lie on the damp ground forever. She'd die if she didn't move.

Her ankle was broken if the loud snapping sound was any indication. "Damn, damn, double damn. Dominic where are you?"

How ironic. She was finally free from Ralph and Charley, and she was going to die not by their hands but by nature. No one would find her for days. Her body would rot out here before another human came along.

The gruesome image helped prod her to her feet. It took her three tries to gain enough balance to stand on one foot. Tessa looked around in the dim light of dawn for something to act as a crutch.

Cypress knees protruded upward from the stagnant pools of water and gnarled branches twined together to form a curtain of wood, but no long straight stick was laying around for her to use.

Tessa let out an audible sigh and dropped down to the ground once more. Frustrated at the hopeless situation, her emotions erupted, and incredible self-pity overwhelmed her. Tessa sobbed and sobbed, so hard in fact, the tears clogged her breathing. She didn't care. Crying felt good.

Tessa cried for her ill brother, cried for her dead father, and cried for never telling Dominic how much he'd come to mean to her.

When no more tears fell, she looked around. More light had edged over the horizon. As if someone had dropped a gift from heaven above, a stick, with a V-shaped top, rested against a log not three feet from her. How could she have missed it? She didn't believe in fairy godmothers, but after the sudden appearance of this aid, she might have to reassess her opinion of the heavenly spirits.

With much effort, Tessa stood and held her foot held above the ground. Taking care not to stumble, she hopped toward her newfound cane. Each jump sent agonizing pain up her body, but Tessa clamped down on her jaw and kept on moving until she reached the wonderful stick.

She tested its strength. Not yet rotted, it gave her the needed support. The top of the stick came to her underarm. Perfect. But its sharp edge poked her to a point where the stick was unusable. Think, Tessa, think. She needed a cushion. Her dripping wet sweatshirt would do more harm on, so off it came.

Standing on one foot, she wrapped the garment around the top of the stick. Renewed by her ingenuity, Tessa took another step, then another until the path came to an end.

A river of sweat poured down her face and stung her eyes, forcing her to stop for a moment. Birds chirped, signaling morning was near.

Tessa took in her surroundings. Tall pines, scum filled pools of water, and briars bordered her. Where had her path gone? She should be able to see the road by now. She couldn't have wandered that far away from the path.

Refusing to let her injuries defeat her, Tessa turned around. She needed to retrace her steps, only this time she'd make sure to watch for the path to the road.

The effort to hop on her right foot, and then lean on the crutch, used a great deal of energy. She'd never make it out of this quagmire in her condition. Her ankle continued to throb whether she moved or stood still, and the blood on her back from the stabbing had mercifully caked. Her right arm lay useless at her side. Her left underarm was beginning to become sore, which would make her journey that much more difficult, but with no other choice, she moved on.

The humidity rose as dawn unfolded. Dragonflies and gnats must have decided she'd be a good breakfast choice and buzzed her face like kids around an ice cream truck. She let them attack, not having the energy to swat the pesky critters away.

So focused on her trek, she heard nothing until a mirage appeared before her. It had to be her imagination, because the image looked like Ralph, and he was dead.

"Hello, Tessa," the watery image said. "Looks like you've had a little accident."

His voice sounded real enough, but she didn't trust her mind. She blinked to clear her sight. "I know you're not really here."

The apparition laughed. "Oh, I'm real all right. Did you think the little knock on the head would kill me? Come on. I'm too thick skulled for that. You of all people should know that."

Every nerve ending exploded. "You're alive?"

"Very much so, but you won't be for long. I blacked out for a few minutes. That's all. When I came to, I witnessed that giant struggling with you as he half dragged you to the kitchen. I figured it was in my best interest to play dead." He smiled, but there was no pleasure on his face.

Ralph closed the gap between them in three long steps and grabbed both her arms. The sharp ache convinced her this was no ghost. Her ankle screamed in protest as he yanked her toward him. Her stomach cramped, as her breath whooshed out of her lungs.

"It can't be," she said, desperate for reality to take another form.

"Trust me, I'm real. And you're about to feel every inch of how real I am."

CHAPTER TWENTY-ONE

"This place better deliver. None of the other trailers the officer marked has given us squat," Phil said.

"Stop here," Dom whispered, pointing to a trailer set deep in the woods whose dim light flickered from inside. "I don't want him to hear us approach."

Phil parked and they both jumped out. Guns drawn, they skulked toward the dilapidated metal box.

"There's a light inside," Phil said, excitement lacing his voice.

"Yeah." Dom pressed his finger to his lips indicating from here on out only hand signals would be used. Phil nodded.

The swamp smelled of stale water and mildew. How could anyone live out here?

Dom motioned for Phil to head around back, while he'd enter by the front. Once Phil disappeared, Dom raced to the entrance, mud splattering his shoes. He pounded on the front door.

"Open up. Police."

He wanted to bust down the door and rush in, but he didn't have a warrant. Please let Tessa be inside.

No sounds came from within. Dom tested the door, and found it unlocked. He pushed it open and barged in, gun drawn.

"Police," he shouted.

Silence.

The door to the bedroom sat open. Dom checked inside the tiny room. Rumpled sheets covered both sides of the double bed, looking as if two people had slept here. Damn, he and Phil must have the wrong place.

He stalked to the back of the trailer and knocked on the window, motioning Phil to come inside.

"Find anything?" Phil asked as he stepped over the threshold.

"Squat." He stabbed a hand over his head.

"Maybe our kidnapper doesn't live here," Phil said in his usual voice-of-reason tone.

The adrenaline rushed out of Dom's system like a deflated balloon. He sat down on the edge of the sofa and dropped his head in his hands. He had to find Tessa, but he didn't know where else to look. She had to be alive. He hadn't fought hard enough to keep his brother at his side all those years ago and the continual guilt nearly destroyed him. He wouldn't let the same thing happen to Tessa.

"Come on," Phil prompted. "Whoever lives here doesn't need to see us when he comes back."

Dom took one last look around. The setting bothered him. The twenty some odd melted candles implied a romantic setting. But where was the woman? Had she fled at five in the morning too? Officer Federer had marked this place with a star. He claimed an old man lived alone. Always had. Something wasn't right.

He stepped over to the mantel and found a picture of a smiling woman and a small child. Could it be the old man's daughter? Tilting the photo toward the lantern, he was surprised at how closely the woman resembled Tessa, and a creepy feeling crawled up his spine.

Dom set the photo down and glanced to the sink. It was clean. The counters were even wiped down. It sure as hell didn't look like an old fart lived here. Dom was tempted to search the closet for confirmation.

"Someone left in a hurry," Dom announced. "You don't leave a propane lamp on and front door unlocked out here."

"Maybe he was afraid the animals might steal something."

"Funny."

"Look, we aren't going to find answers sitting on our asses."

"You're right," Dom said.

As he stood, Dom stopped short. A ring sat on the table next to the sofa. "Phil, wait." He lifted up the dull piece of jewelry and twisted it around. "It's Tessa's."

Phil rushed next to him. "You sure?"

"Sure, I'm sure. It was the same one Ralph took from her place and left at my house." His heart pounded in his chest. "She said her mother gave it to her when Tessa was a kid. Look outside again for signs of her. I'll check more thoroughly in here." The adrenaline renewed the spring in his step.

The search took all of two minutes. There weren't any places to hide other than the bedroom closet. No women's clothes were anywhere, but Tessa had been here. The ring proved it.

Dom rushed outside and yelled to Phil, "Let's go."

Phil joined him at the car. "No sign of any digging or anything out back."

"Good." At least he hadn't killed Tessa and buried her on the property.

Phil took off down the dirt road. The suspension system was no match against the potholes.

"Jesus Christ, don't kill us," Dom said.

Phil slowed as the road narrowed. Ten minutes later the road forked. "Now what?" Phil asked.

"Try calling the officer."

Phil punched in the number Federer had given him. He shrugged and left a message for him to call back. "I wonder where he is."

"Asleep like we should be. Only time is running out for Tessa."

"I'm with ya."

"Okay, turn right," Dom said pointed down a road narrower than the one they were on.

"You sure?"

"No, but the way looks clearer."

"I'll need an undercarriage wash after this expedition. I should have brought my 4-wheel drive."

"You don't own one."

"Oh, yeah."

Dom appreciated Phil's attempt to defuse the tension as they bumped down the uneven road.

"You see something white?" Phil shouted and pointed.

"Oh, shit. It's Charley's van." His heart banged against his chest.

Phil stopped behind the van, and Dom raced out.

***

Tessa hopped backwards as Ralph advanced. "Think what you're doing, Ralph. If you kill me, you'll go back to jail."

"I'll take my chances," Ralph said with a wicked smile as he flicked the knife in his hand. "But first I want to enjoy you. It's been a long time, Tess."

The way he said her name sent shivers up her arms. "Please, Ralph." Tessa despised the whine in her voice.

"Please, Ralph," he mimicked as he lifted up her chin with the blade, nicking her neck.

Tessa took a deep breath. If she was going to die, she wanted to die with dignity. Ralph was an animal. She refused to make it easy for him.

Before she could attack, Ralph grabbed hold of her shirt and pulled it down, ripping it in half. She gasped. Her right arm couldn't move to cover herself and her left arm was grasping the crutch for balance. He reached out a dirty hand and dragged down her bra strap. His mere touch revolted her, but she kept quiet. She understood Ralph's quick temper.

With the slowness of a garden slug leaving a trail of slime through a flowerbed, Ralph dipped his fingers into her bra and pinched her nipple.

Tessa squashed a retort and hopped back on one leg, nearly toppling on the uneven ground. In a flash, he grabbed her waist and dragged her to him, sending the stick to the ground. She screamed as her weight shifted to her left leg. Lifting her ankle, she went limp, forcing Ralph closer to the ground.

"Stand up, bitch," Ralph shouted inches from her face. He yanked up.

"Let go of me," she yelled back as she pushed against his rock hard chest. He didn't budge.

Ralph leaned forward and when he gave her a wet, nasty kiss, she tried to wriggle free, but he wouldn't let go. He'd pinned her good arm to her side, rendering her defenseless.

With his other hand, Ralph pressed his body up against her and ground his erection against her pelvis. His foul breath washed over her.

"Let...me...go, you bastard."

Ralph dropped his arms and stepped back in one movement. Before Tessa could regain her balance, Ralph hauled off and slapped her. Her head whipped to the side, and blood trickled down her chin from the cut lip.

A gun cocked behind her. "Let go of her or I'll shoot and ask questions later," her savior said in a wonderfully threatening tone.

Tessa nearly collapsed from the joy. Her heart beat so fast in her chest, she was sure it would jump out.

Ralph tensed, closed the gap between them faster than she could swallow. He spun Tessa around, clasped a hand over her mouth and drew the knife to her throat.

She drank in the sight of Dominic—strong, wonderful, and powerful Dom. She loved him.

"Leave or I'll kill her in front of you," Ralph said.

"You'll still die," Dominic said with amazing calm.

Tears streamed down her cheeks from the joy mixing with pain. How had he found her? If she'd been able, she'd have thrown herself in his arms. Tessa wriggled in Ralph's grasp, but he held on tight.

A crackling branch sounded behind them, and Ralph turned with Tessa still in his arms. On instinct, she kicked back her right leg forcing her to put pressure on her broken ankle. She screamed and collapsed to the ground. Ralph let go.

The second she smashed into the ground, a gun blast deafened her, and she held her breath.

Ralph's foot contacted her back as he dropped to the ground behind her. As she turned to her tormentor, he yanked her head back by her hair, and a second shot rent through the air. Her head swam, her mind blurred, and all noise faded.

"Tessa, Tessa, are you okay?" Dominic asked.

When Dominic's voice reached her brain, she opened her eyes. What a beautiful sight. "Hi."

Dominic smiled. "Hi, yourself. What hurts the most?"

He gathered her in his arms and stood up. She held on tight, afraid that if she let go, the nightmare would return. "My ankle is broken."

"My God, you're bleeding too." He held out his hand from under her knees.

"Charley stabbed me."

"Charley? Where is he?"

"He's dead. Really dead, not like I thought Ralph was."

"You can tell me all about it later. We need to get you to a hospital."

Another man appeared from the other side of the swamp and nodded to Dominic. "Why don't you put Tessa in the car and I'll call this in." He nodded at Ralph.

"Thanks, Phil."

"Is he your partner?"

"Yes, now put your head on my chest and rest."

"Tes...sa," came a strangled cry.

She strained her head to the left. Ralph was gasping for breath, and the sight sickened her. She feared him, but she hadn't wanted their relationship to end in a gunfight.

"I can't move," he said, his lips parched white.

Ralph wiggled his fingers and moved his arm an inch above the ground, and then dropped down, his body at an odd angle.

"Go. Take care of Tessa," Dominic's partner said.

Dom turned and carried her away from the horrible sight. Ralph yelled a piercing, shrill, screech, and Tessa buried her head in Dominic's chest. He squeezed her tighter.

Once they were away from the scene of the attack, Tessa lifted her head. "How did you find me?"

"I guess you could say Eleanor gave us the first clue. Then Judd told us about this trailer in the Green Swamp, and from there we followed one lead after another."

With every bounce and jostle, pain raced up her leg, stealing her breath. She took short puffs through her mouth to keep from screaming, but the overwhelming security of being in Dominic's arms convinced her she wouldn't want to be any place else.

***

Tessa had insisted Dominic bring her to Tampa General, instead of to a nearby Lakeland hospital which was an hour from home. She wanted to keep an eye on Judd as well as Chelsea—and she wanted to be closer to Dominic. Besides, being treated in a hospital anywhere near the Green Swamp made her shiver.

The emergency staff whisked her into the examination room as soon as Dominic wheeled her in. He insisted on being with her, hovering like an expectant father as the doctor checked her over.

"I'll have the plastic surgeon close the knife wound and then X-ray your ankle, but I'd say you're one lucky lady from what the detective told me you went through," the much-too-young doctor announced.

"Thanks." She didn't feel lucky. She was dirty, cold, and achy from head to toe. Then add in about ten thousand bug bites and scratches.

"We'll give you something to ease the pain shortly."

Only a general anesthetic would do the trick in her mind.

"I see you're in good hands, Tessa," Dominic said. "I need to head back to the crime scene. I want to make sure there are no other surprises. We don't need Charley rising from the dead."

"That won't happen, I promise." Tessa gritted her teeth as the two attendants lifted her onto a gurney. She grabbed his hand and absorbed his warmth and comfort. "How can I thank you?"

"It's all in a day's work." Dominic leaned over and kissed her full on the mouth, and her heart hammered from his touch. She couldn't believe he found her attractive all covered in dirt and blood.

When his words sunk in, her joy at being free faded. Dominic had saved her, not because he loved her, but because his job demanded it.

She tried to push aside his rejection and concentrate on healing. The next two hours proved to be not only uncomfortable, but also lonely. By the time the doctors finished X-raying her foot and tending to her stab wound, it was past noon. They wanted to wait until the swelling went down in her ankle before putting on a permanent cast. Right now, her foot rested in an air cast.

"We'll want to keep you overnight for observation," a different doctor said after flipping through a chart. "We don't want the wound to get infected."

"That's fine." Even if her toiletries hadn't been at Dominic's, she wouldn't have wanted to spend a night alone at her place, especially since using the bathroom required assistance. She also would need some help cooking in the next few days—some Thanksgiving this turned out to be.

A jaunty, full-figured woman entered her room. "Hello. My name's Winnie, and I'm going to be one of your nurses." She carried in a tray of food.

"Is there any way I could take a shower?" Tessa smelled so bad, she couldn't believe everyone didn't wrinkle her nose at her.

"I'll ask the doctor, but first you have to eat. Looks like you could use a few pounds."

Tessa had to smile. She glanced at her hands. "Can I wash my hands at least?"

"Just you wait." Winnie scurried into the bathroom and brought back a wet washrag. "Here ya go."

It was better than nothing. At least the nurses had cleaned her up superficially. If only she'd been able to stand on her own two feet, she'd have insisted on a shower.

Tessa forced down the food even though hunger wasn't on her mind. Charley thrashing about in the lake tormented her, but what could she have done? Reaching out to him would have meant death for her too. Had Charley not died, he would have killed her. He'd been a sick man.

And Ralph? His strangled cry echoed in her head but guilt didn't fill her. Jail had made him crack.

Wasn't she batting a thousand? Here were two men she'd trusted at one time and both had gone bad. Both were crazy, vindictive, and decided they wanted her dead.

Some psychologist she was going to make. Obviously, she didn't understand the human psyche at all.

A knock sounded on her door and Tessa looked up. "Come in," she called.

Annie and Mandy bustled through the door, and joy spread through her like wildfire. "Mandy! Annie, you found her."

"Oh, Tessa, I feel so guilty, especially with what happened. Ralph never took her."

Relief and horror smashed together. "I don't understand."

"Ralph came into the house and held me at gunpoint. He made me call you. He said if I called the police or told you the truth, he'd kill my kids."

"Oh, Annie. I'm so sorry for all the agony you've been through."

Tessa held out her arm for the squirming wonder. Annie placed the baby on Tessa's stomach where she gathered the precious bundle into her arms and rained kisses all over her tiny face.

Annie pulled up a chair. "I feel terrible deceiving you like that, but I had no choice. You must have been beside yourself with worry."

"It's all in the past now." Mandy reached up and grabbed a lock of Tessa's hair.

A huge wave of need overcame her. She wanted a baby worse than anything—but only with Dominic. Her practical side surfaced the second that thought flew into her head. Hard headed and gun shy, Dominic would take lots of work. She'd get her degree, open her own practice and hope by then he'd come to see that being with her was right.

Annie and she chatted for close to an hour while Mandy slept on her lap.

Her friend finally stood. "I need to get going. I'll stop by Judd's room and bring him his adorable child. Hopefully, seeing her will cheer him up."

Once her friend left, Tessa's depression returned. She checked her watch every few minutes hoping Dominic would stop by. How long could it take to check out a crime scene?

Winnie stopped in around two. "Time for a snack. You didn't eat much of your lunch."

"Thank you. Do you know if Detective Rossi has stopped back?" Maybe he'd come by to check on Chelsea.

"You mean that tall, dark handsome man who brought you in?"

"Yes."

"I'll see what I can find out." A smile lit her face. "But I do know that someone with the last name of Redman just came out of surgery."

"Judd had surgery?"

"Yes. One of my friends is his nurse. She says the transplant went very well."

Just as Tessa relaxed against the pillow and smiled, a sharp pain caused her to gasp.

Winnie rushed to her side. "Do you need more pain medication?"

"Maybe a little." She'd suffered enough.

"You drink some water and rest. I'll see what I can do."

After Winnie disappeared, Tessa closed her eyes, and Dominic's face appeared. Her savior. Even though he'd explained the series of events that led him to Charley's trailer, she couldn't believe his incredible timing. Nor did she understand how Ralph had found her in the first place, unless he'd followed either Charley to the swamp or Dominic to the trailer.

The nurse returned a long half hour later and gave her a pill to help with the pain. Tessa figured she'd take a short nap and wait for Dominic's return.

***

"Tessa said an alligator killed Charley, or rather Morton Richter, at a lake," Dom told Phil and Carl Cantori. "Let's fan out and see if we can find a body of water that fits her description. She said there would be a wooden dock leading up from the path to the water, surrounded by dense trees on three sides. She couldn't have gone too far with the knife wound."

Dom planned to mark the spot where Charley fell in, and then call in divers to fish out his body. He doubted an alligator would eat a whole person, but he was no expert on man-eating reptiles. The image of dying under those circumstances gave him the willies even though the sicko deserved to die—just not that way.

Slopping through the cold mud and tangled branches did nothing for his already black mood. If he weren't so desperate to put this case to rest, he'd be at Tessa's side making sure she was okay. However, in a couple of hours, he needed to get on the plane to see his brother, assuming the swamp bugs didn't eat him alive first.

The first available flight didn't take off until eight tonight. Given the three-hour time difference between Tampa and Los Angeles, he'd be lucky to get in by ten California time.

"Yo, over here," Cantori yelled through the thickets.

Dom turned around and headed in the direction of Carl's voice. He caught sight of the path covered by a fallen log and jogged to the lake. Charley Madsen had washed up on the bank, his body torn to shreds.

"He's dead all right," Phil chimed in.

"I'll call it in," Dom said.

"Good. Oh, I forgot to mention that after you took Tessa to the hospital, I called the Fish and Game station. They sent a man out to Craig Federer's house. His throat was cut. Sound familiar?"

"Dear God. Do you think it was Tessa's ex who did this?" Dom asked.

"Could be," Phil said. "Though Madsen might have been the culprit."

"I'll put my money on Ralph. I guess we now know why we never heard back from Federer," Dom said. He glanced at his watch. "If you two can wait for the rest of the team, I've got a plane to catch."

"No problem. Good luck. I hope Alex is...okay."

"Thanks." Dom started to leave, stopped and turned. "Any word on Ralph's condition?"

"I didn't bother to check. When the paramedics arrived, Ralph hadn't moved a muscle. I'm guessing the bullet did some serious damage."

Dom nodded. Tessa would be relieved to know her ex-husband would never be able to come after her again.

On the way to the airport, Dom called the number Watkins had given him and was able to speak with the nurse in charge of Alex's care.

"You say you're Alex's brother?"

"Yes."

"He's lost a lot of blood from the accident and suffered from multiple fractures, but he's holding his own. It's quite a miracle, if you ask me."

"I appreciate the update. I'm catching the next flight out."

"Good, but don't get your...never mind. I'll keep an eye out for you."

Just a little longer, brother. Don't die on me yet.

***

Traveling on the day before Thanksgiving had been riddled with delays. It was, after all, the busiest traveling day of the year. He'd paid more than twice what first class cost, but it was worth it.

When Dom arrived in L.A., none of the rental car companies had any midsize or full sedans available, so he'd had to rent a luxury car at twice the cost. Dom didn't care. He'd have bought the damn car if he'd had to.

After entering the address into the car's GPS, Dom headed to the hospital. Because Los Angeles was chillier than Tampa this time of year, he dialed up the car's heater. Remembering how Tessa shivered when the air was below seventy made him smile. What she did to his soul.

He parked in the hospital parking garage and raced inside. Decorated with pumpkins and cut out turkeys for the Thanksgiving holiday, the lobby was quiet as a tomb.

"I'm here to see Alex Sheffield." The name change still grated on Dom's nerves. They were brothers, dammit, and should have the same last name.

The receptionist clicked away. Dom prayed Alex was still alive. "He's in the I.C.U., room 235, but visiting hours are over. Are you a relative?"

"Yes, I'm his brother. I just flew in from Tampa."

"Well, then, take the first bank of elevators to the second floor."

"Happy Thanksgiving," he threw out as he headed toward his brother.

Now that Tessa was safe, he could focus on connecting to his only living relative. Sure, his foster parents had loved Dom, but they'd divorced five years ago, and he rarely heard from them. Alex was all he had left.

Then Tessa's face surfaced. Correction. He had Tessa, assuming she'd be willing to put up with the likes of him.

Dom punched the button for the second floor, his hands suddenly sweaty. Would he even recognize his brother? Would Alex know who he was? It didn't matter. He needed to see Alex alive.

The elevator dumped him on the second floor. Dom blocked out the usual sickening smells as he hurried to the room, refusing to glance in any other room since he didn't want to see people close to death. Dead bodies didn't bother him as much as those ready to enter the grave.

He stopped in front of 235, knocked, and stepped in. The young man in the bed had his eyes closed. The overhead lights were out, but a light over the mirror was lit. Alex's face was partially wrapped in gauze and his right leg and right arm were in a cast. Dom's heart broke.

A steady rhythm emanated from the machine attached to Alex's arm.

"Alex?"

No response.

Dom pulled up a chair next to the bed and examined Alex's face to see if his brother looked like an older version of the little boy he'd last seen. He didn't, but maybe his puffy face prevented seeing the real Alex.

Given Dom had no place to go, he figured he'd stay the night and surprise his little brother in the morning.

CHAPTER TWENTY-TWO

Wilma bustled into Tessa's room. "Ready to go home today?"

"I guess so, but I want to say goodbye to my brother and check in on Chelsea."

"Isn't she something? All that time in a coma, and she wakes up just like that." Wilma snapped her fingers.

Tessa bet Wilma had seen many such miracles. "I think it was her mother's voice that did the trick."

"I think so too," Wilma whispered and smiled. "I'll find you a wheel chair and take you where you want to go. Okay?"

"Thanks, Wilma."

Dominic had promised he'd find Chelsea's parents. Apparently, he was true to his word. Not that Tessa had spoken with Dominic since he'd dropped her off her three days ago. She contributed some of her depression to not seeing him.

Dominic, Dominic. Where are you? *Don't you care about me?*

Tessa needed to face reality. She was part of a closed case and didn't mean any more to him than a good lay. What a jerk she'd been.

Phil, his partner, had checked in once yesterday, but he claimed he didn't know where Dominic was. Right. Partners always knew each other's whereabouts.

Wilma pushed in a wheelchair. "Let me help you."

"Thanks, Wilma. I don't know what I would have done without you."

The nurse waved a dismissive hand. "You were no trouble at all and a real delight to treat."

Wilma took her to Judd's room first. There was almost no room left once the nurse put her wheelchair next to his bed. Judd looked up and smiled.

"Hi, sis."

His attitude had improved dramatically since the operation, as had his color. "How are you feeling?"

"Stronger each day. And guess what?" he said with a grin.

"What?"

"The bill's been paid."

"Really?"

Judd pushed down on the mattress and sat up straighter. "As if you didn't know. Did you sell Dad's house or something?"

"Hardly. I've been stalked, kidnapped, and stabbed. I haven't exactly had time to make real estate deals."

"Then how?"

"I have no idea."

Judd grinned. "Well, I'm not complaining."

Tessa couldn't imagine how something like this could have occurred. The money Judd had saved in his account could now pay for his medications. Once they opened the restaurant, the profits would sustain him for years, but he hardly had enough to cover the operation even after the insurance kicked in a portion.

Judd leaned over and took a sip of water.

"When did they say you could go home?" she asked.

"This week. Of course, I'll have to rest, but I'm thinking I'll be back at the restaurant full-time in another month."

"That's great." She couldn't put her finger on her emotion. Perhaps she'd grown fond on the place. It was almost as if she'd never belonged anywhere before.

"You don't sound overjoyed," he said.

"No, I am, it's just that..."

"It's just what?" he said in a tone reminiscent of the times when they'd sit in front of the fire and talk. Her older brother always had a way to draw her out.

Tessa didn't want to explain her need for a family of her own—like a husband and a child.

"Who is he?"

Was she that transparent? No use avoiding the issue, even though Dominic might never ask her out. "The detective."

"The guy who saved you? Come on, Tess. Didn't you call that trans-ference or something?"

"So you're the psychologist now? You've got your terms mixed up. Yes, he put me into protective custody at his house and then saved my life, but I like him for who he is. Once you get to know him, you'll see Dominic is really nice."

"The guy was single minded and tough when he came to talk to me."

Tessa didn't need to convince her brother of Dominic's good points. Even before Dominic had rescued her from certain death, she'd fallen for him, but she planned to keep that fact to herself. Dominic's unexpected tenderness in bed the one time they'd make love, convinced her he was the man for her, though Tess was the first to admit she didn't need a man to *complete her* as so many of her friends had claimed. She wanted Dominic because he made her feel special and wanted as a woman. Even though her brother had a child, she didn't think he'd understand.

"Dominic mentioned you helped him find me," Tessa said, wanting to change the subject.

"I did?"

"You told him about the Green Swamp, and from there he traced Charley's whereabouts."

"Cool. I guess when Charley asked me there, he never planned to kidnap you."

"No, I think his brain confused me with a woman who he'd loved and lost."

"Sad." Judd took another sip of water. "How's your friend Chelsea doing?"

"Better. She's out of the ICU. Speaking of which, I need to let you rest and go check on her. I'm going home afterwards."

"They've released you?"

"Yup. My shoulder is healing, but I'll need therapy to get back full range of motion. And my ankle will take a good six weeks in this cast."

Judd yawned and Tessa could tell it was best to let him rest. "Don't let the bed bugs bite."

Judd groaned and Tessa backed her wheelchair out of his room. She wondered if it was acceptable hospital practice to be out and about by herself.

Both of Chelsea's parents were by her side when Tessa rolled in.

"Claire, let's let the girls chat. There isn't room for all four of us."

Guilty she was kicking them out, she wanted to leave, but Chelsea's parents were up and out before she could protest. Tessa never would have guessed Chelsea's dad was a Virginia Senator. Her mom looked the part of the politician's wife, all dressed up in an elegant suit complete with pearls, and a Gucci bag on her lap.

Once Chelsea's parents left, Tessa wheeled closer to Chelsea's bed.

"I know this whole mess has been terrible for you, Chelsea, but can you tell me what happened?"

She closed her eyes and said nothing for the next minute. Had her friend fallen asleep?

"I've gone over this in my mind so many times, hoping with each passing I'd get a better idea of what went down, but nothing changes."

"What did you see?"

"I've told the police everything. Trace saw that guy from the bar pull out of the parking lot, just as we'd started kissing. I heard wheels screech and the next thing I know Trace hops in the car and we take off. I gotta tell you, I was mad."

"About what?"

"I was really hot for that guy, and he blows me off. He was more interested in a car chase than in me. I feel real bad about that attitude now." She looked up at Tessa, seemingly ready to cry. "He's dead, isn't he?"

"I'm afraid so. I'm sorry, Chels. I know you liked him, but the best thing now is to help the police find his killer. Do you remember the car?"

"The one racing out the lot?"

"I guess so."

"I think it was white. Yeah, a white van."

Tessa gripped the wheelchair until her fingers cramped. "Charley had a white van. Did he do this to you?"

"Charley?"

"Yes, our Charley."

Chelsea grabbed her chest and winced in pain. She grabbed a pump and gave herself a shot. "Sorry. I can't remember. It was dark. The streetlights were behind his face. I remember the gun going off and that's all." Chelsea's hand trembled.

Tessa grabbed her hand. "Charley is dead, hon. He can't hurt you anymore."

"Dead? How? When?"

Tessa told her about Ralph and Charley. As she finished, Chelsea's parents returned, concern lacing their features. Tessa turned back to Chelsea. "I need to let you rest. I'll try to stop by tomorrow if I can."

"Thanks, Tessa."

Tessa waved goodbye, and then wheeled out to find Wilma. The nurse spent twenty minutes going over every procedure from medication, rest, and a litany of other instructions. Once Tessa signed the paper to indicate she understood, she was free to leave.

The biggest problem was that she had no way home. "Damn it." Tessa immediately slapped a hand over her mouth. "Sorry, but I just remembered I don't have my purse, which means, I don't have my keys to my house."

Wilma smiled. "I'll be right back." A moment later she returned with a key chain. "You know the friend of your detective, the one who brought you in?"

"Detective Rossi's partner?"

"Yes. Well, he said that Detective Rossi gave these to him to give to you. They're the keys to his house. He thought you might be needing them. Seems he had to be somewhere for a while."

Tessa smiled. Maybe her bad luck was at an end. "You wouldn't happen to know where he was, now would you?"

"No, dear. Did you think I'm some kind of snoop?"

"Not at all. Thanks, Wilma."

"Do you need me to call you a cab?"

"That would be great."

* * *

Dominic awoke with a jerk. He must have dozed off. The last thing he remembered, he'd been watching Alex's chest rise and fall. Friday, his brother had opened his eyes, but with the tube in his throat, he couldn't say a word. The doctors and nurses had bustled Dom out so fast, he wasn't able to let Alex know he was there for him.

Alex's hand twitched, and Dom straightened. "Alex, can you hear me?" He'd been talking to Alex for hours, hoping his voice would rouse him.

His brother's eyelids fluttered, opened, and then closed again. Dom reached over and pressed the button for the nurse.

The room door flew open, and she rushed to Alex's side. He opened his eyes once more and lifted his hand an inch off the bed before falling limp.

"Alex," Dom pleaded. "Can you hear me?"

A low guttural sound emitted from his brother's throat.

"Let me call the doctor," the young nurse said as she raced out of the room.

Dom's heart raced as Alex's gaze found his. Dom grasped his brother's hand. "It's me. Dominic."

Alex's brows pinched together, and his brother's look of intelligence thrilled Dom. The doctors hadn't been sure if there'd be any brain damage. Alex applied pressure to Dom's hand. To him, it was the best handshake in the world.

"Excuse me, I need to see to Alex," a man in a white coat said.

"Sure." Dom let go and moved out of the way.

"If you wouldn't mind waiting outside," the doctor said, as he turned back to Alex.

Not wanting to interfere, Dom stepped from the room and headed straight to the coffee machine. Alex was going to make it. Dom could feel it in his gut.

He'd been gone three days and had never contacted the Captain. Not that he really cared if he found out the man had fired him, but he should check in. He slugged down the coffee and located the exit. Standing outside the front entrance, he made his call to Florida. Given the hour, he'd rather speak with Phil.

"Hello?"

"Hey, Phil. It Dom."

"Good to hear your voice. I thought you'd left the force or something. How's Alex doing?"

"I think he's going to be okay." Dom swallowed hard to remove the lump in his throat.

"So when are you coming back? Or are you?"

Dom didn't like Phil's tone. "Has something happened to Tessa?"

"No, no, she's fine. It's the Captain. He's hoppin' mad you left without a word. He didn't believe me when I said you'd left to visit your brother who'd been in an accident."

A month ago, he wouldn't have believed it of himself either. The force once meant everything to him. Not any longer—not since he'd met Tessa and found out Alex was alive. The idea of a family had crept into his soul and stolen his heart again.

"That's why I called. I need to stay with Alex a little longer to make sure he's going to make it. If you want, I can tell him."

"I'll do it. You just take care of yourself."

"How's Tessa?" Dom held his breath.

"I told you she was fine. She's banged up a little, but with rehab, she'll be good as new."

His shoulders relaxed. Dom wanted to ask if she'd asked about him, but working through a mediator never worked. "Thanks. And Ralph?"

"He didn't make it."

"What a shame."

Phil huffed out a laugh. "You got that right. Hurry home."

"Yeah." Dom hung up. He'd return when he was good and ready.

Dom returned to Alex's room, and the nurse looked up. "You can see him now. The doctor has removed the throat tube. Alex is breathing on his own but don't tax him. He's weak."

"Thanks."

Dom's palm sweated again. Why was he nervous? Even if Alex didn't remember him, they could spend time together and be brothers again. So what if they lived across country?

Alex's breaths were coming out fast—too fast. The nurse stood at the end of the bed taking notes on the machine readouts.

"Dom?" Alex croaked.

His voice sounded scratchy. The nurse grabbed a cup of water and fed Alex a drink.

"Yeah, it's me. I finally found you."

Alex cleared this throat. "What took you so long?" A small smile lifted his lips.

A tear ran down Dom's cheek and he wiped it away. "I've been trying, bro. I've been trying."

Alex's eyelids fluttered. Dom's heart sped up, and he looked up at the nurse.

"He's tired. He's been through a lot. Maybe you should let him rest."

Dom leaned over the bed. "Once you're better, we're going to spend some time together. I've got someone I want you to meet. I'm putting my card on your table. When you're ready to do some catching up, call me. I'll fly back out here in a heartbeat."

Alex opened his eyes. "You can count on it."

CHAPTER TWENTY-THREE

After stopping home first, and seeing Tessa's things gone, he headed over to her house. He spotted her Toyota in the drive and sighed. He needed to remember to thank Phil for bringing her car here from The Blue Moon.

Dom had thought about calling a million times, but speaking over the phone was too impersonal. With his family back together again, he was ready to move on with his life. And he wanted Tessa in it, one way or another. Not knowing if she wanted him was another reason why he needed to see her face-to-face.

Sure he'd been disappointed she'd removed all of her possessions from his house, but at least she'd left a note. Given he hadn't contacted her, he was glad she hadn't trashed his place, not that doing so would have been Tessa's style.

Dom took a deep breath and rolled out of his truck.

"Here goes," he said to the clear blue sky.

He rang the bell and waited.

A moment later the door swung open. With crutches under her arms, Tessa looked amazing. Breathtakingly beautiful, actually, despite her injured state. She smiled and his heart did a summersault.

"Hi," Dom said.

"Hi, yourself. Come in."

Nervous as a teenager on a first date, Dom inched past her, not wanting to bump her. His gaze caught sight of Mandy's empty playpen and a longing tugged at him. He missed the little girl. Sure, when Phil had told him Mandy had never been in danger, his relief had been immense, but now, he wished she were back here. He liked holding her.

Had he suddenly turned into a family man? Maybe. Reconnecting with Alex might have freed his inhibitions. In all honesty, he'd never believed he'd ever have a family, let alone keep one. He'd lost his folks, and then believed Alex to be out of his life for good. When he lost his fiancé to cancer, Dom had decided he'd spend the rest of his life alone.

Then came Tessa.

Sweet, wonderful, Tessa.

As gently as he could, he leaned over and gave her a chaste kiss, needing to test the waters before rushing forward.

She hobbled over to the sofa and plopped down without saying a word. Dom grabbed the crutches before they crashed to the ground and leaned them against the sofa arm.

"How are you feeling?" Dom asked as he sat as close as he dared.

She lifted her cast that covered her foot. "Only five more weeks to go." She raised her left arm parallel to the ground. "I started physical therapy two days ago and already I have a lot of the movement back."

"That's great. And how are Judd and Chelsea?"

Tessa laughed, the sound delighting his senses. He wanted her. Broken ankle and all.

"Judd's operation was a great success, and he's doing fine. Chelsea should be leaving the hospital this week. Her parents were so happy to see her. I wanted to thank you for finding them."

So much had happened, he felt like he'd been away for weeks. "No problem. Actually, I have a private investigator do the leg work. He's pretty good." Dom draped her arm along the back of the sofa and curled a bit of her hair around his finger. "Did you ever find out why she left home?"

"No, but maybe someday I will." Her smile left her face. "Have you heard anything about Ralph's condition?"

Dom didn't want to spoil the night with talk about her ex. He wanted the night to consume only them, but Tessa deserved to know.

He was surprised no one had contacted her. "He passed away."

She looked up at the ceiling for a moment, and then back at him. "I loved him once, you know, but he changed into a man I didn't recognize once he started to gamble. I'm happy he can't hurt anyone ever again."

Her sad eyes tore him up inside. "Me too."

"Oh, I almost forgot to mention the miracle," she said, her eyes sparkling.

"What miracle?"

"Some angel paid for Judd's operation. He wouldn't have been able to afford it otherwise."

Dom kept quiet. He reached up and caressed her face.

She stiffened. "It was you, wasn't it?"

"Maybe."

She twisted on the seat to face him, and her eyes shone with excitement. "It makes sense now. I overheard you talking on the phone at your house. You were giving someone information about an account and didn't want a certain female to learn about it. That female was me, right?"

He knew she'd press him until she found out. "Yes. I know how much Judd's health meant to you. I had the funds, so I transferred some into his name."

"Why?"

"You can't figure it out?"

Her innocent look made him hornier than hell.

"You did it...for me?"

"Come here." Dom slipped his arm under her knees and around her back, and then stood. "You sound as if I don't care about you. Let me show you just how much I do."

She giggled. "Oh, Dominic." Tessa laid her head on his shoulder and his heart did a double take. He knew he'd never been so happy.

***

As soon as Dominic lifted her up, shivers of delight spread through to her toes, and she forgave him for not being around these last few days.

He carried her into the bedroom and placed her on the bed as if she were a fragile flower, and her heart hammered away in her chest.

Standing at the end, he faced her, his gaze locked onto her face. He said nothing as he slipped off his shirt, baring his muscular chest. Just looking at him had her heart dropping to her stomach and her mouth turning dry. Tessa didn't drag her gaze away from his muscular chest until his fingers dropped to his waist. Then she licked her lips.

Yes, she'd seen him naked before, but this time seemed different. The first time they'd make love, it had been purely physical. Well, mostly physical. This time was for real.

It shouldn't matter he hadn't told her he loved her—yet. His actions implied he cared deeply. No man would pay for a brother's operation unless he thought there would be a future for them—or was she putting positive thoughts in her head?

Stop analyzing his actions. Enjoy!

Dominic bent down, untied his shoes, and slipped them off, never taking his gaze from her. Desire pooled in his eyes as he dropped his pants. He was hers, in every way, and she planned to keep him.

Like a lion who hadn't eaten in days, Dominic crawled onto the bed sending shimmers of joy skittering down her spine. He reached out, pulled out her hair tie, and then brought a tendril to his nose and inhaled. He smiled and let it fall back in place.

"Much better." His words held a smile.

His touch robbed her of speech. Dominic's lingering gaze was more than a caress, and she itched to touch every inch of him. As she reached up to his face, he grabbed her hand.

"Just wait."

"Such a delicious promise."

As he kissed the palm of her hand, then each knuckle, her heart sped up. Oh, how she wanted him.

Dominic drew the tip of his index finger down the side of her cheek and along the column of her throat. She urged his hand to dip lower.

"I don't think you need that sweatshirt anymore, do you?" he asked. Glazed eyes peered through his thick lashes.

She swallowed, shook her head and let him lift it over her head. Dominic scooted forward and unbuttoned the top three buttons of her shirt. He leaned over and kissed her skin between the opened blouse, and his clean scent teased her nostrils. Tessa threaded the fingers on her right hand through his hair, marveling at its rich, shiny texture.

"Oh, Dominic, what you do to me," she panted.

"Tell me."

"You excite me like no one ever has. When you touch my skin, every part of my being ignites."

"You do the same for me."

He unbuttoned her blouse all the way and slipped it off over her shoulder. With little fanfare, he unhooked her bra and tossed it on the floor, before he tackled her split-legged sweatpants, socks, and shoe.

Only her panties remained. His gaze dropped to her breasts, and when he leaned over her, his hot breath fanned her nipple. Tessa pressed her chest upward to gain contact.

Dominic pounced, taking one breast into his mouth and sucking on it, while kneading the other. She thought she'd died and found eternal bliss. First he devoured the right breast, then the left. His lips drove her crazy. She grabbed his bicep and ran her hand up and down his arm, enjoying the sinewy tautness of his muscles. She couldn't wait until she could use both her arms to wrap around his broad back.

He flicked his tongue across her tips, and she couldn't help but moan. How long would she have to endure this torture? This glorious, burning, thrilling torture?

Tremors of awareness coursed through her. "I love when you touch me like that."

"How about like this?" He kneaded her right breast, and then grabbed the tip of her nub between his teeth and pulled. Tension shot straight to her groin. "Or like this?" His mouth encompassed her other breast, and he sucked on her nipple she thought she'd go insane.

***

Dominic couldn't get enough of her. He drew his mouth upward along her delicate throat and captured her lips with his. She tasted like roasted honey—sweet, tangy, and so very delicious. When she opened her mouth to let in his tongue, his erection strained against his cotton briefs. He didn't know how much longer he could last.

Dom pulled away to douse the heat that ran rampant through his body, not wanting to come it before he'd had her.

"Please don't stop," Tessa huffed.

He loved hearing her beg. Regaining his composure, he trailed kisses down her throat, memorizing the curves and planes of her body. Want pulsed through him like a wild fire. Hungrily, he ran his tongue over her flat stomach and down between her thighs before sucking on her silk panties.

Tessa grabbed his shoulder and pressed him to her. Her rapid breathing and moans told him she was hanging by a thread, and her desire fueled him. The way she moved, the way she moaned, and the way she gave of herself convinced him she must love him. She was the woman of his dreams.

Dominic sat up and straddled her, careful not to lean against her healing ankle. He grabbed her tiny waist with both hands and marveled at her shape. He drew his hands up to her breasts and cupped them once again. Tessa placed one hand on his chest and heat whipped through his veins, pooling in his groin.

With a quick flick of his wrist, he lifted her rear, pulled off her panties, and deposited them in the same pile as the rest of her clothes. He'd never be able to look at the floor again without remembering their decadent love.

Dominic moved to the side and sank a finger into her wet folds. "I love you, Tessa Redman."

Her eyes widened. "What did you say?"

He nibbled her lips. "You heard me. When that bastard took you I thought I'd never see you again. You make me feel whole."

The smile on her face made the sun look dull.

"I can't believe it."

How could she sound so incredulous? "I guess I'll have to show you how much I love you then."

Dominic rolled to the side, pulled down his briefs and lay next to her. When she reached out and touched his erection, a powerful tremor shot through his body. He grabbed her wrist. "If you touch too much, I might lose it. I'm already on the edge."

She got a devil look in her eye. "Oh, yeah?"

"Yeah."

"I want you now then," she breathed. "I'll perish if you don't take me."

Dominic didn't answer. Instead, he plunged a finger into her wetness and kissed her hard. If she'd been more mobile, he'd have found more exotic poses, but he reasoned they had years to explore every pleasure.

"I've only just begun." He wanted to please her first to give her something to remember. The first time they'd made love, he'd rushed.

With his knee, he gently opened her legs and dipped down between her thighs. She tasted so sweet. Tessa grabbed his head and gasped as he plunged his tongue in and out. Her musky sex scented the air.

She arched her back and yelled his name. "Dominic! That's all. . . I can . . .take."

Joy burst through him at her desperate plea, and liquid heat engorged his sex. He wanted her, but he wanted her to want him more.

"Kiss me again," she said, panting.

That he could do.

Careful to avoid her casted foot, Dominic cradled her in his arms and delved into her mouth, tempting her tongue to mate with his. She held the power to become one with him.

When he knew he couldn't wait any longer, Dominic pressed her legs closer together in order to straddle her. He opened her folds with his cock and plunged into her, reveling in her wet slickness.

"Oh, Tessa," he murmured.

Once he was fully sheathed inside her, Tessa pulled his chest to hers and pumped her hips up and down. Blood pounded in his ears as she bucked and rolled under him. Her moans turned into cries, and her fingers dug into his back. For the next few minutes, they became lost in total bliss. When his orgasm exploded, she opened her mouth and arched her back as her climax took her.

Heavy breathing, slick sweat, and sweet sex filled the room. Dominic rolled onto his back, taking Tessa with him. He kissed her eyelids and raked his hands through her beautiful hair, reveling in their joining. "This roller coaster of emotions is going to kill me."

"Me too," she said.

Dominic rolled to the side, and Tessa leaned up on her elbow. "So where have you been these last couple of days?"

He threw her a sheepish look. "Yeah, I'm sorry about cutting out on you. You see, I hired a private detective to find Alex. And he did."

"Alex?"

"My brother."

Tessa sat up. "Really? Where? Did he recognize you?"

"Eventually." Dom told her of the bad timing of Alex's accident in California.

"And you came after me instead of going right away to see your brother? He could have died."

Dom reached up and cradled her chin. "So could you."

"Yes, but your partner could have come looking for me, or someone else on the force."

"I know, but I wanted to find you. No, I needed to find you. To make sure you were safe."

"You do love me." Tessa pressed a hand over his heart.

He laughed. "That's what I've been trying to convince you for the last hour."

"I love you too."

He believed it. "That's the best homecoming present a guy could have."

Dominic grabbed her to him and showered her with love again. After he'd thoroughly kissed her, he leaned back.

"When your ankle is healed and your brother is back in charge of the restaurant again, how would you like to take a trip to California with me to meet Alex?"

She beamed. "I'd love to, but what about work? Can you take the time off?"

He laughed. "Family is the most important thing to me now, not the Force—at least not anymore. And speaking of family, as soon as we're married I'd like to have a few young ones around."

"Marriage? Oh, my."

"What do you say?" He held his breath.

"Yes! I can hardly believe my good luck. Oh, Dominic, you make me so happy."

He kissed her hard, reveling in the fact he'd found happiness at last.

***

Don't forget to sign up for my newsletter to receive three free books, as well as up-to-date information on my stories. If you prefer to only receive notices regarding my releases, follow me on BookBub.

The End

ABOUT THE AUTHOR

Love it HOT and STEAMY? Sign up for my newsletter and receive MONTANA DESIRE for FREE. Click here

OR Are you a fan of quirky PARANORMAL COZY MYSTER-IES? Sign up for this newsletter. Click Here

Not only do I love to read, write, and dream, I'm an extrovert. I enjoy being around people and am always trying to understand what makes them tick. Not only must my romance books have a happily ever after, I need characters I can relate to. My men are wonderful, dynamic, smart, strong, and the best lovers in the world (of course).

My Paranormal Cozy Mysteries are where I let my imagination run wild with witches and a talking pink iguana who believes he's a real sleuth.

I believe I am the luckiest woman. I do what I love and I have a wonderful, supportive husband, who happens to be hot!

Fun facts about me
(1) I'm a math nerd who loves spreadsheets. Give me numbers and I'll find a pattern.
(2) I live on a Costa Rica beach!
(3) I also like to exercise. Yes, I know I'm odd.

I love hearing from readers either on FB or via email (hint, hint).

Social Media Sites

Website: www.velladay.com
FB: www.facebook.com/vella.day.90
Twitter: velladay4
Gmail: velladayauthor@gmail.com
Tiktok: Velladayauthor1

ALSO BY VELLA DAY

SILVER LAKE SERIES (3 OF THEM)

(1). <u>HIDDEN REALMS OF SILVER LAKE</u> (Paranormal Romance)

Awakened By Flames (book 1)

Seduced By Flames (book 2)

Kissed By Flames (book 3)

Destiny In Flames (book 4)

Box Set (books 1-4)

Passionate Flames (book 5)

Ignited By Flames (book 6)

Touched By Flames (book 7)

Box Set (books 5-7)

Bound By Flames (book 8)

Fueled By Flames (book 9)

Scorched By Flames (book 10)

(2). <u>GODDESSES OF DESTINY</u> Paranormal Romance)

Slade (book 1)

Rafe (book 2)

Will (book 3)

Josh (book 4)

Box Set (books 1-4)

Jace (book 5)

Tanner (book 6)

(3). <u>WERES AND WITCHES OF SILVER LAKE</u> (Paranormal Romance)

A Magical Shift (book 1)

Catching Her Bear (book 2)

Surge of Magic (book 3)

The Bear's Forbidden Wolf (book 4)

Her Reluctant Bear (book 5)

Freeing His Tiger (book 6)

Protecting His Wolf (book 7)

Waking His Bear (book 8)

Melting Her Wolf's Heart (book 9)

Her Wolf's Guarded Heart (book 10)

His Rogue Bear (book 11)

Box Set (books 1-4)

Box Set (books 5-8)

Reawakening Their Bears (book 12)

OTHER PARANORMAL SERIES

<u>**PACK WARS**</u> (Paranormal Romance)

Training Their Mate (book 1)

Claiming Their Mate (book 2)

Rescuing Their Virgin Mate (book 3)

Box Set (books 1-3)

Loving Their Vixen Mate (book 4)

Fighting For Their Mate (book 5)

Enticing Their Mate (book 6)

Box Set (books 1-4)

Their Huntress Mate (book 7)

Craving Their Mate (book 8)

<u>PACK WARS-THE GRANGERS</u>

Meant for them (book 1)

Meant for wolves (book 2)

Meant for forever (book 3)

Meant for her (book 4)

HIDDEN HILLS SHIFTERS (Paranormal Romance)

An Unexpected Diversion (book 1)

Bare Instincts (book 2)

Shifting Destinies (book 3)

Embracing Fate (book 4)

Promises Unbroken (book 5)

Bare 'N Dirty (book 6)

Hidden Hills Shifters Complete Box Set (books 1-6)

CONTEMPORARY SERIES

MONTANA PROMISES (Full length contemporary Romance)

Promises of Mercy (book 1)

Foundations For Three (book 2)

Montana Fire (book 3)

Montana Promises Box Set (books 1-3)

Hart To Hart (Book 4)

Burning Seduction (Book 5)

Montana Promises Complete Box Set (books 1-5)

Novellas:

Montana Desire (book 1)

Awakening Passions (book 2)

PLEDGED TO PROTECT (contemporary romantic suspense)

From Panic To Passion (book 1)

From Danger To Desire (book 2)

From Terror To Temptation (book 3)

BURIED SERIES (contemporary romantic suspense)

Buried Alive (book 1)

Buried Secrets (book 2)

Buried Deep (book 3)

The Buried Series Complete Box Set (books 1-3)

A NASH MYSTERY (Contemporary Romance)

Sidearms and Silk(book 1)

Black Ops and Lingerie(book 2)

A Nash Mystery Box Set (books 1-2)

STARTER SETS (Romance)

Contemporary

Paranormal